VOSPER'S REVENGE

Book Three of the Dragon Stone Saga

Kristian Alva

Eusebian Publishing

Other Books By Kristian Alva

Dragon Stone Saga
Book 1: Dragon Stones
Book 2: The Return of the Dragon Riders
Book 3: Vosper's Revenge
Book 4: The Balborite Curse
Book 5: Rise of the Blood Masters
Book 6: Kathir's Redemption
Book 7: The Shadow Grid Returns
Book 8: The Fall of Miklagard
Book 9: Sisren's Betrayal

Stand-Alone Novellas
Brinsop's Brood
Mugla's Magic

Collections
Dragon Stone Trilogy (Books 1-3)
Chronicles of Tallin (Books 4-6)
The Shadow Grid Trilogy (Books 7-9)

All books are available on Kindle Unlimited.

Frigid
Waste

Snowmarsh

Gut-Burr

The Abundant Sea

Brighthollow
(unexplored)

Elves

Northhurst
Downs

Miklagard

Wheatbridge

Everwood Forest

Lopt
River

White Bay

Stonehill
Bog

Freydale

Dead Man's Pass

Trautt
Plains

Mount Heldeofol

Pine
Grunge

Highmill

Pinemount

Syrd

Lake Wren

Highport Mts

Dead
Forest

Sleita Border
(Disputed)

Aonach Tower (Ruins)

Mount Velik

Blackhaven

Ironport

Hrlinda

The Death Sands

Fairfort

Morholt

Mistfair

Ravenwood

Lysa

Parthos

Nomadic
Tribe

Lockdell
Barrens

Orvasse River

Dyrr

Rignus

Fallwick

Mallowgate

Balbor

Enrilina Mts.

Vertlake

Grofhaven

Persis

Jutland

Elder
Willow

Faeriden

Hwit Rock

Redmoor Island

Buttermead

Gardarshlom

Darkmouth Forest

Welley
Island

The Black Sea

Starryford

The Lofa Sea

Durn

3

Dedicated to my children, the sweetest little dragons of all.

1. SANDSTORMS IN THE DESERT

E lias and his young dragon, Nydeired, trained on the walls of Parthos. Nydeired weaved through the air while Elias threw fireballs.

They circled each other, Nydeired narrowly avoiding the attacks. Tallin directed their training close by, shouting terse commands. "Elias! Move your right leg back—watch your balance," he said. "Nydeired, tuck your wings in closer to your body; you're leaving yourself vulnerable to attack." Tallin spoke entirely in *dragon-tongue*, which Nydeired and Elias both understood.

"Yes, Master Tallin," replied Elias, sweat dripping from his brow. Nydeired hovered in the air, pumping his massive wings; he nodded but said nothing. The young dragon was still learning how to speak.

Nydeired was covered with scratches from countless falls. Some of his wounds were scabbed over and some were fresh, a testament to months of brutal training. Elias also had his share of scrapes and bruises.

Elias adjusted his stance and clenched his fists, getting ready for another round of attacks. "*Hringr-Incêndio!*" he cried, throwing another fireball. This time, it hit Nydeired directly on the shoulder. The dragon recoiled, his right wing collapsing as he tumbled to the ground. Elias looked stricken, but he did not move from his position.

Nydeired groaned, lifting his enormous body up. He grabbed his injured shoulder, dark blood pouring out between his clawed fingers.

"Stop," said Tallin, frowning. He walked over to Nydeired and examined the wound. "Tsk. Elias, tend to that."

Elias nodded, stepping forward to touch Nydeired's injured shoulder. This, at least, he knew how to do well. *"Curatio!"* he said, feeling a familiar surge of energy as the healing spell began to work. Elias' healing abilities were exceptional, a testament to the years of training he had received from his late grandmother Carina.

Nydeired exhaled as his skin and muscles knit back together underneath Elias' glowing palm. A few minutes later, Elias removed his hand, and Nydeired carefully moved his shoulder. The wound was healed, although the flesh was still pink.

"Thank you, Elias," said Nydeired, his gravelly voice stilted and hesitant.

"You're welcome," said Elias, wiping his palm on his tunic. Elias pulled a carved dragon stone out of the pouch around his neck. It was the emerald dragon stone that he had found over a year ago in Darkmouth Forest. He had taken to wearing it all the time since it allowed him to understand dragontongue. However, he was forced to speak out loud—he was still unable to communicate telepathically with Nydeired, and he would be unable to do so until after their binding ceremony.

Duskeye, Tallin's dragon, slumbered nearby. Duskeye offered advice to the younger dragon occasionally, but for the most part, he merely observed.

Hot air swirled on the ramparts, kicking up sand. Elias coughed. He still wasn't accustomed to the heat, even though he had been living in Parthos for a year. On the horizon, clouds of brownish dust swirled on the dunes.

"I think another storm is coming," Elias said, coughing again. He tasted grit in his mouth. "Master Tallin, may we get some water?"

"Go ahead," said Tallin. "I'll pause your training for a moment."

"Thanks," said Elias, and he and Nydeired walked over to a covered barrel and used a metal ladle to scoop out some water. They had been practicing drills for hours. Elias felt bone-weary, aching in every muscle.

Elias offered water to Nydeired first, who drank deeply.

Tallin watched the pair with wonder. Nydeired was *enormous*. Only a year old, he already towered over all the other dragons in Parthos. His dragon stone was also twice as large. The gleaming diamond had finally grown in last month, erupting at the base of Nydeired's throat. Now that he had his dragon stone, Elias and Nydeired could be joined permanently in their formal binding ritual.

Sela, the leader of the dragon riders, would perform the ceremony. Everyone was just waiting for her return from her mission to Mount Velik.

Sela and her son, King Rali, had been negotiating with the dwarves for weeks, trying to convince the clans to ally their forces with Parthos. According to their frequent communications, the negotiations were not going well.

"Still worried about this weather, old friend?" said Duskeye, moving up behind his rider.

Tallin reached over and patted Duskeye's neck. "Yes. The sandstorm is worsening. It'll probably last all night." He squinted, shielding his eyes as he looked out upon the desert. The number of sand-storms had been steadily increasing. The gritty wind blasted the city walls, sometimes for days at a time.

During the storms, trade ground to a halt, as people were forced to remain indoors. More importantly, the frequency of the sandstorms was starting to affect the citizens' morale. "We've been living in the Death Sands for a long time, Duskeye. Do you ever remember seeing *this many* sandstorms in a single season?"

"No," said Duskeye. *"It's never been this bad. The winds feel unnatural. During the storms, I feel magic tugging at my dragon stone."*

"I feel it, too. I can't determine its origin. The energy feels oddly familiar but alien at the same time. It would take enormous amounts of magical power to sustain these storms, day after day. Who has this kind of power, save the emperor himself? But it can't be him. Our intelligence is sound. We know that Vosper hasn't left Morholt."

"Perhaps you're looking at this the wrong way," said Duskeye. *"What does Vosper have to gain by making Parthos inhospitable?"*

"I have no idea. I'm baffled by it, frankly. If anything, Parthos is *safer* during the storms. If these storms are the work of our enemies, then it seems rather counterintuitive."

The wind whipped around them, filled with dust. Elias and Nydeired sneezed. They walked back to where Tallin and Duskeye were standing, looking over the city walls.

"Master Tallin? Shall we continue?" asked Elias. He coughed again. Nydeired waited patiently by Elias' side, his pebble-black eyes watching everything.

"No, Elias, we're finished for today," said Tallin. "You and Nydeired should go inside and get out of this weather."

Nydeired nodded, his giant white head bobbing up and down. The young dragon turned to Elias. *"I'm hungry. Let's see if the palace cooks have something for us to eat."*

"Good idea. My stomach has been growling for the past hour," said Elias as they left the rooftop. Nydeired moved through the doorway sideways, barely squeezing himself through the opening. Dust trickled down where his scaly hide scraped the wall.

"Look at that," said Duskeye. *"Nydeired is still grow-*

ing. They'll have to expand the entrances if he's going to continue to roam about inside the castle. I've never seen a fledgling so large."

"I know," said Tallin. "Nydeired is the largest dragon on the continent, by far. But his size is deceptive. I sometimes forget that he's still basically a hatchling."

"Yes. He's already double my size. But he's ungainly, like a newborn calf. As he is now, Nydeired must remain in the city. The Death Sands are too dangerous for him."

"I agree," said Tallin. "Logistically, it's a nightmare. His size makes him impossible to hide, and he's an irresistible target for our enemies. He's bound to be the most powerful dragon in a century —but only if we can keep him alive until he reaches adulthood."

Another sand-laden gust of wind hit them, and Tallin covered his face with his sleeve. He peered down at the city streets below and noticed street merchants frantically packing up their things. People scurried into their tiny mud-brick homes, anticipating another long tempest.

"It's time for us to leave, Duskeye, or we'll be stuck in Parthos tonight. Can you fly us above the storm? I don't want to stay inside the city walls."

"Of course, my friend," said Duskeye, smiling, his red tongue idling between his razor-sharp teeth. "The storm is moving south, so we shall go north."

"Good idea. Let's go to Salamander Cavern. It's a safe place for us to rest," said Tallin. "Once we reach the caverns, I'll contact Sela telepathically and let her know about the sandstorms."

Tallin draped a camel hide across Duskeye's back and hopped on. Duskeye pumped his muscled blue wings, and within minutes they had risen above the storm. As soon as they were high enough, Tallin looked down and observed the winds. The sandstorm beat down upon the city, but nowhere else. The radius of the cloud was small and concentrated only on the city.

"Duskeye—do you see that?"

"Yes. There's no mistaking it. The dust cloud isn't moving."

"It's more obvious than ever," said Tallin. "There's definitely magic afoot. I just wish I knew who was responsible for it, and why."

"You and me both," said Duskeye. They flew deep into the desert, away from the city.

Meanwhile, Elias and Nydeired were walking down to the palace kitchens. As they entered, all the workers froze, except for the surly head chef, Marlson. Elias strolled in, ignoring Marlson's sour expression. "Hi, Marlson! What's good tonight?" he said.

"Humph!" snorted the chef, trying to ignore the intruders. Marlson was fat, loud, and fearless. He didn't suffer fools in his kitchen. Unlike the other palace staff, Marlson wasn't intimidated by any of the riders or their dragons. "We're *trying* to work, boy. What do you want?"

Elias smiled. "Just visiting. It smells great in here." Dozens of prepared chickens lay spread on the butcher's block. Elias grabbed a chicken by its feet. "Catch this!" he said, throwing the chicken into the air.

Nydeired snapped it up, swallowing it in one gulp. Elias laughed and threw two more dead birds into the air. Nydeired stretched his enormous neck, catching both at the same time. His giant head swiveled back and hit a hanging pot, clanging against the pan like a bell.

The startled cooks jumped at the noise, and Marlson shouted, "Watch it, *watch it!* Be careful with those pots and pans!"

Nydeired burped, rubbing his stomach. "*These birds taste good.*"

Marlson's portly face reddened with anger. Work came to a standstill. The kitchen staff stood and stared, darting frightened looks at the enormous dragon whose thrashing tail had become a workplace hazard.

The long-suffering cook couldn't take it anymore. "That's *enough!* Stop this horseplay this *instant!*" he yelled, wagging his chubby finger at Elias. "You two are *supposed* to be in training, not scattering food all over the place. I won't accept this kind of rough-housing in my kitchen, dragon rider or not!"

Elias bit his lip and tried not to smile. Underneath that stern façade, he knew that Marlson was just a big softie. "I apologize, sir. We meant no disrespect. Nydeired hasn't had much to eat today. May we take a few more of these birds? Then I promise we'll get out of your way."

"Humph!" said the chef, scowling.

"Please?" asked Elias again.

Marlson glowered, trying to maintain his anger, but then his plump face softened. "Aye, boy. You can take them. We were plucking them for you anyway." He pointed a fat index finger toward Nydeired. "That dragon of yours has an appetite like nothing I've ever seen. Fifty chickens a day, three camels a week! He's a bottomless pit!"

Nydeired narrowed his pebble-black eyes and stared at the cook for a moment. The young dragon still struggled to understand human communication, and he couldn't tell if Marlson was kidding or not.

Elias grabbed four more chickens, two in each hand, and turned to leave. "Thanks, Marlson! You're the best. Will you please send up a plate of your delicious roast?" Elias said, pointing to the steaming hunk of camel meat that Marlson had just pulled out of the oven. "I'll be in my room with Nydeired. I'm sure he'd appreciate a few chunks of meat, as well. Or a fresh camel liver, if you have it."

"Aye, aye, I'll send the food up to your room. Now *scoot*, both of you! Or my cooks won't get any work done today!" said Marlson, waving them off. He clapped his hands loudly in the center of the kitchen. "The show is over, folks! Everyone get back to work! I'm not paying you to stand around with your mouths hanging open."

The kitchen came alive again, everyone chopping and cleaning while looking over their shoulders at the retreating dragon and his rider.

"*The fat human seems angry,*" said Nydeired.

Elias chuckled. "He's not, really. Marlson doesn't mean anything by it. It's just bravado."

"*What's 'bravado'?*" Nydeired asked.

Elias paused, searching for a way to define the word in a way the young dragon would understand. "It's all hot air—a lot of bluster," he explained in dragon-tongue. "He yells and complains, but inside he's as gentle as a lamb. He's also the best chef in Parthos, so it's worth putting up with his little outbursts."

They moved through the castle, making their way to their rooms. Soon they reached a vast atrium outside the throne room, where they spotted members of King Rali's private guard, *The Nine*. The men were dark and muscled, with heavily tattooed skin.

Only a single guard had accompanied King Rali to Mount Velik: their leader, *Aor*. The rest of the guardsmen remained in Parthos and spent most of their time keeping fit. They had moved their sparring practice inside because of the dust storms.

Elias marveled at Rali's guards. They dodged back and forth in the vast hallway in active swordplay. The guardsmen dripped with sweat, the moisture soaking through their undyed wool tunics.

One guard swung his broadsword, while another

attacked from behind. The swordsman struck out with his foot, swinging it in a low arc. The other man fell, hit in the stomach by a well-placed kick. The fallen guard sprung back up instantly, leaping from the ground like a cat.

The guards came to attention as Elias approached. They each gave him a slight bow.

"Good evening, rider," said Annarr, who was the second-in-command. Even though Elias was not officially a rider yet, after saving the city from the orc horde, he was treated with deference by the palace staff, including *The Nine*.

The Nine did not use traditional names. Instead, they were named according to their rank in the old language. The first-in-command was simply referred to as "First" (*Aor*, in the ancient tongue), and so on.

"Good evening, Annarr," said Elias. The man nodded but said nothing else. The guardsmen waited until Elias and Nydeired left the area before resuming their practice. Unlike the palace servants, *The Nine* didn't gape at the riders or their dragons. They treated the riders with respect, but never with fear or awe.

Elias walked to his chamber and was pleased to find his dinner already laid out for him on a table. An oil lamp filled the room with soft light. There was a steaming plate of roasted meat and vegetables for him, along with a massive tub of raw camel meat for Nydeired.

"That was fast. This food smells fantastic. Sorry,

buddy, it looks like Marlson didn't have any liver for you tonight," said Elias, throwing the remaining chickens in the air. Nydeired caught three but missed the last one. It landed on the ground with a splat. Nydeired leaned down and scooped it up with his jaws, swallowing it.

"It's fine. The camel meat will satisfy my hunger."

They settled down to eat, Elias at the edge of the bed and Nydeired on the floor, taking up most of the space in the room. Outside, the din of the sandstorm rose and fell, the howling wind whipping against the tiny window. They ate in silence for a moment, and then Nydeired started scratching his stomach and arms.

"Elias, I'm itchy all over. These sandstorms make my scales tingle."

"I know. I feel it, too. The dragon stone that I carry—the one I found in Darkmouth Forest—vibrates when the storms come. The storms have some magical origin."

"Does that concern you?" asked Nydeired.

Elias nodded. "It does, a little. But as long as King Rali is at Mount Velik with Sela, I don't worry as much. Our most important job is to protect the king, and I know that Rali and Sela are safe among the dwarves."

"What about Tallin and Duskeye? Do you think they realize that the sandstorms aren't natural?"

"I'm sure they figured it out long ago, but they didn't feel like it was necessary to share the information with us. Tallin is secretive about *everything*, not just this. He and Duskeye rarely share their thoughts with anyone, except perhaps the king. Did you see them leave? They flew into the desert tonight during the height of the storm."

"How will they be able to see anything? The air is choked with dust."

Elias shrugged. "They'll manage. I stopped trying to second-guess Tallin a long time ago. I can't predict what he's going to do. The only thing I don't do is underestimate him."

Nydeired finished his meal and stretched, curling his white tail around his body. He burped, then yawned, revealing razor-sharp teeth as long as Elias' hand.

Nydeired's yawn was contagious, and Elias answered with one of his own.

He flopped down on the bed. "It's still early, but these storms make it impossible to do anything outside. There's not much to do except sleep."

Nydeired craned his neck toward the tiny window. *"I can't see anything. It's very dark outside."*

"It's the storm. There's a full moon tonight, but the city's under a blanket of sand. Duskeye and Tallin are out there somewhere, probably searching for the source of the storm," said Elias.

"Aren't you the least bit curious? Why don't we find out for ourselves?"

Elias laughed and then stopped. The dragon's expression was serious. "Really? You're not kidding? You want to fly into the storm?"

"Well… Tallin didn't prohibit it, right?"

"No, no... not *specifically*," said Elias. "I'll grant you it could be exciting, but I can't imagine that they'd be *pleased* about us flying into the desert by ourselves, especially at night."

"*Perhaps you're right. We should just stay inside, like baby ducklings,*" said Nydeired, cocking his head to one side.

Elias stared at him for a moment, unsure of how to respond. Nydeired was actually *goading* him, to see how far he'd go. "Are you honestly proposing that we fly out into the desert during this storm?"

"*Why not? We'll only stay out for a little while. We'll come back before anyone even realizes we're gone.*"

Elias wasn't much of a thrill-seeker, but he had to admit he was curious. His lips twitched. "Okay, you've convinced me. We'll go—but not too far from the city. I know that you've practiced carrying me, but never during a storm. Are you sure you can do it?"

"*Yes. I feel strong. I can carry you easily. But we should grab one of the larger saddles, just in case. It's safer that way. I'll feel more comfortable if you have proper stirrups and handholds.*" Nydeired paused, suddenly concerned. "*Do you expect us to encounter any danger? I'm not afraid for myself, but I don't want to put you at risk.*"

"I certainly hope not. I'm more afraid of Tallin's wrath than anything we'd encounter in the desert."

Nydeired smiled, his teeth glinting in the dim light. "*Shall we?*"

Elias chuckled, despite his apprehension. "I still

think this is crazy. Let's leave before I change my mind."

They headed to the sandblasted rooftop to fly out into the desert.

2. THE DWARVES

S ela and Rali sat in the dwarves' vast mead hall at an arranged feast. The clan leaders all sat at the table, arguing back and forth. The rest of the table was occupied by members of the dwarf king's entourage. The dwarf king, Hergung Lindisfarne, sat at the head of the table, drinking mead from an ornate chalice.

Sela leaned over to speak in her son's ear. "This is ridiculous. I can't believe we're still here," she whispered with exasperation.

"I agree, Mother," said Rali, who was equally frustrated. "It's insane how stubborn they are." The clans were no closer to signing a treaty than the day they arrived.

Hergung seemed unperturbed by the chaos. In fact, he seemed to be enjoying it.

Sela slumped back in her chair, struggling to keep a pleasant expression. This was worse than when she went to Redmoor. The first days, they had feasted, and there had been no talk of a treaty or any other type of negotiation. Later, there had been another celebration honoring the dragon riders. It was several days before the dwarf king addressed some of their concerns.

It had quickly become apparent that this diplomatic mission was going to take *much* longer than Rali and Sela had anticipated.

Rali's guard, Aor, stood directly behind him, as erect as a statue. Aor was an imposing figure, even among humans. Compared to the dwarves, he looked like a giant. Some of the clansmen gaped at him openly.

One dwarf was bold enough to approach him during the feast, reaching up to poke Aor's tattooed leg. Aor turned his head and stared silently at the dwarf, who gawked at him until King Hergung ordered him back to his seat.

Thorin Ulfarsson, Elias' old friend, sat near Rali during the meeting, offering whispered advice and answering questions. Thorin had volunteered to act as an additional guard, but he served as more of an ambassador than anything else.

"All this gossip is giving me a headache," Rali mumbled.

The conversation at the table grew heated for a moment. Two leaders were arguing over some procedural matters regarding trade policy.

Their voices droned on and on. It seemed to go on for ages.

Rali picked at his food and ignored everyone until he realized that all the clan leaders were staring at him. He had a feeling that the subject of conversation had changed suddenly.

A heavily-armored dwarf stood up to speak. It was Lord Sundergos, the leader of *Odenskapr*, the warrior clan. Sundergos was taller than the other dwarves at the table, although still shorter than a human.

"Cousins, where is your backbone?" said Sundergos, pounding his mailed fist on the table for emphasis. "Our people are the noblest race in all of Durn! We must honor our alliances. Why tarnish our spotless reputation?"

The lone female dwarf at the table lurched up out of her chair. It was Lady Bolrakei, the leader of *Klora-Kanna,* the jewelcutters' clan. The fat on her arms rippled, and her fingers glistened with goose fat from the feast. Despite her greasy arms and overall grubby appearance, her dress was made of fine silk, and she wore many pieces of expensive jewelry.

She gulped loudly, swallowing the food in her mouth before speaking. "Nay, nay!" she said. "I disagree with Sundergos! It is not our job to defend the humans!"

Thorin leaned forward to whisper in Rali's ear. "She's a salty one! All dwarves enjoy fine things, but ye'll never find a greedier clan than *Klora-Kanna,* and Bolrakei is the greediest of them all. She'll never risk 'er neck to help anyone else unless there's some profit in it for her."

Bolrakei ripped another leg from the goose in the center of the table, sniffed loudly, and then took her seat. She tore into the meat with relish, sucking noisily.

Sundergos wagged an accusing finger at her. "Bolrakei is cowardly! If we fail to help the humans, who will come to our aid when Vosper attacks Mount

Velik? Who will defend us?"

There was a murmur around the table, and a few of the other dwarves nodded. Bolrakei rolled her eyes.

"Sundergos, do you believe that we should send our armies to Parthos? What does our kingdom have to gain from such an alliance? What is *Odenskapr*'s official position?" asked King Hergung.

"My lord, we cannot ignore our human allies. Brighthollow is not a friend of our people. We cannot expect the elves to come to our aid. We know that Vosper is power-hungry. The emperor will never allow Mount Velik to remain neutral. Vosper will come: make no mistake."

"Sundergos glorifies battle!" said Bolrakei. "His clan is bloodthirsty. *Odenskapr* craves only war."

"That is not true. I prefer to avoid bloodshed," said Sundergos, "but war is inevitable."

Bolrakei waved her hand in the air. Her silver bangles chimed. "Foolishness! *Odenskapr* desires battle, and the spoils of war."

Sundergos shot her a withering look. "Watch your tongue, woman! It is the duty of our clan to *defend* this mountain. We take that responsibility very seriously. In the last war, we lost thousands of good soldiers; I lost my own father and two of my brothers during the battle."

"You are fear-mongering," said Bolrakei. "Nothing more."

"I speak the truth, and I won't be silenced!" Sundergos shouted. "We shall resist the empire to our last man." Sundergos sat back down, his armor clinking against the seat. "*Odenskapr* votes for a renewed alliance with the humans."

"And what say you, Utan?" said Hergung, pointing to the leader of the *Vardmiter* clan. The Vardmiters were the largest clan in terms of actual numbers, but the weakest in terms of wealth and political influence.

Utan remained seated. "*Vardmiter* abstains from opinion at this time," he grunted quietly.

Rali tried to read Utan's face, but his expression was an unreadable mask. Rali knew that most of the Vardmiter clan was desperately poor. They lived on the lowest levels of the mountain, crammed into a few small caves. They were social outcasts. Utan didn't have the political strength to oppose any of the other clans openly.

"And what say you, Akkeri?" asked Hergung, pointing to the leader of *Strikeforge*, the weaponsmiths' clan.

Akkeri stood up. He was lean and short with cunning eyes. Akkeri was also young, at least in dwarf terms. His face was smooth and unlined.

Strikeforge's membership was composed primarily of highly skilled metalworkers. The clan was small but had always been influential.

Akkeri must be a truly exceptional smith if he was elected to power at such a young age, thought Rali.

Akkeri spoke quietly, but with crisp authority. "*Strikeforge* is sympathetic to the plight of the humans. Parthos has always been a trusted ally. Of course, caution is warranted—assurances would have to be made, and oaths renewed. King Rali is young and untested—but weren't we all, at some point?"

"So, what is *Strikeforge*'s official position?" asked King Hergung.

Akkeri raised his cup and gazed directly at Rali. "*Strikeforge* supports an alliance with Parthos. My clan supports a treaty with the humans." Akkeri nodded at him, almost imperceptibly.

Thorin moved his mouth near Rali's ear again and whispered, "Akkeri is honorable. He's the youngest clan leader ever to be elected, but ye should see his weaponcraftin' skills! Never have I seen such a gifted smith. He's a marvel to watch! Like a tiny genius, he is."

Akkeri sat down, and the last clan leader rose from his seat, stroking his grizzled beard. The old dwarf's skin was wrinkled like an old potato. His knuckles were layered with thick calluses, hardened from years of mining.

"That's Skemtun," Thorin continued. "He's the leader of my own clan, *Marretaela.* He's lived through two wars, so he's wary, but he also supports a treaty with the humans."

Skemtun crossed his gnarled hands in front of him before he spoke. "My clan refrains from voting at this time. However, *Marretaela* supports a compassionate solution to this issue. That is all." He looked somberly at all the clan leaders for a moment, then sat down.

The room fell silent for a minute. Then the chatter started again. All the dwarves talked over each other, arguing back and forth.

Hergung stood up, striking his chalice with the back of his knife. *Tap! Tap! Tap!*

"Everyone, please, please... quiet!" Once everyone settled down, Hergung cleared his throat and turned to Rali. "Your Highness, it seems we are at another impasse. Our clans must come to an agreement on this matter, but it won't be tonight. I suggest we all enjoy the remainder of the feast and revisit this issue again in a few days."

Rali suppressed a groan. Blast! The next meeting will be another yelling match, with the same outcome as today.

Rali glanced at Sela, whose mouth was set in a tight line. His mother didn't attempt to hide her displeasure. Neither said anything—their hands were tied.

They *needed* this alliance, and they both knew it. Parthos wasn't strong enough to challenge the empire alone. Vosper was just too powerful. They were stuck here, at least for the time being.

Rali and Sela suffered through another hour of boring conversation, then Sela rose from her seat. "King Hergung, your feast has been wonderful. While I appreciate your hospitality, I must leave. Brinsop has not been fed today, and I must tend to my dragon's needs. Please forgive me."

The dwarf king waved his hand. "Of course, of

course! No apologies are necessary, Mistress Sela. Don't let us keep you from your duties."

As Sela left the table, she bowed to her son, addressing him formally in front of the clan leaders. "King Rali, I bid you good night. I shall meet you in your quarters tomorrow to discuss these matters."

Rali nodded, dismissing his mother. He knew that Sela had fabricated an excuse to leave, but he couldn't blame her. He would have left, too, if he could have. As it was, Rali would be stuck at the table until the wee hours of the morning, bored out of his wits. There was no reason why both of them should have to suffer.

Behind him, Thorin had straightened up his chair. The old dwarf was gazing wistfully at Sela's retreating figure, a dreamy expression on his face.

Thorin sighed. "What a *woman!*" he exclaimed softly.

Rali locked eyes with him, and Thorin's face turned a deep shade of red. Thorin dropped his gaze, embarrassed at being caught.

Rali raised an eyebrow. Was it possible? Was Thorin infatuated with Sela?

Thorin cleared his throat and pointedly struck up a conversation with a servant standing behind him.

Interesting, Rali thought. He had *assumed* that King Hergung assigned Thorin to act as their guide and counselor, but now he knew the real reason why Thorin was following them around.

Rali tucked his chin down, hiding his grin. *By*

Baghra's garters—Thorin is in love with my mother!

3. THE ELVES

Nydeired arched his back and flew straight up into the desert sky. A few times, he slowed down or lost altitude suddenly. It wasn't because of weakness—quite the opposite. Nydeired's wings were so powerful that he had difficulty controlling his speed.

Elias rubbed his irritated eyes. "This sandstorm is awful. I can hardly see anything."

"I'll try to get some more altitude," said Nydeired, straining against the wind.

Elias hooked his arm tighter onto the saddle's leather straps, trying to hold on. Nydeired faltered, dipping and weaving while he struggled to control his trajectory.

"Nydeired, this flight is pretty rough. You need more practice flying, and that includes practice carrying a rider."

"Sorry. The sand isn't bothering me, but the wind makes it hard for me to maneuver. Shall I turn around?" said Nydeired.

Elias paused for a moment, looking out upon the horizon. The storm was now behind them, and the desert was beautiful. They flew for another minute, into the stillness of the desert. "No, let's stay out for a while. I don't want to return to that tiny room, just to sit and do nothing. I just hope that Tallin doesn't spot us, or he'll be furious."

"*Tallin worries too much,*" said Nydeired. "*I wish he allowed us to explore the Death Sands more often. How will we ever learn how to fly together if we're not allowed to practice?*"

"In his defense, Tallin has valid reasons to worry. The desert is a treacherous place."

They flew on, passing away from the sandstorm and into the desert.

"*Hud-leyna!*" said Elias, casting a concealment spell around them. A year ago, it would have been impossible for him to maintain the spell around himself and a creature as large as Nydeired, but his powers had improved with practice.

"*It's an odd sensation when you cast that spell,*" said Nydeired. "*I feel like I'm back inside my egg.*"

"Tallin explained it to me—the spell is actually an illusion. The magic creates an invisible barrier around us, and the shield reflects the environment."

"*Like a mirror?*" said Nydeired.

Elias gave a thoughtful nod. "That's probably a good comparison. I performed my first concealment spell over a year ago. At first, I could barely hold the shield around myself, much less another person. Now I can easily conceal myself, as well as other objects."

They continued to fly north for about an hour and eventually came to an area with dozens of plateaus. Elias noticed an outcropping that would conceal them somewhat. Elias motioned for Nydeired to land. "Let's stop here, underneath that rock."

Nydeired swooped down, his enormous wings scraping the mountainside. They landed hard, and Nydeired stumbled into the dirt. Elias was thrown from the saddle, but he rolled and jumped up like a fighter. Elias was accustomed to these imperfect landings.

"Sorry about that. Smooth landings are tough. Are you all right?"

"I'm fine," said Elias, dusting himself off. "Let's crawl underneath this rock. We should stay out of sight. I'm maintaining the concealment spell around us for now, but I need to rest for a minute."

Elias and Nydeired crept under the outcropping. Elias could see Parthos in the distance, surrounded by a dust cloud. "Look at the storm. It's not moving across the desert like a natural sandstorm. It's staying right above the city. That's definitely the work of a spellcaster. Tallin and Duskeye must be searching for the mage who's causing the storms right now."

Nydeired's white scales gleamed in the moonlight, casting gentle reflections on the rocks. *"Do you think they'll find him?"*

Elias nodded. "They've been out almost every night this month. I'm sure they'll find out who's causing it eventually. The two of them make a good investigative team."

"Do you have a hunch? Who do you think is responsible for the storms?"

"Honestly, I have no idea. It might be more than

one person. I can't imagine how a single spellcaster could sustain a spell like that for so long. Spells that influence the weather are difficult to perform, much less maintain, for such a long period."

They sat quietly for a few minutes. "*Shall we do some exploring?*" asked Nydeired.

Elias chuckled, scratching underneath the dragon's massive chin. Nydeired purred. "Sure, why not? I'm enjoying this fresh air. I'll maintain the concealment spell around us so we won't be seen, but we have to return to Parthos soon. I don't want to risk getting caught out here by Tallin. Agreed?"

"*Agreed,*" said Nydeired, smiling. His red tongue flicked out.

Elias jumped on Nydeired's back and immediately saw a flash of silver, like a flicking mirror in the distance. "Do you see that?"

"*What? What did you see?*"

"I saw a glint of light—like a reflection." His brow wrinkled a little. "It's probably just my imagination... but even so, let's get out of here."

They took off into the sky. "*Hud-leyna!*" Elias said, casting a concealment spell as they left the ground.

Elias now saw several sparkling lights a short distance away. Larger than fireflies, but smaller than a fist, they ranged in color and intensity, pulsing silently in the air. The lights trailed after them, even though Elias had already cast his concealment spell.

"Nydeired, do you see those lights?" said Elias.

"*Yes. They're following us. And that's not all. I smell*

something." The dragon's nostrils flared as he inhaled the desert air.

Elias' heart started to pound. "What? Do you sense danger? Is it orcs?"

"No. I sense the fragrance of other dragons, both male and female." Nydeired inhaled deeply. *"Their scents are unfamiliar. These dragons are unknown to me."*

Elias' eyebrows shot up. "Are you sure?"

No one had seen another dragon in a long time—the last wild dragon Tallin found was Nagendra, a young carnelian female that had accepted Duskeye as a mate. That was over a year ago.

Elias opened his mouth to ask a question, but he felt a push. "Ugh! Nydeired! Someone is trying to pierce my barrier. I feel like I'm getting punched in the stomach; my spell is weakening!" The dragon stone that Elias carried began to vibrate, as it always did when he was in danger.

"What can I do?" Nydeired asked, his voice anxious.

"I feel dizzy—I can't concentrate. We have to land," said Elias.

Nydeired landed on a nearby hill, stumbling as he did so. He tried to steady himself but tripped over his own tail. Nydeired swayed in place for a moment and then toppled to the ground, his face planting in the dirt.

Elias jumped from the saddle, again landing on his feet.

"Letta-hud-leyna!" he said, releasing the concealment spell, pulling his magic back. It was useless

to try to hide; whoever was out there already knew their location.

"*This is my fault,*" Nydeired cried. "*We never should have come out here!*"

Elias was too dizzy to respond. He stumbled as a wave of nausea hit him. The whole world was spinning. Nydeired caught Elias as he fell, wrapping his tail around him before his body hit the ground.

In the distance, the spheres began a slow ascension toward their location. A soft melody filled the air, like the sound of songbirds. It was hypnotic. The lights floated lazily, bobbing and weaving around each other. As the glowing orbs approached, they changed shape. Elias watched the lights. As he stared, his expression became almost euphoric.

Panting with fear, Nydeired maneuvered his enormous body in a protective position around Elias' body.

"Isn't it lovely?" said Elias, sagging against Nydeired's body. The lights stopped a few paces away from them, right at the rock's edge.

Nydeired wasn't affected, and he wrapped his body tighter around Elias. A low growl rumbled in his throat. He spread his wings in warning. "*Elias! Snap out of it! Talk to me!*" said Nydeired, desperation in his voice.

This wasn't an enemy you could fight. Neither of them was prepared for anything like this.

The globes shimmered, then expanded. They took different shapes: some larger, some smaller. One of the lights took the form of a man, glowing rosy-white. It approached Elias, reaching out with its luminous arms.

Elias reached out too, straining against Nydeired's protective grip. Nydeired growled, jerking Elias back. His body flopped like a rag doll.

Other figures took shape: a female and another male. Three other globes grew larger, forming into the shape of dragons, all different colors.

The figures stopped advancing and held their positions. Nydeired opened his jaws, breathing fire toward the closest man. The glowing figure stood motionless, unaffected inside the flames.

Nydeired roared again, not knowing what to do. Seconds ticked by. Elias yawned and then closed his eyes. Nydeired laid the limp body of his friend on the ground and straddled it, covering Elias' body with his own.

"Stay back; do not come any closer!" growled Nydeired.

One of the figures responded in perfect *dragontongue.* "I am a friend, Nydeired. You need not be afraid of us."

"How do you know my name? What are you?" asked Nydeired.

"You are known throughout our kingdom, Nydeired. The first white dragon in generations. We are here to help you—we mean you no harm." The figure took another step forward.

"Stop! Do not come any closer!" Nydeired crawled back, dragging Elias' limp body with him.

"Calm yourself. You cannot harm me," said the

man. "It is useless to try."

"*What have you done to Elias?*" said Nydeired.

The man gave a low chuckle. "Nothing, really. Your friend has been charmed. Humans who are unused to our presence react oddly at times. Do not worry. The effect is only temporary."

Just then, the air shimmered, and the night sky filled with brilliant light. Nydeired looked up to see Tallin and Duskeye swooping down from the sky.

Nydeired exhaled a sigh of relief. He had never been so happy to see anyone in his life.

"Nydeired, move out of the way!" shouted Tallin as he and Duskeye landed.

Nydeired scooped Elias up and covered him with his wing. Elias was mumbling incoherently, still delirious.

Tallin faced the glowing man. "That's far enough!" he shouted, drawing his falchion.

Duskeye opened his sapphire jaws, shooting a river of flame toward the figures. The strangers stepped back a few paces but otherwise remained unaffected.

Duskeye swung his head and addressed Nydeired angrily. "*Foolish fledgling! You have put yourself and your rider in incredible danger. This little 'excursion' of yours was as foolish as anything you've ever done. I'll deal with you when we get back to Parthos. Believe me, you will pay for this disobedience. But for now, step back and keep Elias safe.*"

Nydeired tucked his head down, chastised. He was humiliated but still incredibly relieved.

Nydeired dragged Elias back a safe distance while Tallin and Duskeye faced off against the shining figures.

Tallin pointed his sword and addressed the group: "I order you to drop your *glamour*, all of you!"

"Ha! Such boldness!" The glowing man chuckled. "Do not presume to bark orders at me, *dwarf*. I am not a common servant. You can't control me with your shouted commands." The last sentence was tinged with ice.

"I recognize that voice," snarled Tallin. "Reveal yourself, Carnesîr. I won't play your *glamour-games*. Not here. This desert is my home, and it would be a mistake to test my mettle in this place."

The man let out a heavy sigh. "Very well," he said, waving his right hand in a high arc. Rose-colored sparkles filled the air, and the *glamour* dissipated, revealing three elves.

"I knew it was you," Tallin hissed.

Carnesîr was the eldest of the three, with silver-gray hair that ran down the small of his back. The other male elf was younger, with blond hair cropped at the shoulder. The last elf was a young female with silvery blonde hair. Her skin was milky-white, but her eyes and eyebrows were the deepest shade of black.

To Tallin's surprise, the elves were accompanied by four dragons—three adults and one little green hatchling. The hatchling clung desperately to his mother, a carnelian dragon with familiar scars on one leg.

"By Baghra!" said Tallin. "Nagendra, is that you? And you have a hatchling!"

Nagendra raised her head proudly. "*Yes, it is I,*" she said. Tallin approached Nagendra slowly. She did not wince as she had during their meeting in the desert over a year ago.

"I see you have been bound to a rider," said Tallin. "Congratulations, little sister."

"*Thank you, fleshling,*" she said, staring at Dusk-eye intently. "*After our meeting in the desert, I traveled north, hoping to find Brighthollow, the enchanted land that you described. It was an arduous journey, but worth it. Brighthollow is lovelier than I ever imagined. There are no humans, no orcs, and no dragon hunters there. It is a true paradise.*"

"Living among the elves has been a positive thing for you. How did you manage to find Brighthollow?"

"*The journey to Brighthollow was treacherous, and I encountered many dangers. It was difficult, but I persevered. Once I arrived in their enchanted land, I was welcomed by the elves and eventually matched with Amandila, my rider. We went through the binding ceremony mere weeks ago, right after my hatchling emerged from his egg.*"

Amandila bowed. The female elf carried her half of the dragon stone implanted in her chest. The stone gleamed dark crimson in the moonlight.

The elf's dragon stone was set in gold, with a thin ring of the precious metal visible at the circumference of the implant. The other two elves had identical implants embedded in their chests, their onyx stones ringed by a circle of gold.

The little green hatchling played happily with Nagendra's tail, which swished back and forth in the sand. Amandila stroked Nagendra's neck while staring intently at Tallin with her black eyes.

Nagendra looked at Duskeye and inclined her head to him.

Duskeye knew instantly that he had sired Nagendra's fledgling. He did not approach his former mate or the hatchling—it would have been a breach of etiquette. Instead, he bowed his head and purred, greeting her formally. "*Nagendra, it pleases me greatly to see you in such good health.*"

"*Thank you,*" she nodded, acknowledging Duskeye's greeting. Her tongue flicked out demurely, then she wrapped her wing around her hatchling, lifting the tiny dragon off the ground. She flexed open her wing, displaying the hatchling for Duskeye to see. The little dragon was perfect—brilliant green, like the first leaves of spring. Duskeye's chest expanded with pride, but he said nothing.

The other two dragons present were both onyx males. They were larger than Duskeye but smaller than Nydeired, who towered over all the others by at least a third.

Tallin turned to Duskeye and asked quietly, "Did you know that Nagendra was living among the elves?"

"*Truthfully, I did not,*" answered Duskeye. "*But she asked me many questions about Brighthollow. I answered them to the best of my ability. I always suspected that some of our kin had escaped to Brighthollow to live in isolation with the elves. Nagendra must have risked the dangerous journey to Brighthollow to ensure the safety of her hatchling."*

Carnesîr turned and introduced the others. He pointed to the female elf. "You've already met Amandila and her dragon, Nagendra. Fëanor and Blacktooth are behind me, and this is my dragon-companion, Poth."

Carnesîr pointed at the oldest dragon. Poth yawned, lifting one wing in greeting. Poth was *ancient*; most of his teeth were missing, and his eyes were cloudy-cataract blue. His scales were faded, more charcoal gray than black. The other onyx dragon was much younger and paired with the blond male elf.

"How many other dragons live in Brighthollow?" asked Tallin.

"We are not at liberty to disclose that information," said Carnesîr. "Queen Xiiltharra has given specific orders to that effect."

Tallin rolled his eyes. "Fine, don't tell us. Why does it matter if we know, anyway?"

Carnesîr shrugged. "Maybe it doesn't matter, but we cannot disobey a direct order from our queen."

"We can tell you that there are very few," said Amandila, ignoring Carnesîr's angry glare. "The magic of Brighthollow hinders dragon fertility. Nagendra arrived at Brighthollow already bearing her egg. She would not have been able to have her hatchling otherwise."

"All right, enough about that." Carnesîr cleared his throat and changed the subject. "Master Tallin! I'm pleased to see that you were able to extricate yourself from the *predicament* that you were in."

Tallin narrowed his eyes at him. "What do you mean?"

Carnesîr's steely blue eyes were mocking. "I'm referring to your unfortunate capture and subsequent incarceration. I'm pleased that you were able to escape Vosper's dungeons. How did you manage it?"

The elf's voice lilted like birdsong; it was mesmerizing, even when the words cut like a knife.

Forcing his voice to calmness, Tallin said, "If you're referring to my months in captivity in Morholt, then yes, I escaped. Duskeye and I were very lucky."

"Well, that's *wonderful* news," said Carnesîr.

There was no *obvious* hint of sarcasm in the elf's voice, but Tallin knew Carnesîr was baiting him. Tallin bit back a reply. As always, it was the nature of the elves to play with mortal emotions.

Tallin reflected on the first time he met Carnesîr. It was during the Dragon Wars. Carnesîr, along with a few other elves, arrived at Mount Velik to aid the dwarves against their battle with Vosper. The elves fought valiantly, and their powerful spellcasters saved many lives.

Although the dwarves were ultimately grateful for their aid, it was always challenging to be in their presence. The elves were arrogant, callous, and cruel. Some of the elves fathered children with dwarf women, only to leave when the war was over. Now, as before, Tallin could feel his patience wearing thin.

"So you're here officially then?" said Tallin. "I must admit some surprise. Has your ice queen finally softened?"

Carnesîr fixed him with a lightly contemptuous stare and replied blandly, "The official position of Queen Xiiltharra remains unchanged. We are here merely as an interested group, not in any official capacity."

"I see," said Tallin. "So Brighthollow remains neutral, as always?"

"Yes, and so it shall remain. But rest assured, our queen is sympathetic to your cause. Brighthollow knows about the murder of the elf-rider, Riona, and her dragon, Stormshard. We also know about your traitor, Hanko, and how his shameful treachery directly contributed to Riona's death."

Tallin's eyebrows shot up. "How do you know about Hanko? We never sent messengers to Xiiltharra."

Carnesîr snorted. "Don't be so naïve. You have your informants, as do we. Is it not true that one of your riders turned traitor?"

"Unfortunately, yes... it is true," Tallin admitted. "Hanko turned traitor for the empire last year. A Balborite assassin stole his dragon stone, and Vosper blackmailed him."

"Is there any doubt of his guilt?"

"No," Tallin grimly admitted. "He confessed."

43

Carnesîr nodded slightly. "Where is your traitor now?"

"He's not in Parthos. Hanko is a prisoner of the High Council; he awaits trial in Miklagard. If your intent is to kill him, you won't satisfy your vengeance here."

Carnesîr scoffed, waving his hand. "Don't be silly. Elves do not lust for *revenge*. That is strictly a mortal failing. It is against our nature."

"Then why *are* you here?" said Tallin.

Carnesîr didn't seem to notice Tallin's anger, or wasn't worried about it if he did. "The queen recognizes that Parthos is experiencing certain *difficulties*. It would be remiss to ignore the implications of that. That is why we're here."

"And just what 'difficulties' would you be referring to?" said Tallin, this time through clenched teeth. He didn't like the elves even in the best of times, but now he was really starting to lose his patience.

Carnesîr sighed, brushing imaginary dust off his clothing. "Well, Mitca was killed, only to be replaced by a child-king. Riona, the only elf-rider on Durn, was brutally murdered, along with her dragon. And one of your *human* riders turned traitor. You must admit that the situation is grave."

"It's not as bad as it sounds," Tallin proclaimed, not rising to the bait but still feeling the need to defend his people. "Parthos is strong. We have two new dragon riders, Galti and Holf, who are training in Miklagard now. Sela and Rali are negotiating a treaty with the dwarves as we speak."

"And how are the treaty negotiations progressing?" asked Carnesîr.

Tallin crossed his arms over his chest and frowned. "I don't see how that's any of your business." In truth, the negotiations were not going very well. But he wasn't about to tell Carnesîr any of that. He could keep secrets, too.

"Oh, my mortal friend, I can see that you do not realize the gravity of the situation. The emperor plans to conquer both Mount Velik and Parthos; his preparations are nearly complete."

"Yes, we know," said Tallin. "That information is not news to us."

Carnesîr shook his head and sighed, as though astounded by Tallin's stupidity. "Then how can you ignore the danger? Vosper is the most power-hungry emperor in a millennium. It's tragic, really. The mortal races are prone to such feebleness of character... so much misery and suffering for nothing."

"Is that a question or a statement? I didn't ask for a history lesson, Carnesîr. Parthos has done a fine job defending itself so far, and *without* the elves' help. Speaking of which—are you causing the sandstorms?"

"Yes, it's our doing," Carnesîr admitted. "We've been steadily increasing the frequency of the sandstorms for months. It's a protective measure. Parthos is safer during the storms. We've also been monitoring the desert for other dangers. Amandila and Nagendra captured a Balborite assassin just a few days ago."

Tallin was going to ask about the assassin, but Elias interrupted their conversation with a loud moan. "Ugh… my head. What happened?"

"You were charmed by elvish magic," said Tallin. "Cast your wards, Elias. Do not move any closer until you're protected."

Elias staggered to his feet, and Nydeired put his tail around his waist to keep him from falling.

"Are you all right?" Nydeired asked quietly. *"Your skin looks very white."*

"I feel dreadful," said Elias. "My body itches all over." He shook his head and took a deep breath, trying to clear his mind. "How long was I out?"

"Only a short while. The elves cast a spell on you." Nydeired quickly explained what happened.

"Traust-nand-rammlingr," Elias said, quickly reciting the wards that would protect him from the elves' enchantments.

A short distance away, the terse exchange between Tallin and Carnesîr continued. Elias was astounded by how attractive the elves were. He had never seen such beautiful creatures. Their skin was flawless. Even Carnesîr, who was obviously the eldest of the three, had no wrinkles on his face.

Each of the elves' dragons, save the hatchling, wore an exquisite saddle made from spun silver. Their dragons had an air of dignity and serenity that seemed almost regal.

Duskeye and Nydeired, tired and covered with dust, looked like grimy ragamuffins in comparison.

Tallin turned away from Carnesîr, lowering his voice to a whisper. "Elias, it's not safe for you here. I want you and Nydeired to return to Parthos immediately."

"I'm so sorry," Elias blurted. "I didn't mean to cause trouble."

Tallin held up his hand. "I know you didn't. Don't worry about that, and don't say another word. The elves can hear everything we say—they have better hearing than bats. We'll talk later. Just get out of here. Fly straight to Parthos, and don't stop. The sandstorm is waning."

Elias obeyed, silently mounting Nydeired's back.

Tallin turned to face the elves. They all had the same placid expression on their faces. It made him want to scream. He waited until Elias and Nydeired had flown some distance, and then he mounted Duskeye and flew away from the plateau.

When he looked back, the elves had disappeared. Colored orbs floated in their place. The elves had restored their glamour. The globes floated upward, rotating around each other like fireflies.

When they reached Parthos, Tallin and Duskeye disappeared without saying anything to Elias or Nydeired.

At the very least, Elias had expected to receive a firm scolding. Tallin's silence puzzled him more.

Whether they liked it or not, the elves had come to the desert. Was their presence a blessing... or a *curse?*

4. GREED

Back at Mount Velik, Rali walked wearily back to his quarters, exhausted after another long night of fruitless negotiations. Days had turned into weeks. Now a month had passed without any real progress. Aor and Thorin followed silently behind him. Thorin struggled to keep up while juggling his ever-present pipe.

Eventually, they arrived at their suite. The two dwarf soldiers stationed at the entrance stepped aside, making room for Aor and Rali to pass. Thorin stumbled inside seconds later, gasping for breath.

Rali collapsed into a chair, rubbing his temples. "By Baghra, what a mess. I was hoping we could return to Parthos weeks ago. Do the clans always argue like this?"

Thorin nodded. "Aye—the clans are rarely in agreement, especially at the beginnin' of these negotiations."

"The *beginning* of negotiations?" said Rali incredulously. "Golka's curses! It's been a bloody *month* already, and we're no closer to a treaty now than when we arrived. At this rate, my beard will be gray, and Vosper will have conquered all of Durn before the clans come to an agreement."

"Now, now, yer highness, it's not as bad as all that.

Ye must admit that we've made *some* progress."

Rali groaned. "I certainly don't see it, and we're running out of time. The intelligence reports coming from Morholt aren't good. No one knows for sure when Vosper will attempt another attack, but I expect it sooner rather than later."

Just then, Sela arrived, followed closely by her dragon. Brinsop crawled in sideways to pass through the narrow entrance. Sela had stopped attending the negotiations, although she decided to stay at Mount Velik to offer advisory support and additional security.

Sela walked over to Rali and kissed him gently on the forehead, ignoring honorifics while they were in private. "Hello, son. How did the negotiations go today?"

"More of the same, unfortunately," said Rali. "We're at an impasse. The clans refuse to sign a treaty. The clans can't even agree on the terms."

"Don't get discouraged," said Sela. "Everything moves slower here, son. For the dwarves, no decision is taken lightly."

"I know, I know," said Rali, putting his face in his hands. "That's what everyone keeps telling me, but I'm still dreading the next meeting. The talks began well enough—everyone polite, talking pleasantries. But it always ends in a screaming match."

"I'm sorry, but we have no choice," said Sela. "We must stay. The elves will never agree to a treaty with us. And since I was unable to secure a treaty with King Selwyn, that leaves only the dwarves as potential allies. "

Rali sighed. "It wouldn't be so bad, if it wasn't for Bolrakei. She fights us at every turn. She's positively dreadful."

Thorin nodded in agreement. "Bolrakei's doin' everythin' she can to derail these talks. And she's very convincin' when she wants to be."

"Indeed," said Rali. "I've seen the evidence of her *persuasiveness* every day since we've arrived."

"She'll be the last holdout," said Thorin. "She always is."

"Well, Thorin, you're familiar with dwarf politics," said Sela. "What do you suggest we do to move these negotiations along? I may be forced to return to Parthos soon, and I would hate to leave Rali here to fend for himself."

"I understand, Miss Sela. May I make a suggestion?"

"Yes, of course," said Rali. "Anything to get us out of here sooner would be a blessing."

"Bolrakei is crafty, but deep in her heart, she's a businesswoman. There's more to her refusals than simple politics. Find out what she really wants, and she'll cooperate. The truth is, if war comes to Mount Velik, it affects *Klora-Kanna* less than the other clans. The jewelcutters' clan continues making money, even durin' the war. They did durin' the Dragon Wars and durin' the Orc Wars, too. Business will continue as usual for them, whether we're at war, or not."

"If she has nothing to lose, why is she opposing the treaty?" asked Sela. "Is it on philosophical grounds? Or does she simply dislike humans in general?"

"Nay," said Thorin. "She's holdin' out for some type of concession. Ye must have somethin' she wants."

"Hmm. I didn't think of that," said Rali. "We ask for an audience with her, then?"

"Nay, nay, that's not how ye do it," said Thorin. "Ye can't let the other clan leaders know that ye've reached out to her. She won't respond to ye directly."

"Well, how do we find out what she wants if she won't talk to us?" said Rali with exasperation. "Baghra's garters! Nothing is ever easy with the dwarves."

"Get used to it, son," Sela chuckled. "Believe me, it's not much easier with other leaders. Human politics are equally frustrating at times."

"So, Thorin, what do you suggest?" said Rali.

Thorin grinned. "Give me until tomorrow. At the very least, ye'll be a wee bit closer to a resolution. I'll speak to a few of me kin, and we'll get somethin' goin' for ye," said Thorin, winking. Then he turned on his heel and left the chamber, whistling down the hallway.

Rali turned to Sela. "Do you have any idea what he's going to do?"

"I haven't the foggiest," said Sela. "But Thorin is an experienced negotiator. I trust him. Whatever his plan, as long as it helps to break this gridlock, it's a good thing."

Brinsop, who had been lying quietly in one corner, piped up. "Perhaps the old dwarf plans to bribe the fat one. Fat humans are like dragons. They like eating lots of food. He could offer her some cake. Humans like cake."

"Perhaps," said Sela, laughing.

"But what could she want?" asked Rali. "Money? She couldn't possibly need more. Bolrakei's already dripping with gold and jewels."

Sela sighed. "Greed takes many forms, son. I would not be surprised if Thorin returns with some outlandish request from that woman."

Early the next day, Thorin stood outside the private chambers of Bolrakei Shalevault, the leader of the jewelcutters' clan. Bolrakei's guards announced his presence and escorted Thorin into her luxurious private room. The walls were embedded with semi-precious gems, set in mosaics in swirling designs.

In the center of the room, Bolrakei reclined on an enormous upholstered sofa. All the furniture was draped in red velvet, and Bolrakei herself was dressed in red robes. As always, her neck and wrists were adorned with jewels.

Although Bolrakei had changed her clothes from the previous evening, she hadn't bothered to bathe —her arms, hands, and face still glistened with fat from the banquet.

"Good day, mistress," said Thorin, bowing deeply.

"Well, well… if it isn't Thorin, one of King Hergung's favorites. To what do I owe the pleasure of this visit?"

"Mistress Bolrakei, I've been sent here to speak with ye regardin' a private issue."

Bolrakei wiggled to the end of the couch, belching loudly once she was upright. She scratched absently at her distended belly. "Would this have something to do with our visitors, the dragon rider and her royal whelp?"

"Aye, mistress," said Thorin. "King Rali was wonderin' if ye would consider a compromise."

"Ah, I see," said Bolrakei, licking her lips. "You're here to negotiate. As a matter of fact, there *is* something I desire from your human friends." Then she paused, her face eager.

Thorin waited for a moment, and when Bolrakei did not elaborate, he asked, "Well? What is it that ye want exactly?"

Bolrakei demurred. "Thorin, look at all my jewels." She swept her flabby arms in the air, pointing at the gem-encrusted walls. "Aren't they breathtaking? These, as well as the thousands in my vault, are my legacy. *Klora-Kanna* is the wealthiest clan in all of Mount Velik—our precious stones are the finest in the land, sought after by kings and commoners alike!" Her voice rose at the end, and she beat her fist against her chest with pride.

"Is that what you want?" asked Thorin. "More

jewels?"

Bolrakei rose up and twirled on her heel. He was shocked by how fast she could move, considering her size. "More jewels? No... not really. I'm interested in a single jewel. The rarest gemstone of all. The only gemstone that I don't currently own."

"What is that exactly?" asked Thorin, his expression puzzled.

"I want a *living* dragon stone," she said.

"A living dragon stone? But that's impossible," Thorin said incredulously.

She smirked slightly. "No, it's not, actually. I own several dragon stones already. The problem is that they're all *dead stones*—from deceased riders and dead dragons. They're shattered, cracked, or splintered. They're gray and ugly. What good is a stone like that? No, they just won't do. I need a dragon stone from a *live* dragon rider for my collection."

"It cannot be done, Mistress Bolrakei."

"Yes, it can! Don't lie to me. Rali can arrange this if he so chooses. He's the leader of Parthos, is he not? His realm is the last dragon sanctuary, and his own mother is a dragon rider!"

Thorin protested again. "My lady, it's an evil thing to separate a rider from his stone."

"Bah! Who says it's evil? The dragon riders? Their power has all but disappeared from this land. All negotiations have a price—and this is mine. I want that stone!" She seemed to stop herself and closed her eyes for a moment.

"This talk is unseemly, my lady," said Thorin,

frowning.

"Who are *you* to tell me what's 'unseemly,' eh, *earth-digger?*" she spat, using an offensive epithet for Thorin's clan, *Marretaela*.

Thorin bristled at the insult, but he had determined not to lose his temper.

Bolrakei detected his discomfort and laughed. Then she walked back to her sofa and sank into the plush cushions, watching him with contemptuous eyes.

Thorin tried again to reason with her. "Ye won't reconsider? Ye want a *living* dragon stone? Is that really the price for yer cooperation, my lady?"

"Yes. Now stop looking so surprised, and go tell your human friends that I'll continue to block treaty negotiations until I get my stone."

"And if they don't agree?" said Thorin.

"Then I know the humans aren't serious about their desire for a treaty with us. Don't forget, Thorin... no one can hide secrets from me. I have spies everywhere. I know about the mageborn boy. He carries an emerald dragon stone from another rider. That stone would suit me just fine."

"How do ye know this information?" asked Thorin.

"Humans are easy to bribe, almost pathetically so, and I can afford the best informants. *Klora-Kanna* has spies throughout the empire, even in Morholt. My spies make these political negotiations more enjoyable, at least for me."

Thorin knew she wasn't going to change her

mind. "All right then," he said. "I will relay yer message to King Rali and Sela. But there ain't no guarantees."

"Of course," said Bolrakei, waving him off. "You're just a simple messenger, after all."

Thorin bowed, backing out of the chamber. Once he reached the exit, Bolrakei called him back. "Thorin!"

"Yes, mistress?" asked Thorin, looking over his shoulder.

"This conversation *never happened*—understood?" she said, her eyes narrowing into slits. "If you tell Hergung, I'll have you branded a liar. No one will ever believe your word against mine."

"Understood, my lady," he replied.

Thorin left the chamber. As soon as he was a safe distance away, Thorin stopped, taking a deep breath.

She wants a livin' dragon stone! he thought. A dragon stone torn from the chest of a *livin'* rider!

The very idea made his stomach churn. Thorin pulled out his pipe and filled it with smokeleaf. His hands were shaking. Now he had to relay this dreadful request to King Rali and Sela.

Thorin realized something. Bolrakei Shalevault, the leader of *Klora-Kanna*, was the dragon riders' enemy.

5. CARNESÎR

T he next morning, the sun rose on the city of Parthos. That was when the elves decided to arrive.

"The elves are here! The elves are here!" screamed a frantic palace servant, running downstairs to alert the rest of the staff. The elves and their dragons materialized in the sky over the city like jeweled giants.

Amandila and Nagendra arrived first, followed closely by Fëanor and Blacktooth. Several minutes later, Carnesîr and the elder dragon Poth arrived, flying slower than the others. The citizens of Parthos came out and observed them with wonder.

Tallin and Duskeye were already waiting on the palace rooftop. Tallin wore his finest leather armor. Duskeye had been outfitted with an elaborate dragon saddle. Elias stood close by, dressed in a clean tunic and new breeches.

Tallin had awakened Elias before dawn; he had correctly predicted that the elves would make their formal appearance in Parthos today.

As they stood on the ramparts, Elias watched Tallin's lips move silently. He was spellcasting—setting his protective wards before the elves landed. Elias followed suit, also casting his wards. Tallin had warned him ahead of time.

Carnesîr and Poth flew in and landed softly. The other dragons landed silently as well, except for Nagendra's hatchling, who stumbled when he jumped down from Nagendra's saddle. Nagendra gathered the hatchling into her wing.

The three dragons clustered together, with Poth at the head of the group. Elias wondered how old Poth was; he looked so different from the others.

Carnesîr smiled and raised his hand in greeting. Tallin did not return the greeting. Instead, he stood quietly, his mouth set in a tight line.

"Tallin?" said Carnesîr, his voice like birdsong again. "What a surprise to see you again. I expected King Rali to greet us. Is he not present?"

"No, not at the moment," Tallin replied cautiously. "King Rali is on a diplomatic mission. I am the acting steward in his absence."

Carnesîr waited for Tallin to elaborate, but Tallin said nothing.

The elf made an exasperated expression. "And Sela? Where is she? I would like to speak with her."

"Sela is not here either," said Tallin.

Elias remained silent during the exchange, which was getting frostier by the second.

"Well, why don't you tell me where they are?" Carnesîr said, his voice deceptively mild. "You know that I can easily scry their location."

"Then *do* it, Carnesîr," said Tallin. "It's not my place to disclose the location of my king and my superior officer. Besides, I suspect that you've already determined their location."

Carnesîr laughed; the sound was like wind chimes. "You're right, dwarf. We already know that Rali and Sela are at Mount Velik."

"I dislike playing games with the fair folk, Carnesîr," said Tallin.

"Who's playing games?" Carnesîr asked, innocent-like.

"Are we going to keep dancing around like this?" asked Tallin. "Because I don't have all day to stand here and play word games with you. Unlike you, I actually have work to do."

The elf gave a snort of laughter. "Very well. You're right...we already know that Rali is attempting to forge an alliance with the dwarves. And it is our understanding that the treaty talks are on the verge of collapse."

"That's a bold statement," said Tallin. "Negotiating with dwarves is always a delicate affair. But Parthos is committed to an alliance with Mount Velik."

"A *delicate affair*? Is that how you see it? That's an *optimistic* way of looking at the situation. Of course, you're a dwarf, so your opinion of these matters is somewhat subjective." The other two elves nodded in agreement.

Tallin was about to lose his patience. He gritted his teeth. A wisp of smoke escaped from Duskeye's nostrils. The dragon had tensed during the discussion, sensing Tallin's discomfort.

The elves' dragons said nothing, but at one point,

Poth snorted and shook his head as though he and Carnesîr were sharing some private joke.

Elias started to understand Tallin's distaste for the elves. Everything Carnesîr said was condescending, rude, or pompous, in a blasé, offhand way. The elves treated mortals like ignorant children.

Tallin leaned in and whispered in Elias' ear. "Speak softly or not at all, and keep refreshing your wards. I can feel Carnesîr trying to pierce mine—it's subtle, but I know it's happening. They're trying to sway our emotions, trying to gather more information. It's a passive attack. Elves are masters at this type of spellcasting. Don't let your guard down for a second."

Carnesîr caught Elias' eye, and Elias felt something like an itch on the back of his neck. His protective wards activated, and he felt a subtle drain of energy. Like their first encounter in the desert, Elias felt nauseated.

"I feel sick—like I'm going to vomit," whispered Elias.

"That's normal," replied Tallin quietly. "Just relax and try to concentrate. It's a reaction to the elves' magic pushing against your wards. Just concentrate. Once they leave, the feeling will go away."

Elias bit his lip and tried to keep his breakfast from coming up.

Tallin faced the elves again. He needed to end this conversation. And fast, before Elias threw up. "Carnesîr, what is the official reason for your visit?"

Carnesîr waved his hand nonchalantly. "Of

course. How silly of me; I get distracted so easily. We've come to help guard the city."

"I see. Well, thank you, but no. We're managing fine without your help," said Tallin. "I have no intention of leaving Parthos at this time, and I haven't received any orders to the contrary."

"Tsk, tsk, Tallin," said Carnesîr, wagging his finger as though he was scolding a child. "Think carefully. You're the only dwarf rider in the entire kingdom. Your presence at Mount Velik is *imperative* for treaty talks to succeed. Rali needs your support. You must realize this."

Tallin frowned. Carnesîr had a point. "I'm aware of the current dilemma, but I have my duties here. I must continue to train Elias and Nydeired."

"Come now. Be reasonable. Let's put aside our petty disagreements for a moment. I'm fully capable of defending a little mortal city like Parthos. And don't you think it's time for Elias to move to the next step in his training?"

"Next step? What do you mean?" asked Tallin.

"Shouldn't the boy be training with his father?"

"What?" asked Elias, the blood draining from his face.

Tallin groaned. "Carnesîr, don't..."

"What does he mean?" asked Elias. "Tallin, what is he talking about?"

Carnesîr held his gaze. "So, the boy still doesn't know about Chua? Typical. You mortals and your foolish sentiments."

Tallin turned to Elias. "I'm sorry. I didn't want

you to find out like this."

"My father is *alive?*" Another wave of nausea hit him, and Elias clutched his stomach. He struggled to maintain his wards.

"Yes, it's true," Tallin admitted. "Your father is alive. He lives in the east."

Elias' face was stricken, almost as though he was in physical pain. "W-why didn't you tell me? How could you keep something like this a secret?"

"Elias, I had good reasons for keeping this information from you," said Tallin, "not the least of which was your father's own request to keep his existence a secret."

"But…" said Elias.

"I'm sorry, Elias," said Tallin quietly. "But this conversation must wait. This was an attempt to shock you and weaken your protective wards. Don't let them break through your shielding. As soon as the elves leave, I'll answer all of your questions, I promise."

Elias nodded, gagging through another wave of nausea. Tallin was right—the elves were trying to fracture his wards. He tried to focus.

Tallin faced Carnesîr. "How did you know that Chua was alive?"

Carnesîr broke into a lilting laugh. "Oh, Tallin, surely you can't think that our queen would be ignorant of Chua's existence? He's the *living oracle!* His magic affects that entire region. We've known about him for a dozen years."

"But how…?" asked Tallin.

Carnesîr rolled his eyes. "Tallin, the Elder Willow is *thousands* of years old. Its existence predates mortal records. That sacred grove was planted by *my people*, not yours. You must have suspected this. The tree sprites are cousins to the elves; those that safeguard the grove have been providing Queen Xiiltharra with regular reports."

"If you knew this all along, why get involved now?" asked Tallin.

"Because of the prophecy... a mageborn boy and a white dragon." Carnesîr tipped his hand in Elias' direction. "There could be no other. Until now, the elves have observed but declined to get involved. All was well until Chua decided to surrender his dragon stone to the boy. That changed everything. Even now, I can feel the presence of Chua's stone." Carnesîr's piercing eyes fixated on the leather pouch hanging from Elias' neck. "You have it on your person, don't you, boy?"

"Yes," said Elias, not bothering to lie. "I'm carrying the stone. I always have it with me. Nydeired and I haven't gone through our binding ceremony yet."

"Of course you haven't," said Carnesîr. "But soon, you shall. And then you'll be bound to Nydeired forever. After that, the prophecy will unfold like a bedroll. It was a brilliant move on Chua's part, leaving his dragon stone where his son could find it. What a thoughtful and inventive way to start a war, don't you think?"

"It was never Chua's intent to start a war," said

Tallin. "Chua was only trying to protect his son."

"Protect his son?" Carnesîr put a hand on his chest, as if shocked. "At the expense of the entire mortal kingdom? It boggles the mind how short-sighted you mortals are. Chua is a *seer*—he *knew* what would happen if he planted his dragon stone in the forest, and he chose to do it anyway. He bears the fault in this, and there's an element of revenge in his actions. Chua was tortured and disfigured by the emperor, and this is his chance for retribution."

"You're wrong," snapped Tallin, more harshly than intended. He was letting Carnesîr get to him. "This is not about revenge. Chua was merely doing what he thought was right."

Carnesîr went on as if he hadn't spoken. "The emperor has always been rather unstable, you know. But now, with news of the prophecy spreading like wildfire, Vosper has been whipped into a frenzy. It's just a matter of time before he attacks your precious city in earnest."

"Vosper's victory isn't guaranteed. Chua told me as much, and you must know it too," said Tallin.

"Victory or no, Vosper won't rest until Elias and Nydeired are dead, and Parthos is destroyed."

Tallin smiled thinly. "We are perfectly capable of defending this city. In fact, we defended Parthos against an orc siege quite recently. And we did it *without* your help—or that of your queen."

"You were lucky," said Carnesîr. "The attacks on Parthos shall escalate. You can't defend Parthos alone. Admit it. You need our help, Tallin. To refuse our goodwill would be a mistake."

"We're not *asking* for your assistance!" Tallin shouted. He was so angry he could barely talk.

Duskeye locked eyes with Tallin, reaching out silently with his mind. *"My friend, set aside your anger. I know that the elves are insufferable, but we could use their help. Someone needs to watch the city. The elves are strong enough to defend it. With them here, you could go to Mount Velik and help Rali. And even though you may not want to hear it, it's time for Elias to meet his father."*

"Golka's curses," said Tallin, running his fingers through his red curls. As much as he disliked it, Duskeye had a point. "Give me until sundown. I must contact Sela and Rali. The final decision is theirs."

"Good," Carnesîr said, nodding. "That's a much better attitude. I'll expect your answer tonight then. If you prefer to speak with me in person, I'll meet you at Salamander Caverns after sundown." The elf smiled and turned to leave. A few seconds later, they were gone, leaving Elias and Tallin on the rooftop in the blistering heat.

As soon as the elves were a safe distance away, Elias walked to the wall and vomited over the ramparts.

"Sorry, Elias. I should have prepared you better for this," said Tallin sympathetically. "Learning to resist elf magic is difficult, especially if they are trying to target you specifically. It will get easier with practice."

Elias couldn't face him. His head pounded, and his nausea was almost overwhelming. "So it's true,

Tallin? What Carnesîr said? My father is still alive?"

"Yes, it's true. Chua is alive, and so is Starclaw, his dragon. They live inside the Elder Willow. Your father is the oracle of the east."

"Why didn't you tell me this before?" said Elias, his voice breaking.

Tallin sighed. "I made a promise to your father. And you weren't ready. In fact, you still aren't. But there is nothing we can do about it now. It's time for you to meet him and learn about your past."

Elias wanted to ask more questions, but his head felt like it was going to burst. Another wave of nausea hit him. He retched into a nearby trash bin.

"Why don't you go lie down in your quarters? The nausea will pass in a few hours. There's no remedy for it—you just need to sleep it off. I'll come to your room later and answer any questions you have."

"Okay," said Elias, nodding. Although he desperately wanted to know more about his father, his head felt like it was going to split open like a ripe melon. It seemed impossible that his headache could actually get worse, but once the elves disappeared on the horizon, the pounding between his ears got even louder. Elias left the sweltering rooftop, followed by Nydeired, who offered his wing to steady his swaying rider.

"He'll feel better in a few hours," said Tallin, watching Elias leave the roof. "Let's go, Duskeye. It'll be easier for me to concentrate away from the city. I have to contact Sela—the sooner, the better."

Duskeye nodded, and the two of them took flight, moving in the opposite direction that the elves had gone. Tallin would contact Sela telepathically and give her a brief description of what was going on, and then he would prepare a more detailed message and send it along with a bird messenger. He knew that Sela's limited telepathic skills would not allow for a full description of what was happening, and it was just as well.

The bigger question was—what would happen when Elias met his father?

In the capital city of Morholt, empire troops assembled in the morning sun. Hundreds of soldiers marched in formation through the streets, their steps in perfect tandem. As they marched past the castle walls, the soldiers looked up and issued a sharp salute.

The emperor's sprawling castle overlooked the metropolis. The castle was a fortress, made of iron and brick with extraordinarily high walls.

There, in his throne room, sat Emperor Vosper dressed in flowing black robes. He reclined in an enormous carved chair, his ragged breath echoing softly in the chamber. A thin spellcaster stood on his right side, observing the emperor intensely.

Vosper's black eyes were sunken, and his papery skin was pale—a side effect of the charms that lengthened his life. Vosper coughed into his hand,

and a spider web of bloody spittle appeared on his palm. He wheezed for a few minutes before settling back down in his chair.

The spellcaster said, "My lord, let me see your hand."

Vosper wiped his palm on his robe. "I am fine, Qildor."

"Forgive me, your highness, but your longevity charms are failing. Please allow me to strengthen them."

"Qildor, don't be an idiot," hissed the emperor. "If you strengthen the charms any further, I shall die. My insomnia is already crippling, and I have lost the desire to consume food. You must find another solution."

"But sire, your health..." said Qildor.

"Shut up, you fool!" said the emperor. He glanced anxiously at the two necromancers swaying in the corner of the throne room.

The necromancers' mouths constantly gnawed, a byproduct of the magic that kept them "alive." They levitated silently in place, just off the ground, staring silently at nothing. The *necros* never slept, never ate, and rarely spoke. They smelled faintly of licorice and rotting flesh.

Both necromancers had recovered from their short captivity. Komu, the leader of the High Council, had succeeded in capturing them in the desert. For a while, the necromancers were entirely at Komu's mercy.

But not for long, Vosper thought, smiling. It was

a testament to Komu's ineptitude that both necromancers escaped mere days after their capture. That, coupled with the fact that Councilmember Delthen was sympathetic to the empire, ensured that Komu or Miklagard would never be a real threat.

Although Vosper was glad to have them back, having them present at the palace was a mixed blessing. The necromancers always made him uncomfortable.

Vosper whistled. The necromancers snapped to attention, turning their ghostly-white faces toward the emperor. "Yessss...your highnessss?" they asked in unison, their raspy voices echoing through the chamber.

"Come here," said the emperor, waving his hand.

The necromancers floated slowly over to him, their red teeth gnashing back and forth inside their blackened mouths.

Qildor stepped away, giving the necromancers a wide berth.

"I have an important task for you. Something both of you will enjoy." Vosper wanted them out of the throne room, and it was always easier to dismiss them when he gave them an interesting job to do.

"A young nobleman was captured and brought here today. He's the governor of Pine Grange. Well... not anymore. Now he's our prisoner. We discovered he was working for the Shadow Grid."

The necromancers perked up. "What issss... your... bidding, ssssire?"

"I want you to question him. Thoroughly. He promises to be full of useful information."

"Yessss, your highnessss," they replied, bowing deeply.

"Don't be too eager. You know the punishment I reserve for traitors, correct? But I want you to question him thoroughly *before* he dies, understood?"

"We hear... and obey, ssssire..." said the necromancers.

"Excellent. You are dismissed. Do not return until the prisoner is dead," said Vosper.

The necromancers bowed and left the room, floating soundlessly down the hallway. As soon as they were out of earshot, Vosper turned on Qildor and hit him on the side of the head.

Vosper's signet ring caught on Qildor's skin, tearing open his cheek. Qildor screamed, tumbling to the floor.

"You useless fool!" spat the emperor.

"Y-your Highness—w-what did I do?" said Qildor, reaching up to touch his injured cheek. Rivulets of blood streamed down his face.

"How many times? How many times must I remind you?" said Vosper, placing his foot menacingly near Qildor's head. "Do *not* speak of my weakened condition in front of the necromancers."

"Forgive me, sire! P-please, sire—I meant no disrespect," said Qildor. The spellcaster trembled violently.

"It's a miracle that I haven't killed you already," said Vosper, rising to strike again.

Qildor recoiled, covering his face with his hands. The mage braced himself for another blow, but it never came. Instead, Vosper hissed and turned around, his black robes trailing behind him.

Vosper placed his hands behind his back and walked over to the window. He watched the marching soldiers below in silence. Minutes ticked by.

"S-sire?" said Qildor, still on the ground.

"Qildor, be quiet. You haven't offered me a useful piece of advice in months."

"Y-yes, sire."

Vosper took a deep breath and spoke again, his voice calm. "Qildor, observe these men, my soldiers. They are willing to die for me, to the last man. If I asked any one of them to fling themselves from the nearest cliff, they would do so, at my command. Would you be willing to do the same?"

"O-of course, sire. I am... *devoted* to the empire," said Qildor, rising up cautiously from the floor.

"Good, good... I'm pleased to hear it. Leave me, Qildor. I need to rest. Tell my staff that I am not to be disturbed until nightfall."

"As you command, sire," said Qildor, backing out of the throne room quietly. Once he reached the hallway, he exhaled, clutching his stomach. His heart pounded in his chest. Qildor relayed Vosper's order to the guards before rushing downstairs.

As he walked through the corridors, the palace servants stopped and bowed. Everyone respected and feared Qildor. He was the leader of Vosper's spellcasters, after all.

71

The only people who didn't respect him were the necromancers... and Vosper himself. Qildor passed a mirror and paused, stunned by his appearance. The right side of his face was already turning purple. Streaks of dried blood ran down his cheek, disappearing into his robe. He touched his cheek gingerly and winced. The bump was pulsing with its own heartbeat.

Another spellcaster walked into the hallway and noticed Qildor's swollen face. It was Islar, a talented young mage who had just recently been promoted to Master.

"What the heck happened to you?" he asked. "Vosper punched you in the face *again?* What did you say to him this time?"

Qildor shot Islar a withering look. "I merely suggested that he strengthen his longevity charms. He lost his temper."

"Ah... well, did you say it in front of those *deadrats* of his?" said Islar. "You know how much he hates it when you talk about his age in front of the *necros.*"

"Uh... no," Qildor lied. "Uldreiyn and Uevareth... weren't present."

"Right," Islar said skeptically. "Too bad for you, chum. It looks like you just caught him on a bad day, eh? I'm glad I'm not his *favorite.*"

"I need a healer," said Qildor, touching his throbbing cheek again. He groaned. The bump was the size of a duck's egg. "Come on; let's finish this conversation inside the mage's chambers. I don't want to discuss the emperor out here."

Qildor and Islar walked down a short hallway and passed into an atrium. From there, they took another door into a sealed room. The room was vast, but windowless, illuminated only by light crystals. The crystals suffused the chamber with dim artificial light. Qildor closed the door behind him, ensuring their privacy.

There was another spellcaster in the room—a gray-haired female who was practicing spells in the corner. She frowned as they walked in.

"Come, Parnaiba," said Qildor, as he motioned for her to join them. They all sat down on a sprawling leather sofa in the center of the room.

"Vosper wants me to find another solution for his weakened state," said Qildor. "He doesn't want to reinforce his longevity charms anymore."

"There's not much we can do," said Islar. "He's *old*. Really old. And he's not an elf, so his time is almost done. There's only a certain amount of sand in the hourglass of our lives."

"Well, that's helpful," said Qildor sarcastically. "Are *you* going to tell him the bad news? Just *look* at my face. I need help with this, or next time he's going to kill me!"

"He's probably going to kill you anyway," said Parnaiba. "There is no solution. We all know that Vosper isn't very good at accepting bad news."

"Parnaiba, do you have anything useful to say, or just your usual sarcasm?" said Qildor.

"Don't play stupid," said Parnaiba. "Both of you know the answer. We all do. It's just a question of when Vosper will finally admit it. He's dying."

"She's right," said Islar. "Vosper's time is almost done. His longevity charms are failing at an alarming rate. He must choose between death and necromancy. There are no other options."

"How much time do you think he has left?" said Qildor.

"A few cycles. Perhaps less," said Parnaiba.

"He's coughing blood now," said Qildor. "I saw it this afternoon. He has no appetite, and he rarely sleeps anymore."

"That's good, in a way," said Parnaiba. "If Vosper decides to cross over, then he won't sleep or eat ever again. He needs to prepare himself for the side effects. It must give him pause, even one as power-hungry as him. It's a ghastly solution."

"I think he's already decided," said Qildor.

"Oh? What makes you so sure?" asked Parnaiba.

"Vosper asked if I was willing to die for him," said Qildor. "He's never asked me anything like that before, at least not directly. He usually just ignores me."

Islar's face fell. "So it's true then. The emperor plans to become a necromancer."

"Yes. He's decided to cross over. And when he does, he must choose three spellcasters to sacrifice. He'll choose the strongest mageborns in the kingdom. I'm going to be one of them," said Qildor. "Of this, I'm certain."

"It's going to be the three of us," said Parnaiba. "The other palace spellcasters are marginal, at best.

No one else even comes close to our combined powers."

Islar's face turned white as the reality dawned on him. "What? Vosper plans to sacrifice our lives?" The young spellcaster had just celebrated his eighteenth cycle. "But I'm not ready to die! Can Vosper force me to do it, even if I don't want to?"

"No… he can't *force* you," said Qildor. "The mages who are sacrificed for *the Necromancer's Oath* must be willing."

Islar exhaled. "Thank goodness! That's a relief."

Parnaiba sighed and shook her head. "Islar, don't be an idiot. Think about it. To refuse the oath will mean death. Vosper considers self-sacrifice to be a great honor. Either way, you're going to die."

"What about you, Parnaiba?" asked Qildor. "What will you do?"

Parnaiba sighed again. "I have reflected on this possibility for many years. I have been a spellcaster at Morholt for a long time, and before that, I was a Master at Aonach Tower. I always suspected that Vosper would take the *Necromancer's Oath.* I knew that if I lived to see that day, I would be chosen as one of the sacrifices. If this is to be my fate, I accept it. I will not disobey my emperor's wishes."

"How can you be *so calm?*" asked Islar. "Aren't you the least bit afraid?"

Parnaiba waved a weary hand. "I am afraid of many things, but not of death. I'm a tired old woman. I lived through the destruction of Aonach Tower, and the loss of my entire family. There is no one left. I cannot remember... the last time I was truly happy. I have seen over eighty winters, and I am ready to leave this world."

"And you, Qildor?" asked Islar. "You have a young daughter and a wife. What will you do?"

Qildor hesitated. Then he hung his head. "I have no choice," he whispered. "Vosper will kill me if I refuse, and probably my wife and child, too. I must do it."

Parnaiba turned to Islar. Her face, hardened by years of loneliness and strife, softened for a moment. She placed her wrinkled hand on the young man's shoulder. "Islar... Qildor and I must do this. Our fate is sealed. But you are a young man... the age my grandson would have been... had he survived. Your life has only just begun. You are young and unmarried. Vosper has nothing to blackmail you with. You can escape this fate."

"She's right," said Qildor, nodding in agreement. "If you want to live, you'd better find a way out of Morholt—and fast."

6. STONEWALLED

Sela sat down, exhausted from repeated telepathic communications with Tallin. He had contacted her *three times* today already, each time with more urgent news. Sela was unable to maintain the contact for more than a few seconds, so Tallin waited hours between each contact so she could regain her strength.

"How do you feel, Mother?" said Rali, who was sitting nearby. As a second-degree mage, Rali's limited magical abilities allowed him to *listen* in to the communications between Tallin and Sela, but he was unable to respond or add to the conversation.

"Still tired, but better. Tallin will contact me again before nightfall, so I must preserve my strength." A few minutes later, Sela felt a familiar itch on the back of her neck. Tallin was trying to contact her again. It was too soon, and she felt dizzy when she tried to stand.

"Brinsop! Lend me your strength," said Sela.

"*Of course, my friend,*" said Brinsop, reaching out with her dragon mind, joining the spell.

Rali stood up as well, offering Sela his support. He couldn't do much to help, but at least he could keep her from falling over.

She opened her mind to Tallin's contact, and her dragon stone began to glow.

"Sela!" said Tallin, his voice echoing from far away. "Three elves have arrived at Parthos. Carnesîr is leading them. They've offered to take over the city's defenses while you and Rali are away."

"That's absurd," said Sela. "We can't leave Parthos in the hands of outlanders."

"What is your answer?" asked Tallin. "I think I could be more helpful to you there."

She bit her lip, thinking furiously. "Let *The Nine* take over stewardship of the city. Only Aor is here, so the remaining eight guardsmen can manage Parthos in his absence. Notify Annarr, the second-in-command, and he shall take over. *The Nine* are trained well enough to do it. Their tattoos will provide enough protection against the elves' charms."

"Shall I come to Mount Velik, then?" asked Tallin.

"Yes. We really need you here. The clans are bullying us, and you would be invaluable during the negotiations. Rali must stay at Mount Velik until treaty negotiations are complete." Sela started to tremble with the strain.

"Understood," said Tallin. He didn't sound happy about it. "I shall leave for Mount Velik immediately. What about the elves?"

"The elves may act as sentinels. They're permitted to guard the city walls, but that's all. If they don't like it, they're welcome to leave."

"And Elias? Carnesîr revealed Chua's existence to the boy," said Tallin.

"That's unfortunate, but it was bound to happen sooner or later," whispered Sela. She struggled to maintain consciousness. "It's time... for Elias to meet his father. Prepare Elias... and Nydeired for the journey to the Elder Willow. Then come to Mount Velik." Her voice trailed off, and Sela collapsed.

"Mother!" said Rali, catching his mother's limp body before she hit the floor. She had maintained the telepathic contact for too long. It drained her past her limit.

"Are you still there?" asked Tallin, his voice reverberating in Rali's mind.

Sela was unconscious, but Tallin still felt the mental link with the young king. "Rali, I know you can't respond, but I want you to *listen*. Don't worry about your mother—Sela will regain consciousness soon. Lay her down on the floor and observe her until she awakens. She'll be exhausted, but unhurt. I'm sorry for pushing her so hard. I'll see you in a few days. Until then, await a bird messenger with full details."

"I will," said Rali out loud, not knowing if Tallin could hear him or not. Then he felt Tallin's consciousness disengage and slip away.

Rali laid his mother's limp body on the floor. Brinsop crawled over and nuzzled Sela's neck with her snout. Brinsop didn't seem overly distressed; perhaps she had seen this all before. Rali wished again that he could understand dragon-tongue, so he could ask Brinsop what to do.

"Sela? Mother?" asked Rali, patting her face

gently.

There was no response at first, but a few minutes later, Sela groaned. Her eyes fluttered open. "Rali? What happened?"

"You fainted, Mother. Tallin told me to watch you until you regained consciousness. Do you remember the conversation?"

Sela closed her eyes and nodded. "Yes... I remember. By *Baghra*, that last contact finished me. I won't be able to cast any spells for a good while." The multiple telepathy spells would leave her drained for days. She inhaled deeply, touching Brinsop's nose.

"*Take some of my strength, old friend,*" said Brinsop, reaching out to lift up her exhausted rider. Sela drew on Brinsop's formidable power, using the dragon stone as a focal point. Both of their stones glowed, and Sela felt the borrowed energy trickling back into her limbs. She was able to stand unassisted a few minutes later. She stumbled to the couch and plopped down.

Brinsop knew that the worst was over, so she went back to sleep near the fireplace.

"Mother, Tallin spoke to me after you fainted."

"Really?" asked Sela, somewhat surprised. She hadn't realized that Rali was strong enough to maintain a telepathic contact by himself.

"Yes. I could still hear his voice. It sounded weaker, like a whisper in the distance. I don't know if he heard me, but I could definitely hear him."

Sela beamed, pleased at her son's abilities. "That's impressive, since I was the one maintaining the original spell. That means your telepathic abilities are stronger than we originally thought. Telepathic contact is extremely difficult for humans, but easier for elves and dwarves. Maybe your father had a touch of elvish or dwarvish blood."

"Maybe," said Rali, shrugging. He tried not to think too much about his late father—the memories were still too painful. "Tallin said he would be here in a few days."

"Excellent," said Sela. "We desperately need his help during these negotiations. I honestly thought it would be easier. Without him, the dwarf clans will continue to toy with us."

"We're at an impasse here, but what about the elves? Just having them in Parthos makes me uneasy."

"The presence of elves in the desert is definitely a mixed blessing. Their arrival complicates things. Tallin dislikes them intensely, so I can't imagine how he's dealing with them in Parthos. Maybe I should return to Parthos to act as its steward. You can't leave—the treaty talks won't continue unless you're present."

"Are you sure you'll be able to handle the elves on your own?" asked Rali.

Sela smiled thinly. "I may not be the most powerful spellcaster in the kingdom, but I can certainly handle a few immortals. Elves neither frighten nor intimidate me. I understand them better than they understand us."

Rali nodded. He marveled at her self-assurance—

his mother was a remarkable woman. "Hopefully, once Tallin gets here, he'll be able to convince Bolrakei to abandon her request for a dragon stone. There's no way I would ever agree to such a ridiculous demand. Perhaps she'll agree to some other concession."

Thorin had told Sela and Rali of Bolrakei's desire to own a dragon stone days ago. Sela was so furious that she hadn't spoken to any of the clan leaders since. Rali and Thorin attended the talks together, but neither of them spoke directly to Bolrakei.

"I avoided telling Tallin about Bolrakei's little attempt at blackmailing us," said Sela. "It would have infuriated him. He's already going to be angry enough when he arrives. We'll tell him later about her *'request.'* She'll be lucky if Tallin doesn't kill her."

Aor stepped into the doorway. "Sire, the dwarf Thorin has arrived. Shall I allow him entry?"

"Yes, Aor," said Rali. "Let him in."

Thorin strode in and bowed. "Good day, Your Highness... and Mistress Sela."

Thorin's tone was nothing but polite, but his gaze lingered a little too long on Sela's face.

"Where have you been all day, Thorin?" asked Rali, jokingly. "Off having fun while we're stuck dealing with the council?"

"Nay, nay," said Thorin, tugging at his beard. "I've been sniffing around a bit, and I have some important news, if you please."

"Go ahead," said Rali.

"First, I apologize for eavesdroppin', but ye know that we dwarves have good hearin'. As I was waitin' outside, I overheard ye discussin' Bolrakei and the matter of the dragon stone."

"And? What is your opinion on our little problem?" asked Rali.

Thorin cleared his throat. "I know it's rather a delicate subject for y'all. But I've known Bolrakei Shalevault for over a century. She's as stubborn and greedy as they come. Once she gets an idea in her head, she's unwillin' to bend. I'm fairly sure she won't change her mind about this."

"Well, what do you suggest we do?" asked Rali. "We can't very well give her Chua's dragon stone. Or anyone else's, for that matter."

"Nay, I'm not suggestin' that," said Thorin. "But there's another *livin'* dragon stone in the kingdom, one that is even now separated from its rider."

"You mean, *Hanko's* dragon stone?" said Sela, lifting her head off the pillow. "Hanko, the traitor?"

"Aye, that one," said Thorin.

Rali folded his arms over his chest. "I don't like the direction that this conversation is going.".

Thorin held up a hand. "Nay, please, hear me out. Instead of givin' her Chua's stone, why not offer Hanko's stone to her instead? That would solve the problem. I'm no expert in these matters, but wouldn't it be an appropriate punishment for a traitor? Ye'd be killin' two birds with one stone, no pun intended. It could just be temporary, until the treaty is signed. I'd find some way to get it back."

"I still don't like it," said Sela. "Hanko is still awaiting trial in Miklagard. He may be a traitor, but it would be unseemly to give his stone to someone who is, in effect, blackmailing us."

"It's moot anyway," said Rali. "We don't even know where Hanko's stone is. He said it was stolen from him."

Thorin looked up at the ceiling. "Well, ye see... that's my news. I *do* know where it is. Hanko's stone is in Morholt. Vosper has it, and I know how we can get it back."

"Are you sure?" asked Rali.

"I'm absolutely sure," said Thorin, grinning wolfishly. "Of this and some other things."

"How did you obtain this information?" asked Sela.

"Well," Thorin fidgeted. He seemed to be weighing whether or not to share his sources. "Just between us, my informant is my cousin, Floki. We grew up together in Mount Velik, but he left our clan when he reached beardhood. Floki's been workin' in Morholt for months. He sent me an encoded message. I just received it today."

"The capital city isn't safe for dwarves. Why did your cousin choose Morholt, of all places?" asked Sela.

"It wasn't really a choice. Floki used to live in Jutland with his family. It was my fault that he left Jutland. I sought his help last year when I was travelin' with Elias. We were all forced to flee the city together. It was sheer luck we escaped alive."

"How did your cousin end up in the capital?" said Sela.

Thorin sighed. "Floki's not a *pure-blood*. He's a halfling. He almost passes for human, so he prefers to live among ye. When Floki left Jutland, he traveled across Durn with his family. But work was scarce, and his wife didn't want to come here. Floki got desperate and sought work in Morholt. He secured a position working in the palace stables. Everythin' was fine until Floki was approached by one of Vosper's spellcasters. The mage knew that Floki was a halfling and passin' as human. The mage threatened to expose him, if Floki didn't help him escape the capital."

"What does the mage want?" asked Rali.

"His name is Islar. He's one of Vosper's Master spellcasters, and he wants to defect to our side—he wants to come to Mount Velik. Floki also wants to leave. He knows it's just a matter of time before he's discovered, and he's afraid for his family."

"We trust *you*," said Sela. "But how can you be sure that this isn't one of Vosper's tricks?"

Thorin shrugged. "I suppose it could be a trap, but I don't think so. Floki certainly believes him. My cousin sent me a message describing everything. The scroll was written in my clan's secret language. It could not have been a forgery."

"But even with this information, how can we get Hanko's dragon stone back?" asked Rali. "Assuming Vosper has it, it's probably under lock and key."

"The spellcaster knows where it is," said Thorin.

"He promised to bring the stone to us, in exchange for his life. Islar is terrified he's going to get killed."

"You know," Sela said thoughtfully, "This crazy plan just might work. I thought Hanko's stone was gone forever. So Vosper's spellcaster has agreed to steal it back?"

"Aye. The mage doesn't want money," said Thorin. "He's asking for sanctuary. He's young and terrified. I don't know all the details, but he's tryin' to escape because Vosper plans to kill him durin' some kind of dark ritual."

Sela gasped. *The Necromancer's Oath! Vosper's actually going to do it. He plans to cross over!* She struggled to hide her shock.

It was soon—too soon. If Vosper took the oath now, they would never be able to defeat him. Elias was still just a boy, and Nydeired was barely a year old. None of the other dragon riders were a match for someone as powerful as Vosper, and much less so if the emperor decided to become a necromancer.

Rali gave her a look of concern. "Are you all right, Mother?" he asked, touching her shoulder.

"Yes, I'm fine. Just tired from earlier," she said. She decided to keep her suspicions to herself, at least for now. "Thorin, please go on."

Thorin cleared his throat and continued. "As I was sayin', Islar wants safe passage. In exchange, he'll cooperate with us fully, and bring us the dragon stone."

"And what about your cousin Floki?" asked Sela. "It must be dangerous for him in Morholt, especially now. What will he do?"

"Floki always knew he'd be forced to return to Mount Velik eventually. The day just came sooner than he thought. Even if he doesn't like it here, he's a talented horse breeder, and my clan will be happy to take him back."

"Have you informed King Hergung?" said Rali. "He should at least know what's going on."

Thorin nodded. "Yes, I told Hergung this morning. He said that since the dwarves are still officially neutral in this matter, that he would leave the decision up to you. So... what do you say, King Rali?"

"I say... let's do it," said Rali. "Assuming Islar isn't an outright spy, it would be foolish to pass up a chance to question one of the emperor's personal spellcasters. And getting Hanko's dragon stone would make the treaty negotiations go more smoothly, if only to trick Bolrakei into believing that we will capitulate to her request."

"It's a great opportunity, but getting Islar and Floki out of Morholt isn't going to be easy. If Vosper catches wind of this, he'll flay them alive," said Sela. "Thorin, where does your cousin wish to rendezvous?"

"In Ironport," Thorin replied. "By boat, it's only a day's travel on the Orvasse River. They'll leave Morholt at night, and we'll meet them in Ironport the next day."

"Mother, will you go?" asked Rali.

"Yes. Thorin and I will go to Ironport by dragonflight. Brinsop can drop us off near the city, and then we'll accompany Floki and Islar back to Mount Velik from there. Hopefully, Vosper won't discover Islar's absence until it's too late. It's doubtful we'll get an opportunity like this again."

Rali felt uncomfortable putting his mother in danger, but he knew her plan was sound. "It's decided then. Elias shall go to the Elder Willow, Tallin shall come here, and you and Thorin shall escort Floki and Islar to safety."

Sela sighed. "The riders are stretched to the breaking point, but we have to take this chance. Vosper's renegade spellcaster might be the key to winning this war. Imagine the information he can give us about the emperor's plans."

"I agree," said Rali. "We must do it. Thorin, arrange the meeting. You and Sela may leave as soon as you're ready."

"As ye command, yer highness," said Thorin, offering a small bow.

Rali sank down into a chair, looking much older than his years.

Thorin also sat down, but he was grinning broadly as he pulled out his smokeleaf pipe.

"What are *you* so pleased about?" asked Sela.

"Well... Let me see if I've got this right," said Thorin, as he counted off on his fingers. "We're on the verge of war, the elves are in Parthos, the dwarf clans are fightin', Bolrakei is crazy, and I have to travel halfway across Durn on the back of a dragon, never mind that I'm afraid of heights!"

"When you put it like that... it sounds pretty

awful," said Sela, baffled by his good mood.

His grin grew wider. "Yup, it surely is. But Mistress Sela, I'm goin' on a quest with the downright *prettiest* dragon rider in the entire kingdom. So... why be worried?" Then he leaned over and *winked* at her.

Sela's eyes got wide, and Rali laughed so hard that he fell off his chair.

7. LEAVING PARTHOS

The following morning, Tallin cheerfully notified Carnesîr that *The Nine* would be taking over temporary stewardship of Parthos.

Carnesîr bristled with anger at the idea that he would be forced to obey orders from *human* guardsmen. "You seriously can't expect us to take orders from a common soldier!" he exclaimed.

"Well, those are King Rali's terms," said Tallin. "If you don't like it, you're all welcome to leave."

Carnesîr seethed but said nothing else. He turned and left to confer with the other elves. Less than an hour later, the elves silently took up patrols above the city. They accepted the decision without further comment, albeit unwillingly.

The Nine took their positions at strategic points in the city, with Annarr quietly taking over palace administration. Tallin marveled at their silent efficiency. Rali's guards rarely spoke, but when they did, no one questioned their authority. Perhaps it was because they were colossal and covered from head to toe in tattoos.

Tallin spent the next few days preparing Elias and Nydeired for their trip to the Elder Willow. Nydeired practiced his flying technique. His mighty wings allowed him to soar faster and longer than any dragon in the kingdom, but he still had trouble landing. Elias and Nydeired trained together, and eventually, Tallin felt comfortable enough to allow them to travel alone.

On the morning of their journey, Elias waited on the palace roof, packed and ready. He carried his grandmother's journal, which contained detailed maps of the countryside. His dagger was tucked into his boot, and Chua's dragon stone hung around his neck, as always.

Nydeired had been fitted with a modified saddle, designed especially for him. A few minutes later, Tallin and Duskeye arrived on the rooftop. Tallin checked Nydeired's saddle, making sure the bindings were tight.

"Elias, are you ready?" asked Tallin.

"As ready as I'll ever be," Elias said. "I'm a bit nervous, but excited too."

"As long as you're cautious, everything will be fine. Stay vigilant, especially when you cross the desert border."

"Shouldn't I send a message to Chua before I leave?" asked Elias. "A bird messenger, or something?"

"That's not necessary, Elias. Chua knows you're coming. He's an *oracle*, remember? I'm sure he'll be waiting for you when you arrive."

"I suppose you're right. It's still hard to believe that my father's alive," said Elias.

"He'll answer all of your questions when you get there. Remember, you must prepare yourself for his appearance. That goes for you too, Nydeired. Starclaw also bears the scars of grave injuries."

Nydeired nodded. "*I am also anxious about meeting my dam*," he said, with a voice like crushed gravel.

Nydeired had grown even larger. He could no longer enter the castle through the regular doorways. Stonemasons had to create a separate entrance for him. Even the elves who had lived long enough to have seen other white dragons were awestruck by Nydeired's extraordinary size.

Tallin continued, "Now, I know you won't like this, but you won't be traveling alone. Fëanor and Blacktooth will accompany you until you reach the southern border. Don't expect either of them to speak to you—they'll likely keep their distance. Once you cross over the Elburgian Mountains, cast your concealment spell and strengthen your wards. The last leg of your journey will be the most dangerous. If you must rest, do it before you leave the desert. Don't attempt to hunt in Darkmouth Forest, and don't stop until you reach the Elder Willow. Southern Durn is crawling with empire soldiers and bounty hunters; it's not safe for you to descend."

Elias mounted Nydeired and grabbed the reins. "Thank you, Tallin... for everything."

"You're welcome. May Golka protect you on your journey," he said.

Nydeired crouched, his legs thicker than tree trunks, and took off into the sky. The gust of wind from their departure was so strong that it lifted pebbles off the ground. As they flew away, the desert sun reflected off Nydeired's glittering white scales, casting rainbow-colored prisms into the air.

Minutes later, Elias looked back. Tallin and Dusk-eye were already gone. Above the city, Carnesîr and Poth patrolled the sky. And behind them, following about a league away, flew Fëanor and Blacktooth.

"Fëanor and Blacktooth are behind us," said Elias. "Tallin was right; they're keeping their distance. I wonder if they'll stay behind us the entire journey?"

"Are you actually surprised? They probably don't want to talk to either of us," said Nydeired. *"They're so snotty with their smart remarks."*

"No... I guess not. Quite honestly, the elves haven't been *that* rude to me, except for our first encounter in the desert. They seem to ignore me. But with Tallin, they don't even *attempt* to be friendly. They treat him with actual contempt, especially Carnesîr. I wonder if there's some old quarrel between those two, or if Carnesîr just treats Tallin that way because he's a dwarf."

"I noticed it, too. The elves' dragons are distant as well. Especially Poth. I tried to speak with him more than once, but he just stared off into the distance like I wasn't even there. Poth is ancient, though. Perhaps he's senile."

Elias snorted. "It's more likely he's just *rude,* like his rider. But who knows? Maybe you're right. Poth could have been bound to Carnesîr hundreds, or even thousands, of years ago. Elves are immortal, after all. The magic of the binding goes both ways."

Elias looked back again, watching Fëanor and

Blacktooth in the distance.

"*Are you nervous about meeting your father?*" asked Nydeired.

"A little. At first, I was angry at Tallin for withholding the information from me, but after he explained his reasoning, I understood. I've fantasized about this meeting my entire life—the things I would say, how I would react. But that was when I thought my father was dead. It's an odd feeling to know that I'll be face-to-face with him in a few days."

"*Do you think their injuries are as bad as Duskeye and Tallin described?*"

"Yes. I'm sure they are. Probably worse. It's not Tallin's nature to exaggerate. It's hard to imagine how Chua and Starclaw could have been so badly wounded and still survived. Then again, it was my grandmother, Carina, that saved them, and she was a gifted healer."

They continued to fly deeper into the southern desert. A few hours before dawn, Elias spotted a group of nomads below, their colored banners and oil lamps bobbing above the dunes. The tribesmen raised their spears and shouted a greeting into the sky. Elias waved, and another shout went up from the group.

"I recognize this tribe's colors," said Elias. "Would you like to go down and say hello?"

"*Sure—maybe they'll offer us something to eat,*" said Nydeired hopefully. "*I'm a bit hungry.*"

"You're *always* hungry," said Elias, laughing.

"*What about Fëanor and Blacktooth?*" asked Nydeired.

"We'll only be a minute. I don't think they'll mind," said Elias.

Nydeired began to descend, and sure enough, Elias felt Fëanor's telepathic contact seconds later. The back of his neck itched, and Elias felt the powerful touch of the elf's unfamiliar mind on his own. Elias allowed the contact but strengthened his wards before responding.

"Elias!" said Fëanor. "Is something wrong? Why are you stopping here?"

"Nothing's wrong. I recognize these tribesmen. I want to stop for a moment and greet them."

"*Fine,*" said the elf, slightly irritated. "Please be brief."

"Understood," said Elias, relieved that Fëanor didn't argue. The elf dropped contact and did not say anything else. Fëanor and Blacktooth landed on a nearby plateau to observe, keeping their distance.

Nydeired circled down and landed. The tribesmen bowed deeply, and a few of their elders approached.

Elias recognized one of the men instantly. "Greetings, Sa'dun! That's your name, isn't it?" He looked thinner than the last time Elias had seen him, and much of his hair had gone gray.

The startled nomad stepped forward and offered his hand. "Yes! I am Sa'dun. Forgive me, esteemed rider, but how do you know my name?"

Elias shook his hand with a firm, steady grip. "I'm

Elias. I met you last year with Tallin and Duskeye—he's the dragon rider with red hair."

Sa'dun appeared confused for a moment, and then a shadow of recognition crossed his face. "Ah, yes... now I remember. That was when Tallin warned us about the orc horde... and the slaughter of the Tribe of Wahid. Please forgive my forgetfulness—it was a sorrowful time for us." His voice trembled a little at the end.

"No apology is necessary, Sa'dun. I understand," said Elias.

"How you've grown, young man! I scarcely recognized you. And you've become a rider, I see. Congratulations."

"Thank you, Sa'dun. If I may ask—were you able to notify the other tribes? Were your people able to avoid the horde?"

The nomad nodded sadly. "Yes. Thanks be to Golka, we were able to warn the other tribes in time. No more of our brethren fell to the orcs, although Tallin was right about the Tribe of Wahid. The greenskins slaughtered them all, even the women and children. There were no survivors. I had many family members in the Tribe of Wahid. Our people mourned for a long time."

Elias swallowed hard. "I'm sorry for your loss. How have you fared since the attack?"

Sa'dun's eyes were filled with sorrow. "Life has been... very challenging," he said sadly. "the orcs invaded the desert, our tribes moved to the south for safety. The move saved my people, but the journey was hard. Many died along the way, especially young children and the elderly. Food is scarce in the south, but we have no choice but to stay. We must move forward, as the sun moves forward in the sky."

"Why is that?" asked Elias. "The orcs were driven back past the Sleita Border; their numbers were cut in half. The Death Sands are safe again."

"That may be so, but the orcs did so much damage to the northern desert that we have been unable to return. The ground is still blackened from their oil fires, and the necromancers poisoned all the wells in the northern part of the desert. There is almost no potable water."

"I'm sorry, Sa'dun. I had no idea," said Elias. His eyes scanned the crowd. The women were covered from head to toe in traditional *carthin*, so Elias could not see their condition, but all the men and the children looked very thin. There were fewer camels, too—where once this tribe had dozens, now only a handful remained. "Is there anything I can do to help?"

Sa'dun thought for a moment, then answered. "Perhaps. We could use a source of clean drinking water in this region. That would help us a lot."

Elias scratched his chin thoughtfully. If Tallin was here, he would know what to do. Then Elias looked at Fëanor, standing off in the distance. *Would he help me?* he thought. "Wait here a moment, Sa'dun. I'll be right back."

Sa'dun bowed, and the other tribesmen followed suit. Sa'dun turned around and spoke to his kinsmen, and the women started chattering excitedly. Some of the children clapped their hands.

Elias sighed. He knew that Sa'dun had just informed his tribe that the "mighty dragon rider" was going to help them. Now he felt even more pressure to do this right. Elias mounted Nydeired and flew in Fëanor's direction.

"Are you going to ask Fëanor and Blacktooth to assist these people?" asked Nydeired.

"Yes. I have to try. Fëanor is a jerk, but he's a more experienced spellcaster. The worst he can say is no."

Nydeired landed near Fëanor a few minutes later. The elf was levitating with his legs crossed. Blacktooth was sitting upright, staring blankly off into the distance. They were meditating.

"Fëanor? Sorry to interrupt, and I know we're in a hurry, but these people need a water source and—."

The elf put his hand up. "Stop," he interrupted. "I already know what you're going to ask."

"Please, Fëanor. *Look* at them. They're starving. They need our help."

Fëanor heaved an exasperated sigh. "Elias, I have orders to escort you to the southern border and nothing more. This is highly irregular."

"I can't just leave them like this! There is barely any food or water. They're *suffering.*"

"Humans are always *suffering*," said Fëanor sarcastically. "Our mission is paramount. We don't have the time for this. You're a dragon rider. You shouldn't allow human emotion to cloud your judgment."

Elias bristled at the insult. "My *judgment* is fine. So, let me put it this way: I'm not leaving until I help these people. With or without you, I'm going to do it. This will go a lot faster with the two of us, so are you going to help me or not?"

Fëanor pursed his lips and frowned. "Fine," he said, "I'll assist you. But you must promise that we won't make any more unscheduled stops after this."

"Thank you," said Elias, smiling. "I promise. No more stops. You have my word."

"Good," said Fëanor. "Let's get this over with then." Fëanor and Blacktooth flew down to where the nomads were waiting.

As soon as the nomads saw the elf, a collective gasp went through the crowd. The men started to pant and look dizzy. Some of the women fainted. Even the camels went into a drunken stupor. It was incredible to watch; just being near Fëanor caused everyone to respond oddly.

Elias recalled what had happened the first time he met the elves in the desert. He whispered a silent prayer under his breath, thankful again for his protective wards.

"So, these people desire a well?" asked Fëanor.

"Yes... if it's possible," said Elias.

"Of course it's possible," said Fëanor. The elf closed his eyes and sniffed the air. Blacktooth snorted, nodding in his rider's direction. They were communicating telepathically.

Elias longed for the day when he and Nydeired would be officially bound to one another, so they would be able to communicate the same way, rather than having to talk to each other out loud.

"Follow me," Fëanor finally said, walking east.

Elias and Nydeired followed, and the entire tribe marched along behind them. It was the strangest procession—the elf and his black dragon in the lead, Elias and his white dragon in the center, and a ragtag group of tribesmen holding up the rear.

They walked for about thirty minutes before Fëanor stopped, this time in a rocky area. He sniffed the air again. "Here. There's water below the surface."

"How do you know?" asked Elias.

"I can smell it," said Fëanor. "There's an aquifer underneath the bedrock. Once I pierce the stone, the water will flow. Stand back, please."

Fëanor closed his eyes and raised his arms. His body started to glow a rosy hue.

Elias was intrigued—necromancers glowed red when performing magic, and mortals usually glowed blue. The elves shone pink when they performed their spells.

"*Stefna-logur!*" Fëanor said, his palms facing upward. Nothing happened. "*Stefna-logur!*" he repeated. Blacktooth crouched nearby, and his dragon stone also started glowing. They were helping each other perform the spell.

Elias made a mental note to ask Chua about that —he wondered if only elves could do this, or if all riders had the power to draw upon their dragon's magic.

At first, nothing happened. Then the ground turned dark with moisture. A trickle of water formed at the surface, which then turned into a puddle, and then a small pool about the size of a dinner plate. Blacktooth, who had been waiting silently nearby, now positioned himself near the spring.

"*Bjarg-rammlingr!*" said Fëanor, and shattered rock shot up from the ground in a spray of pebbles.

Blacktooth opened his jaws, shooting a river of fiery breath. The air sizzled with rising steam, and the fire heated the stone until it was red-hot. Fëanor stared at the molten rock, whispering incantations. The heated stone softened and began to transform.

"*Vatn-Nyr-Lliki,*" he said, reaching out as if to touch the pool. Fëanor's fingers moved, and the molten rock flowed, like a centipede. The stone curled around itself, taking a cylindrical shape.

A few minutes later, Fëanor stepped back. The elf nodded, satisfied with his handiwork.

"*Bjarg-Risa,*" he said, touching the stone one last time. The rock hardened and cooled, and the well was complete.

Fëanor had fashioned the rock into a beautiful geometric pattern: a series of triangles overlapping one another. That part hadn't been necessary, but Elias supposed the elf wanted to add his own touch.

The tribesmen scarcely breathed, standing quietly behind Elias. The children giggled excitedly and craned their necks, trying to sneak a peek around Nydeired's formidable bulk.

Elias walked to the well, scooping up a handful of

water. The water was cloudy but drinkable. "This is amazing, Fëanor. Thank you."

"I'm not finished," said Fëanor. The elf walked toward a cactus growing nearby. The elf reached out with his index finger and touched it, saying, "*Avoxtraogr*." Immediately, the cactus' growth exploded; dozens of cactus fruit appeared and ripened. Fëanor repeated the spell with every plant, tree, and cactus in the area. Everywhere he stepped, fresh grass burst forth from the earth. By the time he was finished, it looked like a thriving garden.

The nomads gasped in wonder. The children ran forward, drinking from the well and grabbing ripe cactus fruit. They bit into the desert fruit with relish, juice dripping down their brown chins.

Fëanor walked back toward the well. "My task is complete. Shall we go?" He didn't look the least bit tired.

"Yes, of course, Fëanor. I am in your debt," said Elias. He meant it. It was much more than he had expected.

Fëanor nodded, his beautiful face expressionless. He turned to go, and almost as an afterthought, he said over his shoulder, "Tell the mortals to care for this oasis; it shall produce water and food for generations, as long as it is maintained properly."

Seconds later, Fëanor took off into the sky. The elf never once spoke or even looked at the tribesmen.

"I will tell them," said Elias, who relayed Fëanor's message to the grateful tribesmen. The men pounded their shields, and the women wept openly. Elias looked up at Fëanor and Blacktooth. They were already circling above, anxious to leave.

"Sa'dun, we must go," said Elias, clasping the man's hand.

Tears were rolling down the nomad's cheeks. "Thank you, dragon rider. Thank you! May the gods bless you in this life and the next. We shall never forget your kindness, I swear it."

As Elias and Nydeired flew into the sky, he looked back at the nomads. The women were picking fruit and filling their waterskins from the spring. The camels were eating grasses and drinking their fill. All the men were dancing in a great circle, giving thanks for the blessing they had received.

Nydeired hovered beside Blacktooth, and Elias waved. Fëanor didn't smile or wave back. Then Elias felt the touch of the elf's mind on his own again.

"Do not trust the humans," said Fëanor.

"What do you mean?" asked Elias puzzled.

"Sa'dun said he would *never forget* your kindness. But he is lying. He will forget, Elias. All of them forget. Mortals always do. It is in your nature to do so," said Fëanor. "Mortals forget past kindnesses, past friends, and, worst of all, their past mistakes. For this reason, you are ill-fated to repeat history. It is the way of mortals."

"If you truly feel this way, then why did you do it? Why help them at all?" asked Elias.

"I helped the humans because it was simpler for me to create the oasis than to argue with you. You are stubborn and obstinate. Not unlike your grandmother, Carina," said Fëanor.

Elias was incredulous. "Wait—you knew my grandmother?"

"Yes, I knew your grandmother well. I fought by her side in Mount Velik many years ago, during the war. She was courageous but ever prideful. You're a lot like her. To your credit, however, you're still far easier to deal with than that *infuriating* dwarf, Tallin."

"But how..." said Elias, but Fëanor broke contact and flew back into his old position, a full league behind Elias and Nydeired.

Fëanor remained behind Elias for the remainder of the journey, not speaking to him again until they reached the southern border of the desert. As soon as they reached the Elburgian Mountains, Fëanor contacted Elias telepathically again.

"We've reached the border," he said. "Our task is finished. Farewell." He turned and flew back in the same direction that they had come.

"That's it? They're leaving?" asked Nydeired.

"Yes," said Elias. They watched as Fëanor cast a concealment spell and disappeared from sight. "They're gone, without another word."

"Tallin was right. Elves **are** *capricious,"* said Nydeired.

Elias shook his head. "It makes me wonder why they've involved themselves in this conflict at all. Why show up now? What do the elves have to gain by helping Parthos in a war against Morholt?"

Neither of them had an answer to that question.

Sela and Thorin arrived in Ironport before dawn. It was still dark when they arrived, so Brinsop landed a few leagues outside the city, near a forested area.

Sela dismounted carefully, but Thorin stumbled out of the saddle and fell on his rump.

"Ouch!" he said, rubbing his backside.

"Careful, Thorin," said Sela. "This is a good spot, Brinsop. We'll try to be back before sundown. Hopefully, Islar and Floki are already inside the city. Try to remain hidden until nightfall and rest if you can."

"*I shall,*" Brinsop said, yawning. "*I'm hungry. I'll try a little hunting before sunrise. Perhaps I'll get lucky and find an osolut. I haven't eaten one in ages. This is their mating season, when they become like walking slabs of bacon.*"

"Sounds delicious," said Sela. The osolut was a large rodent, similar in appearance to a beaver, except it was much larger, and, apparently, tastier to dragons.

"*Mmmm... They are. If I'm lucky enough to find one, I'll save some meat for you,*" said Brinsop. The dragon licked her lips.

"Thanks," said Sela, smiling. "Thorin, I'm going into the city. Hopefully, I'll get lucky and gather some information. What's Ironport like these days? It's been ages since I've been this far east."

"Ironport isn't safe these days, especially at night. The governor is a drunk, and the town is overrun with bad people. My people used to do a fair amount of trade with this city, but most of the dwarves have left. There's naught in Ironport but bandits and thugs."

Sela nodded. "Thanks for the advice. This close to Morholt, I expected some unsavory characters. You're welcome to stay outside the city walls, if you wish."

"Stay here? Nay, nay!" Thorin said huffily. "I'd never let ye go into Ironport by yerself, Mistress Sela! What if somethin' happened while ye was there? I couldn't forgive myself!"

"Okay, okay!" said Sela, laughing. "You've made your point. We shall go together."

Thorin grabbed his cloak and a small axe from his rucksack. He tucked the axe into his belt and straightened his beard, which he had re-braided for the journey. "I'm ready, Mistress Sela."

Sela donned her cloak. "Let's move—I'd like to make it inside the city walls before sunrise," she said, waving goodbye to Brinsop.

The dragon was already sleeping soundly, hidden deep in the underbrush.

Sela and Thorin traveled through the forest, staying off the main path, until the city came into view. They approached the gate just as the rosy fingers of dawn appeared on the horizon.

Scattered groups of travelers trudged silently toward the city gates. The gates were open and unguarded. Sela and Thorin entered without opposition.

As soon as they got inside, Sela drew a sharp intake of breath. The condition of the city was appalling. The roads were filthy; the gutters ran deep with sewage. Countless beggars lined the sidewalks, their arms reaching out for alms. Most of them had grievous injuries—missing limbs, weeping sores, hanging tumors, or leprosy. Animals defecated out in the open near vendors who sold foul-smelling food to passersby.

As each group of travelers entered the city, unkempt children approached, trying to pick pockets and steal food.

"Thorin... this is worse than I imagined. This city has become a cesspit."

"Aye," said Thorin. "Ironport's in a bad state. It's as bad as Faerroe, now—maybe worse."

One skinny boy slunk quietly toward Sela. The child had black hair and blue eyes like her own son, Rali. He couldn't have been older than six or seven. The boy reached for her pocket, trying to steal some money. Sela grabbed his arm, and the boy yelped with alarm.

"Owww! I wasn't goin' to do nothin', Missus! I swear it!" said the boy, squirming against her firm grip. The boy screamed. "Let go of me!"

"Shhh! Be quiet, boy. I'm not going to hurt you," said Sela. She raised the boy's sleeve, revealing a long, infected cut. The wound was open and suppurating freely, and the boy's shirt was stiff with dried pus. "Come with me. I'm going to fix your arm."

The boy looked frightened, but he stopped resisting. They walked behind a building, and Sela placed her hand on the boy's injury.

"Close your eyes, boy," she said.

"No!" he said, shaking his head. He tried again to jerk his arm away. The boy was terrified.

This time, Sela squatted down to meet the boy's gaze. "Don't be afraid," she said. "I'll make you a deal. Just close your eyes, and I promise I'll give you a copper penny."

His eyes lit up. "You promise?" It sounded too good to be true. A copper penny would buy bread for three days. The boy's stomach growled, and he rubbed his distended belly. Sela knew that it had been a long time since this child had enjoyed a good meal.

"I promise," said Sela, crossing her heart.

"Okay," said the boy, who shut his eyes tightly and looked away.

"*Curatio*," she whispered. Her right hand glowed, and the redness on the boy's arm disappeared. The wound sealed up, leaving only a pink scar.

"Ouch!" said the boy. This time, he did jerk his arm away, but the pain was gone. He pulled up his dirty sleeve and looked at the healed wound with disbelief. "How did ye do that, Missus?"

"Magic," said Sela, smiling. "But don't tell anyone. It's a secret."

The boy's eyes grew even wider. "Magic? Really?"

She smiled. "Yes, really. Now tell me your name,

boy."

"Katahl," he said. "What about your promise, Missus? Where's my penny?"

Sela drew two copper coins out of her money pouch. "Katahl, here's your penny," Sela pressed one coin into the boy's outstretched palm. "However... I'll give you a chance to earn another. How well do you know the streets of Ironport? We need a guide. If you escort us around the city, I'll give you one more penny, plus a loaf of bread. What do you say?"

The boy nodded and clapped his hands gleefully. "I'll do it! I know 'em real good, Missus! Better than anyone else, I'll bet!"

"Great," said Sela, removing food from her daypack. "Here's some bread and a piece of cheese."

Katahl grabbed the food and ate ravenously. It only took him a few minutes to finish. When he was done, he asked, "So, where do you want to go?"

"Take us to the city square," said Sela.

"Sure thing!" said the boy, "I know a shortcut!" They turned into an alleyway, which was filled with rotting garbage and the long-dead carcass of a dog. The smell was dreadful, but Katahl seemed unfazed by it.

Katahl looked at Thorin. "Can I ask you something? You're a dwarf, ain't you?"

Thorin nodded. "Aye, I am. My name's Thorin."

"I could tell by your beard. There used to be a lot of dwarves in Ironport, but not anymore. They all went away."

"Why do you think that is?" asked Sela.

Katahl shrugged. "I don't know. A while ago, empire soldiers came. They took the old governor, and then all the dwarves left. Things changed a lot after that. The city used to be cleaner, too."

"How often do you see empire soldiers in Ironport, Katahl?" asked Sela.

"Every day. A whole bunch of them came into the city yesterday. They had horses and everything."

Sela and Thorin exchanged a worried glance. "You say there's a lot of soldiers here right now?" she asked, trying to keep her voice calm.

"Yeah, a lot. I stopped counting after forty, because I can't count any higher than that. Last night, they all went to the *new* governor's office, and now they're going around the city, asking people all kinds of questions. I think they're looking for someone."

"Katahl, did you see anyone *else* arrive with the soldiers?" said Sela. "Perhaps someone who looked a bit strange?"

The boy thought for a moment. "Yes! There were two men in dark clothes. They followed behind the soldiers, but they didn't have any horses."

"Did you happen to see what they looked like?" said Sela.

The boy shook his head. "Naw, they were wearing hoods. I didn't see their faces. But I remember them because their hands looked really weird."

"What do you mean by that?" asked Sela.

"Their hands were so white, like snow. But their fingernails were long and black, like they were painted. They were walking really close together, almost touching. People ran away from them. I don't know why everyone was so scared. I thought they looked funny!"

Necromancers.

Sela cast a worried glance at Thorin, who tucked his beard into his cloak and slowly drew his axe from his belt. "Katahl, do you know where they are now—the men with the black fingernails?"

"No... I haven't seen them since last night."

They heard shouting at the end of the alleyway. Sela and Thorin ducked into a nearby alcove. Two empire soldiers raced by on horseback, outfitted in their familiar yellow and red armor.

Sela's heart raced, and she forgot about the horrible smell in the alleyway.

She turned to Thorin and whispered, "This is bad. I don't know why the empire is here, but there's no way we're getting out of this city through the front gate, now. I suspect our mission has been compromised."

Sela turned to the boy. "Katahl, we've changed our mind about going to the city square. Where's the Whale's Head Pub? We're meeting some of our friends there later."

Katahl pointed west. "It's right past the city square behind the cathedral. See that bell tower? It's about a block away from there. You can't miss it. There's a big whale painted on the sign."

"Thanks for all your help, Katahl," Sela said, handing a coin over to the boy. "I don't think we'll need a guide after all. Here's that extra penny I promised you. Now you can go. I think we're going to stay here and rest for a little while."

"Wow, thanks!" said the boy, happily accepting the coin, oblivious to Thorin and Sela's rising distress.

"Just do me a favor. Don't tell anyone you saw us, okay?" said Sela.

"Okay," said the boy, nodding. Then he ran off in the other direction and disappeared.

As soon as the boy was gone, Sela faced Thorin. "We're in trouble. This is not a coincidence. We must assume the emperor knows about our plan. Even with Brinsop's help, I'm no match for two necromancers. There's no way I could defeat them both, much less an entire cohort of empire soldiers."

"Aye," said Thorin. "Do ye want to leave the city now? We could wait in the forest, and maybe return at nightfall?"

"No, leaving now would be too risky. They're probably watching the gates for us. We need to find your cousin and Vosper's renegade mage, and fast. Hopefully, they're still alive." Sela silently readied herself for any scenario they might encounter, including coming face to face with one of Vosper's necromancers.

"Where should we go now?"

Sela pointed at the bell tower. "There. If we can get to the top of that tower without being noticed, we'll have a view of the entire city. Your eyesight is superb. You might be able to spot the necromancers from there. At the very least, we'll find out where the soldiers are stationed."

"Aye. It's a good plan. But before we go, I think we should try to blend in with the locals." Thorin ripped his sleeves and picked up a handful of dirt, rubbing it onto his face and neck. When he was finished, he looked a lot more like a homeless beggar.

Sela sighed. Thorin was right. "It's a pity. This was my favorite cloak. *Incêndio!*" she said, and dozens of tiny flames burned holes into the wool. Then she also rubbed dirt into her clothing, face, and hands. She undid her neat ponytail and streaked her hair with mud. "Better?"

Thorin smiled. "Better! Ye don't look like an outsider anymore. But even covered in muck, ye're still beautiful."

Sela laughed, despite herself. "Thorin, has anyone ever told you that you're a shameless old flirt?"

"Nay, I only do it when I'm around ye," he said, with a wink.

The sound of galloping horses filled the air. They ducked back into the alcove as soldiers dashed by again, this time traveling in the opposite direction.

Sela popped her head out a few seconds later. "It's all clear. Let's get out of here. This alleyway is a death trap. Thorin, cover your face and try not to call attention to yourself."

They ran toward the end of the alley, staying close to the wall. Once they reached the street, they fell behind a crowd of haggard-looking citizens.

Thorin tucked his head down, faking a pronounced limp. They followed the motley group a few blocks and then ran down a side street, narrowly avoiding another soldier on horseback.

"Whew! That was close," said Sela. "This place is crawling with soldiers, and we're still blocks away from the bell tower."

"How about a concealment spell?" asked Thorin.

Sela shook her head. "No, I want to avoid using any magic unless absolutely necessary. The energy will attract the necromancers. Plus, that type of spell is very tiring, and I need to conserve my strength in case we get attacked."

Thorin cupped his ear, listening for the sound of horses. "I don't hear anythin' now. It's safe to go."

"Okay, let's move," said Sela.

They kept moving cautiously toward the tower, which they reached within the hour.

They jogged down the street and ducked into another alleyway. More soldiers passed, this time with swords drawn. They monitored the road from a doorway for a minute.

A single, drunken beggar sat by the bell tower entrance.

"Stay here," whispered Sela. "I'm going to check the door." She jogged across the street and jiggled the doorknob. It was locked. "*Lauss-lresa!*" she said, and the lock clicked open.

The beggar glanced at Sela, but said nothing. He didn't seem to notice that his drool was falling onto his chest.

She looked back over her shoulder and waved Thorin over. He jogged across the street, and they both ducked inside the building, locking the door behind them.

Thorin put his finger to his lips. "Shhh! I hear somethin' up top," he whispered, pointing to the stairs with his index finger.

Sela couldn't hear anything, but she knew that Thorin's dwarf hearing was superior to hers. "What is it?" she asked softly.

Thorin paused, listening intently. The sound of male voices drifted down. He cupped his hand to his ear, and the conversation became clear.

"Can you believe how long we've been stuck here? I hope our relief comes soon. I'm hungry," said one man.

"You're *always* hungry, Masheck. Stop complaining. Be thankful we don't have to be down there in the streets with all the riff-raff," said another. "Goodness, how I hate Ironport! This city is disgusting. Full of beggars and garbage. It's no better than an outhouse."

"Those *necros* are pretty scary, eh? Did you know they never sleep? During the day, they just stand in a corner, floating in place. Brrr! They give me the chills," the man said. He shivered involuntarily.

"Yeah, me too. They make my skin crawl. Just avoid them. I hope they find that damn spellcaster soon. I'd like to leave this filthy city and get back to the capital tomorrow. I'm wagering on the races next week, and I want to watch my horse win."

The other man laughed. "When was the last time your horse won a race? More likely, you'll be watching your horse *lose*!" The sound of laughter drifted down.

Thorin relayed the conversation to Sela. "There are two men upstairs, both empire soldiers. They sound pretty relaxed. If we're careful, we can probably take 'em by surprise."

Sela nodded, drawing her short sword. The sword rasped quietly against the scabbard; the sound made Sela's heart beat faster. She had been fully trained for battle, but it had been years since she'd experienced hand-to-hand combat.

Thorin grasped his axe with his right hand and a short dagger in the other. They tiptoed up the stairs, stopping just before the top step. Sela peered around the corner. Both soldiers stood with their backs to them, watching the city.

One pointed down at the city and laughed, amused by something in the street. "Masheck! Come 'ere and look at this! The captain is roundin' up the governor's lackeys in the center square. What a bunch of misfits!" The other man came over and peered over the side. He started laughing as well.

"Now!" whispered Sela, and they ran toward the unwitting soldiers.

Thorin jumped up, slicing open the neck of the first man, who fell instantly to his knees. The man clawed speechlessly at the air, blood spurting from his neck like a fountain. He coughed once, then collapsed.

"What?" said the other man, his eyes widening with alarm. He tried to draw his sword, but it was too late. Sela thrust her blade under his chest plate, jamming the point directly into his heart. The man gurgled blood and sank to the floor.

Sela searched the man's vest and was lucky enough to find a printed map of the city. She wiped her sword on her tattered cloak and returned the sword to its scabbard. "Nice job, Thorin," said Sela. "It's a pleasure fighting by your side."

Thorin's face was flushed. "That's champion, Mistress Sela. The pleasure's all mine." He cleaned his axe and his dagger on the dead man's tunic and tucked them back into his belt. "It's been a while since I've seen battle, but some things ye just never forget."

Thorin stepped over to the wall and looked down. "There's a lot more than forty soldiers in the city right now. Just on the streets, I'm seein' at least a hundred."

"Do you see the necromancers?"

"Nay, I don't see them. They might be indoors. They dislike sunlight, ye know."

"I know, but I still think the necromancers are down there somewhere. Why would Vosper send both of his *deadrats* here, only to have them hide all day? No... they may dislike sunlight, but *necros* don't sleep, so they're probably out looking."

"At least we know that they're lookin' for Islar. That boy did a shoddy job concealin' his exit from Morholt."

"Either that, or Islar did it on purpose," said Sela. "We still don't know if we can trust him."

"Aye, that's true," said Thorin, looking down again on the city. "Wait—I see my cousin Floki!"

"Where is he?" said Sela, crouching by the wall.

Thorin pointed down toward the street, by a saloon. There were dozens of men milling around the entrance, and the sound of loud music drifted up toward them. Even at a distance, Thorin could hear it.

"Look there—by the entrance of the Whale's Head Pub. He's not inside; he's back in the alleyway. He's the one wearin' a brown cloak. Ye can't see his face now; he just pulled up 'is hood."

"Are you sure it's him?"

"Positive. It's Floki, all right."

"Is Vosper's mage with him?"

"No… I don't think so. He's standin' alone. Islar might be waitin' somewhere else."

"I hope so," said Sela, stepping over the dead soldiers. "May Golka watch over us. I pray we're not stepping into a trap."

They walked swiftly down the stairs and carefully out the door, locking it behind them. The same beggar extended his hand to Sela. Sela pulled a coin from her purse and dropped it into the beggar's hand.

"You never saw us, understood?" she said.

The man nodded, displaying a toothless grin. He accepted the coin, tucking it into his pocket.

Sela and Thorin crept around the circumference of the watchtower and then strolled in the direction of the pub.

Soon they were across the street from the Whale's Head. As the boy had said, there was a painted sign of a whale hanging near the doorway. The whale in the picture was smiling and drinking an enormous flagon of ale.

"Over there," said Thorin, jerking his chin toward a short man standing outside. "That's Floki."

Thorin coughed loudly, and Floki looked up. A shadow of recognition crossed his face, and he grinned. As Floki stepped off the curb to approach them, three soldiers exited the pub with their swords drawn.

"*Stop!* Stay right where you are!" ordered one of the men.

"It's a trap!" hissed Sela. She grabbed Thorin by the collar and yanked him into the street. She pointed at Floki, "You! Get over here now!" she ordered. Startled, Floki jumped and ran over to them.

As soon as Floki got to the middle of the street, Sela grabbed his collar, too. "*Hud-leyna!*" she said, casting a concealment spell around them. The air shimmered, and the three of them disappeared. A gasp went up from the crowd.

"She's a mage!" said one of the onlookers.

"Sound the alarm!" said one of the soldiers.

"Run!" said Sela, and they sprinted down the street. Sela struggled to concentrate as they moved forward, hidden inside the protective bubble of her spell.

"This is a neat trick," said Floki. "They can't see us?"

"No, they can't see us," said Sela, "but they can still hear us, so keep quiet. We're far from safe. I don't know how long I'll be able to maintain this concealment spell around us. These types of spells aren't my strong suit, and Brinsop isn't here to help me. The sooner we find a place to hide, the better."

"I've got an idea," said Thorin. The old dwarf was struggling to keep up. "I remember an old building at the edge of town. There's an underground escape route that will take us out of the city."

"Yes," said Floki, "I remember it, too. It's the old governor's lodge."

"How far away is it?" asked Sela, still running.

"It's at the city's edge. We still have a ways to go," said Floki. They continued to run for several minutes, zigzagging through alleys, trying to stay off the main roads. In the distance, they heard the deep sound of a war trumpet.

"There goes the alarm," said Sela. "Soldiers are being alerted throughout the city."

A few times, empire soldiers rode right past them, and Floki jumped, forgetting that he was concealed by Sela's magic.

Finally, a massive structure came into view in the distance. It was overgrown with grass and weeds. A few abandoned houses stood nearby.

"Is that it?" asked Sela, squinting into the sunlight. Her face was flushed and streaked with dirt and sweat.

"Aye," said Thorin, huffing loudly. "That's it. It's abandoned. Vosper killed the former governor when he was discovered harboring mageborns. Vosper slaughtered the entire family—his wife and the children. Not even the servants were spared. Nobody lives there now. They say the building is haunted."

They continued until they reached the abandoned mansion. They stepped carefully through the brush and walked to the back of the building. Once they were hidden from the street, Sela released the spell. *"Letta-hud-leyna!"* she said, exhaling deeply.

She paused for a few moments, gathering her strength. "We were lucky to get this far," said Sela. "Floki, how did Vosper's men know your location?"

"I have no idea," said Floki. "I arrived two days ago. I counted at least a dozen empire soldiers when I arrived, but I've tried to stay out of sight. Islar has that dragon stone—that one you wanted. Maybe Vosper discovered the theft."

"But how would he know that Ironport is where we chose to meet?" said Sela. "It's more likely that Vosper allowed both of you to escape in order to set a trap for all of us."

"Vosper couldn't have known about our plan," said Floki. "Our messages weren't intercepted."

"Well, Vosper knows something, or else he wouldn't have sent his necromancers here," said Sela.

Floki's eyes opened wide. "N-necromancers? Vosper's *deadrats* are in the city right now?"

"Yes," said Sela. "They're here. We overheard two soldiers talking earlier today—they're searching for you and for Vosper's renegade spellcaster. Where is he?"

"Islar was so scared, I told him to wait outside the city," said Floki. "He's basically just a kid. I left him in that wooded area a few leagues away from the city. He's got Hanko's dragon stone with him."

It was the first good news they'd had. "Brinsop is out there, too, waiting for us," said Sela. "We have to find a way out of here. Thorin, where's that hidden passage?"

"Not exactly sure, but I believe it's directly underneath this house. It's a shaft that leads outside the city. It was used by the old governor to smuggle mageborn children out of Ironport during the war. We just have to find it."

"How do you know about the passageway?" asked Sela.

Thorin pressed a hand to his chest. "Because I was on the receivin' end. I helped transport the mageborns through the forest, and then into Mount Velik. From there, they were taken to Miklagard. Most of 'em were children. It didn't last long. Vosper found out, and the governor was executed, along with his entire family."

Sela nodded. The story was plausible. "Vosper has spies everywhere, even in Miklagard. Vosper's two *necros* escaped from Miklagard earlier this year, and I'm pretty sure they had assistance. I have my suspicions about who was responsible for helping those two *deadrats* escape."

"There's a traitor at Miklagard?" asked Floki.

"Probably more than one," said Thorin. "Last time I was there, there seemed to be some shady characters on the High Council."

"Enough chattering, you two," said Sela. "Let's look for that passageway. The soldiers already know that I'm a spellcaster, but if they discover that it's me, we're all in much bigger trouble. Vosper will do almost anything to get his hands on a dragon rider."

They began searching for the passageway, lifting rotting boards and pushing aside overgrown bushes. Blackberry brambles grew everywhere. After a few minutes, they were covered in scrapes and cuts from the thorns.

The horn blared again.

"That sound is getting closer," said Floki. "The soldiers are coming in this direction."

"You're right," said Sela grimly. Just then, she felt the touch of Brinsop's mind on her own. "Wait— Brinsop is calling me." She stood up and touched her dragon stone. The ruddy stone began to glow, and Brinsop's voice echoed in her mind.

"Sela! Good news. I've found Vosper's little renegade spellcaster. I almost fried him to a crisp before I realized who he really was. He's just a youngling! I frightened him nearly out of his wits. I think the poor boy may have actually wet himself. Do you want to communicate with him through me? The wretched little thing is crouching on the ground now, trembling like a leaf. He doesn't speak dragon tongue, so you better talk fast, be-

fore he attempts some little spell, and I have to knock the spit out of him."

"Bless you," said Sela. She tried to remember the spell that would allow her to speak *through* her dragon. It had been so long since she'd used it. The communication was done through their dragon stone link, so it wasn't nearly as exhausting as regular telepathic speech.

"Tala-Pekkja," she said, and her body began to glow bluish-white. Her outline wavered like a heat haze and then stabilized. In the forest, over a league away, a glowing image of Sela's body materialized, reflecting outwards like a prism from Brinsop's dragon stone. The vision sharpened, and Sela was able to see the terrified young spellcaster through Brinsop's eyes. *"Islar! I am Sela, leader of the dragon riders. Calm yourself—Brinsop is a friend. My dragon will not harm you."*

Islar, still crouched in a defensive position on the ground, stared at the apparition with wonder.

"Don't be afraid," Sela continued, *"I'm here to save you."*

Islar stood up and approached. He reached out with his fingers; they trailed through Sela's apparition like smoke.

She continued, *"Floki, Thorin, and I are trapped inside Ironport; we're trying to leave the city. Soldiers are watching the gates, and two necromancers are searching for us."*

Islar swallowed hard. "Vosper's *necros* are here?"

"Yes. To make matters worse, we were ambushed at

the Whale's Head by empire soldiers. The whole city's on alert; we're trying to get out of here without being killed."

"Can I do anything to help?" said Islar.

"Remain where you are, but stay alert. Thorin knows of a secret tunnel out of the city, and we're searching for it now. Be prepared for anything. If you see something suspicious, tell Brinsop, and she'll contact me telepathically. She cannot speak to you, but she understands human speech. Can you defend yourself, if necessary?"

Islar nodded. "Yes. I don't have much fighting experience, but I'm an eighth-degree mage. I just completed my Master's training last month. I wouldn't be able to defeat a necromancer, but I can certainly defend myself against a regular soldier."

"Good, because it's likely that you'll need to use your powers today. Keep your mind unguarded, just in case I need to contact you again."

"I will," said Islar.

Sela ended the spell but remained in contact with her dragon.

In the forest, Brinsop stood up, and Islar jumped back, still a little afraid.

"My, my... you're a skittish little thing, aren't you?" she said. Brinsop looked off into the distance, her stone glowing on her chest. "Sela, do you need me to come to the city?"

"No, not yet," Sela replied. "I don't want to risk you being seen. Don't break contact, though, just in case."

"Agreed," said Brinsop, silently maintaining their

connection.

"I found something!" said Floki excitedly. "Look at this!" He pointed to a stone slab near the dilapidated fence. "There are two holes at the top. They aren't natural—they're man-made."

"Ye found the exit!" said Thorin happily. "Those boreholes are how they lifted the block, usin' a pulley system. This is it!"

"But this stone is massive—it would take six men to lift it, at least. We can't lift this alone," said Floki.

"Move out of the way," said Sela, positioning herself in front of the stone.

Floki and Thorin moved back a few steps. Sela looked over her shoulder, mildly exasperated. "Further back!" she commanded firmly.

Startled, Floki and Thorin jogged back to the fence line.

The war horn sounded again. The sound was very close now.

"Mistress Sela, I hear horses," said Thorin. "They'll be here in a few minutes."

"I know," she mumbled, raising her hands. "Let me concentrate." She drew a deep breath and closed her eyes. A nimbus of blue flame developed around her. The grass near her feet started to burn.

The flames grew higher and higher. There was no way to hide it now—her glowing body was like a beacon.

Floki raised his hand, covering his face from the intense heat. "What's she *doing?*"

Sela clenched her right hand and dropped to one

knee. *"Hniga-rof!"* she shouted, dropping her fist onto the slab. The rock shattered, exploding upward like a geyser. Hot gravel rained down everywhere, pelting Thorin and Floki even as they tried to avoid it.

"Look out! Ow!" said Floki. "Owwww!"

Thorin's breath caught in his throat. "What a *woman!*" he whispered.

Sela spun around, her face flushed. "Done," she said, "and not a moment too soon!"

Seconds later, four soldiers on horseback appeared at the property's edge. "Stop! By order of the emperor!" ordered the first soldier, pointing his broadsword.

"Time to go!" said Thorin, yanking Floki's sleeve. The dwarves ran toward the opening and hopped in, disappearing down the hole. They landed with a thud.

Sela stood her ground, a glowing fireball in each hand. She stared at the soldiers, who approached her on horseback. "Stay back—if you want to live."

"Don't let her escape!" said one soldier, spurring his horse. They surrounded her with swords drawn, but did not attempt to engage her in combat.

They're not attacking me—they're waiting for the necromancers to arrive, thought Sela.

Five more soldiers appeared, and behind them, a short distance away, Sela saw a cloaked figure. It had milky-white hands and black nails.

Sela heard Brinsop's distressed voice in her mind. *"Sela! Get out of there!"*

"I'm going," she said, dropping backward into the opening. She twisted in the air, landing on her feet like a cat. Thorin and Floki stood waiting for her inside the tunnel.

"What are you two doing, just standing there?" she said. "*Run!*"

Floki and Thorin jumped and started running single-file down the narrow passageway.

The soldiers shouted from above. Sela heard them dismounting. Then she heard the hissing voice of the necromancer shouting orders. Sela pointed one hand at the opening. "*Skellr-Bresta-Elta!*" she said. A blast of energy erupted from her palm, jerking her back with the recoil. The opening collapsed, dirt filling the chamber. The passage went completely dark.

"Sela?" Thorin called out. "Are ye all right?"

"I'm fine," she replied. "Keep moving."

"Can ye see anythin'?"

"*Fljota-villieldr,*" she said. A floating orb of light materialized before her. "Now I can! *Tvennr!*" she said, and another glowing orb appeared. She threw it down the passage. It flew past the two dwarves, floating in the air, illuminating their way.

"Let's move!" she cried, and all three began running down the passageway. Above them, they could hear the muffled shouts from the soldiers.

"That's not going to hold them for long," Floki said. "The necromancers are going to follow us."

"I know," said Sela, still running. "Prepare yourselves. We're in for the fight of our lives."

8. THE RETURN TO PERSIL

E lias and Nydeired flew through the night. They passed over the Elburgian mountains and continued east. The forest below grew thicker, and soon there was nothing but evergreens below them.

Elias recognized the terrain. He had spent years exploring this forest as a child, and memories flooded back. Just before dawn, Elias noticed a familiar village on the horizon. His heart jumped.

"See that little settlement over there? That's Persil; I used to live there." As they approached, Elias looked down and was shocked by the town's appearance. Most of the houses had been destroyed. Nearby fields, once neatly cultivated, were overgrown and neglected.

"What happened here?" said Nydeired, as they flew over what remained of the small settlement. *"Where are all the people?"*

"Well, it's not dawn yet, maybe they're sleeping," said Elias, but his voice betrayed him. Something awful had happened, and they both knew it.

"Do you want to stop?" asked Nydeired, slowing down.

"No... we really shouldn't. Tallin said it was

dangerous." Elias looked down again. He saw the charred remains of his grandmother's cabin, and his breath caught in his throat. The memory of Carina's death still haunted him.

The cabin's roof had collapsed, and the exterior was overrun with weeds. As they continued on, Elias noticed entire blocks of damaged houses: their windows shattered, doors torn off their hinges. There wasn't a soul in the street. Persil was abandoned.

Then, off in the distance, Elias noticed smoke rising. "I see smoke in the air. Maybe someone is still here."

"I see it; it's that house at the edge of town: the one surrounded by all the garbage. Do you see it?"

Elias saw it too, and his blood ran cold. The only house left occupied—the only person still living in Persil—was Frogar, the loathsome merchant who had betrayed him to the emperor. This was the man responsible for his beloved grandmother's death.

"Elias, is something wrong?"

Elias swallowed the lump in his throat. "Yes... that's Frogar's house. It looks like he's the only one left in the city."

"Do you know him?"

"Unfortunately, yes. He's a junk merchant. After I found the dragon stone in the forest, I showed it to my grandmother. She warned me not to tell anyone, but I wouldn't listen."

"What happened? Tell me."

"I was a stupid kid and made a stupid mistake."

He shook his head, fighting back tears. "We were so poor... I tried to sell the stone, so I could give the money to my grandmother. I took the stone to Frogar, but he refused to buy it. Instead, he got angry and threw me out of his shop. I thought that was the end of it, but a few days later, empire soldiers came to Persil looking for us. The soldiers attacked my grandmother. She died trying to save me, and I barely escaped with my life. Frogar betrayed us. No one else knew about the stone. More than anyone else, I blame him for my grandmother's death."

"What do you want to do?" said Nydeired.

Elias fell silent for a moment. He felt anger rising in him, his arms and shoulders tensing. "Tallin specifically ordered us not to stop, and yet... this might be my only chance to confront Frogar for what he did."

Nydeired didn't respond. He simply circled down. The sun was rising, but Elias didn't bother casting a concealment spell—there wasn't anyone else here. They touched down right in front of Frogar's shop. Nydeired made a good landing, but there was so much refuse on the ground that his wings knocked over some metal boxes. The boxes clanked against each other and then toppled to the ground. The noise was loud, and a light went on inside the filthy shop.

"What in the bloody hell? Hey! Who's there?" called a gruff voice from inside.

Frogar.

Elias' heart pounded. He dismounted and waited

for Frogar to exit.

Sure enough, the old man came to the door. "What in blazes is going on out here?" he said, yanking open the door. Frogar's mouth dropped open when he saw Elias and the enormous dragon on his doorstep. Frogar screamed and slammed the door shut, followed by the sound of furniture being dragged around inside. Frogar was trying to block the door.

Elias waited for a moment. Then he looked at Nydeired. "Can you take care of this for me?"

"*Absolutely*," said Nydeired. The dragon reached out with one enormous clawed paw, yanking the door right off its hinges. The door sailed through the air, landing on the roof with a thud.

Frogar screamed again and rushed behind an old cabinet, trying to hide. "W-what do you want? I don't have any money!" he screeched, his voice desperate.

Elias stepped into the shop and stared at the old man, who was *quivering* with fear.

Frogar didn't seem to recognize him. The old man looked withered and shrunken, dressed only in a threadbare nightgown and a tattered cap.

Frogar's appearance gave him pause. Elias couldn't believe this was the same person who had frightened him so much when he was younger.

"Don't you recognize me?" said Elias, creeping toward the old man. Elias' skin tingled, and his hands began to glow with blue flame. Power surged through him; he knew that he could kill Frogar with a single word.

"I don't know you! I live here alone—I don't bother anybody!" he said.

"Look into my eyes, Frogar. You *do* know me."

The old man stared, confused. Slowly, a look of terrified recognition crossed the old man's face. "Elias?" he whispered. "But that's impossible! I thought you were dead," he said, stepping back. This time, the old man tripped over a pile of old baskets. He went tumbling to the floor, his spindly legs sprawling.

"I'm not dead, *despite* your best efforts," said Elias.

Frogar covered his face with his hands. "Please! Don't hurt me! Just tell me what you want!"

Elias clenched his teeth. He could smell the old man's foul stench—a mixture of cheap whiskey, sweat, and fear. Elias felt fury coursing through him; his whole body glowed with the *mage's flame.*

"I'll tell you what I want, old man. I want my grandmother, Carina, back. Can you bring her back to life?" said Elias, reaching out to grab Frogar by the collar.

The old man yelped, and then shrank down even further, like a turtle trying to hide inside its shell.

Frogar said nothing—he just trembled, his bloodshot eyes wide with fear.

Elias said quietly, "Now you're going to answer some questions for me. And you'd better tell me the truth, or I'll fry you to a crisp. Are we understood?"

Frogar gulped and nodded. "I'll tell you whatever

you want to know."

"Good. First, tell me what happened here. Why is the city empty?"

Frogar swallowed hard. "Vosper wanted your stone. After what happened to your grandmother, the emperor wasn't happy. More soldiers came. And then more. They rifled through your grandmother's cabin, looking for the stone in the ashes of the fire. When they couldn't find it, they assumed one of the townspeople had taken it. The soldiers ransacked the entire village. They searched every house."

"I have the stone in my possession. I always have," said Elias.

"I figured that, and I told them so, but the soldiers wouldn't listen to me! They broke windows and doors, and even burned some of the houses down. They killed anyone who tried to resist. The townspeople thought that was the end of it, until..."

"Until *what*?" asked Elias.

"Until the necromancer came," whispered Frogar.

"A necromancer came *here*? To Persil?" said Elias.

Frogar shuddered. "Yes. It came here searching for *you*. I've never seen anything so frightening in my entire life. Its eyes and fingernails were black. Its teeth were red—sharpened into points. And when it spoke, you felt like you were drowning. The necromancer kept babbling on and on about some prophecy. It questioned everyone in the town, even the children. Some of the people went mad—they simply started screaming and never stopped. No one was the same after that. Then people just left—one by one. It didn't take very long. The town became deserted."

"So why are *you* still here?" said Elias.

"I... don't have anywhere to go," said Frogar, his voice choked with emotion.

Elias stared at the old man. "Why did you do it, Frogar? Why did you tell the empire about the dragon stone?"

"I did it for the money!" Frogar cried. "There! I said it! There was supposed to be a reward! But there wasn't. I never imagined this would happen. I certainly didn't think they would *kill* anyone! I've lived here my entire life, and now Persil is destroyed. I know it's my fault. No one is ever coming back here, and I'm all alone!" The old man put his face in his hands and wept bitterly.

Elias stared. This wasn't the reaction he had expected. Elias tried to stay angry, but he couldn't. Even after everything Frogar had done, Elias felt sorry for him.

Nydeired tucked his massive head inside the doorway. It was the only part of his body that would fit. *"Elias? Are you all right?"*

"Yes, I'm fine," he said. Then he sighed and offered the old man his hand. "Get up, Frogar."

Frogar looked up, startled. "You're not going to kill me?" he asked.

"No, I'm not going to kill you," Elias said. He grabbed Frogar's wrinkled hand and lifted the old man to a standing position. Still terrified, Frogar continued to tremble.

Nydeired blinked his pebble-black eyes at the old man. "*What are you going to do with him? Do you want me to kill him for you?*"

Elias looked at Frogar. The old man was hunched over, staring timidly at Elias and his dragon.

Elias came here wanting revenge, but even after everything that he had suffered, he knew that he couldn't kill an unarmed man, especially one as wretched and miserable as Frogar.

"No," said Elias. "I don't want you to kill him. I'm not going to do anything to him."

Elias turned to Frogar, looking him directly in the eye. "Frogar, I've hated you for a long time. More than anyone I've ever hated in my entire life. I hold you directly responsible for my grandmother's death. She's gone because of what you did. But I don't believe you're an evil man—just greedy and foolish. You'll have to live with the consequences of your actions for the rest of your life, and I think that's punishment enough."

Elias turned to leave. Once he reached the doorway, he paused for a moment, still struggling with his emotions. Elias caressed Nydeired's head gently, thankful for his precious friend. Elias felt a great weight had been lifted. Without looking back, Elias said, "Frogar... I forgive you. Farewell."

Behind him, Elias heard Frogar crying softly.

Nydeired crouched down, and Elias mounted the dragon saddle. Nydeired spread his enormous wings, getting ready to take off. Just then, Frogar rushed outside.

"Wait! Elias! Wait!" In his haste, the old man stumbled on a broken chair in the walkway. He fell down, landing face-first in the dirt.

Elias suppressed a smirk. Despite everything that had happened, watching Frogar scrabble in the dirt gave him a small measure of satisfaction. Elias waited for him to rise. "Yes? What do you want?"

"Here," said the old man, reaching out to hand Elias an ornate crossbow. "Take it—I've had it for years. It's just collecting dust. I don't get many customers anymore."

Elias reached down to accept the weapon. It was lovely—the most exquisite crossbow that he'd ever seen. The wood felt as hard as stone, but it was as light as a feather. It had an ornate gold casing, inlaid with five precious stones: diamond, onyx, sapphire, carnelian, and emerald—all the colors of dragonkin. "How did you get this?"

Frogar shrugged. "People sell me all kinds of things. I've had this crossbow at least a dozen years. An empire soldier sold it to me for a few silver coins. The fool wanted drinking money. He had no idea what he had. It's a peerless weapon, made by elvish hands. I know that much. You'll never find another one finer, you can bet on that."

"It's beautiful, but why are you giving this to me?" said Elias.

Frogar looked down for a minute. His slippered foot played absently with a piece of trash. When he finally spoke, his voice was a whisper. "I'm no saint, that's for sure. And I'm not good at apologies. I'm sorry about what happened to you and your grandmother. I know this gift doesn't make up for what I did, but I hope it aids you on your journey." Then Frogar turned around and disappeared back into his shop.

"Thank you," said Elias, but Frogar was already gone. Elias looked at the crossbow again. It truly was magnificent. He tucked it into his saddlebag, and Nydeired took off into the sky.

"We've lost some time, so I'll cast a concealment spell around us, and we'll make up the hours before we stop to rest. *Hud-leyna!*" he said. The spell surrounded them, and they disappeared from sight.

"*There's magic in that weapon, Elias. I can feel it,*" said Nydeired.

"I can feel it, too," Elias said. "It's enchanted somehow, just like my grandmother's dagger. Despite everything, I feel better. I'm glad we came."

"*I'm proud of you,*" said Nydeired. "*I wouldn't have been so forgiving, but then... I'm a dragon.*"

Elias laughed. He took a deep breath, looking at the horizon. The day was warm, and the sky was cloudless and beautiful. Elias raised his arms to the heavens and closed his eyes.

He knew, at that point, he was ready to face the future.

9. TALLIN

T allin and Duskeye arrived at Mount Velik late in the evening.

King Rali and King Hergung were waiting for them outside the mountain, dressed in royal finery. There were hundreds of other dwarves in the crowd, which included Hergung's sizable entourage, as well as a large group of curious onlookers. They had apparently decided to make a public show of his arrival.

"Look! It's him!" cried one dwarf. "It's the dragon rider!"

"It's Tallin! It's Tallin!" yelled another, running down into the caverns to alert the others.

"Here we go," said Duskeye, landing in a prepared area near the entrance to the dwarf caverns. The ground was littered with flowers in anticipation of their arrival.

"Let's get this over with," said Tallin quietly. He hated these ceremonies. Unfortunately, it was one of the things that the dwarves were known for. Tallin raised his hand, and a hearty cheer went up from the crowd.

Tallin did not dismount. Instead, he stayed seated and entered riding Duskeye. Inside the mountain, hundreds of dwarves lined the walls, cheering and banging shields as they passed.

"This is ridiculous," hissed Tallin under his breath.

"Do they always act this way?" asked Duskeye. *"The last time we were here, I don't remember there being so much hullabaloo."*

"No, they *never* act this way, at least with me. The last time we were here, there were hundreds of dragon riders. Now, there are only a handful of us. They're celebrating because I'm the only remaining dwarf-rider. Considering the way the dwarves treated me before, it's absurd." Tallin's mood soured as he thought about his past.

This was the first time that Tallin had returned to Mount Velik since the war. Because he was a halfling, Tallin had been teased mercilessly as a child. The dwarves save their cruelest bigotries for those of mixed blood, and Tallin suffered persistent bullying throughout his youth.

When he reached puberty, his magical gift was discovered, and the public mockery stopped, but he was still treated like an outsider. It wasn't until Tallin was accepted to Aonach Tower and was matched with Duskeye that he finally felt some measure of happiness and acceptance. But his joy was short-lived.

The Dragon Wars changed everything. Tallin and Duskeye were captured, tortured, and then forced into hiding in the desert. He hadn't returned to Mount Velik since then.

Now the dwarves were welcoming him like a forgotten son. After everything he had endured, their reception seemed hollow and fake. Tallin couldn't forget the past.

King Hergung raised his arm. "Esteemed dragon rider, we greet you!"

Cheers rose from the crowd, which had now become a mob, all of them squeezing forward to catch a glimpse of the dragon and his rider. After living in quiet isolation for so many years in the desert, all of this attention made Tallin deeply uncomfortable.

The king waved his hand in a high arc, pointing at endless rows of tables set up for a lavish banquet. Dancing women in ornate costumes whirled in the center of the vast hall, and musicians played a jolly tune that echoed through the caves.

The crowd moved closer, surrounding them, touching them. Dwarf women lifted their babies toward him, crying out for a blessing. Duskeye struggled to move forward and then stumbled as dozens of children attempted to climb his legs. It was too much, and Tallin became more and more agitated. Finally, he couldn't take it anymore.

"Enough! Everyone move back! *Prongva-hrofk-kva!*" he said, and the entire crowd fell back as if pushed away by an invisible barrier. People screamed, stumbling and tripping on top of each other.

"Stop!" Hergung cried, his face horrified. "Please stop!"

The crowd fell silent.

Tallin raised his chin, defiant. "We are *not* here to

celebrate. We returned to Mount Velik because our land is at war. Is this how my people prepare for *battle?* With lavish banquets and ceremonies?" His voice echoed loudly off the walls.

The dwarf king was sweating profusely in his heavy robes. "Tallin, we meant no disrespect," he said. "This celebration is for you!"

Tallin responded with a withering glare. "I'm not your *puppet*, and this is an inappropriate time for celebration. Vosper *will* attack—of that, you can be certain. It's just a matter of time. When he finally comes to our mountain, he will show no mercy. He will slaughter every man, woman, and child. None will be spared. *All of you will die.* Vosper wants to wipe the dwarves from the face of this earth."

King Hergung's mouth fell open, and a collective gasp went through the crowd.

Tallin knew what he was doing was a *serious* breach of dwarf etiquette. But he simply didn't care.

They all stared at him. Tallin's voice had changed, turning deep. "While Duskeye and I are here, we will not attend any parties, nor take part in any hollow displays of pageantry. I will *not* be attending any banquets. Do you hear me? War is coming, and the time for festivity is *over!*"

King Hergung's face was pale. No one dared to speak.

Rali covered his mouth with one hand, hiding a smile. *Bravo, Tallin,* he thought. It was everything that he wanted to say, but could not, because of his title.

"*Prongva-hrofkkva!*" Tallin said again, more forcefully. He stretched his arms in front of him, and then expanded them slowly as if parting open a curtain. The startled crowd split down the middle, creating a path. Tallin and Duskeye walked forward, leaving the main hall and entering the caverns.

The crowd didn't move or speak, stunned at what had just happened.

Rali left Hergung's side and followed Tallin, with Aor, his honor guard, close behind. Rali caught up with the dragon and his rider a few minutes later.

"That was quite a display," Rali said. "I'm sure they'll be talking about it for a long time."

Tallin's head snapped towards the young king. "Sire, where are your quarters? We must talk."

"On the north side of the mountain, near the mushroom fields," said Rali. "Look for my banner. It's posted outside my suite."

"I'll meet you there," said Tallin, as he tapped his heel into Duskeye's side.

The dragon moved to the edge of the pathway, which dropped off onto a sheer cliff. Duskeye spread his sapphire wings and took flight, soaring above the fields within the mountain. The dwarves on the ground pointed and stared, watching the dragon with wonder. Duskeye circled above for a few minutes, and then landed near the mushroom fields. Tallin dismounted, and they both disappeared into the northern part of the caverns.

Rali and Aor continued to walk, arriving at their quarters much later. Rali didn't see Tallin or Duskeye, but as soon as they arrived at the chamber entrance, Rali heard Tallin's voice.

"*Letta-hud-leyna!*" he said, releasing the concealment spell. They had been waiting for Rali outside the chamber, hidden from view.

Duskeye was too large to enter, so he remained outside, blocking the doorway. Aor walked up to him, but when Duskeye failed to move, the guardsman calmly climbed over him.

Duskeye never stirred, and Aor didn't say a word; he merely took his place directly inside the chamber entrance. Duskeye opened one eye and blew a gentle smoke ring around the stoic guard. Aor didn't move as the smoke drifted down around him, but just for an instant, the corner of Aor's mouth lifted in a tiny smile.

"How was your journey?" asked Rali, removing his heavy robes. After a year of wearing light tunics in the desert, it felt odd to wear the type of gaudy imperial clothing that the dwarves expected.

"Interesting," said Tallin. "On the way here, I took a quick detour and decided to pass over the ruins of Aonach Tower. There's some activity there."

"Is it Vosper's men?"

"No, I don't think so. It looked like regular villagers. They're rebuilding the tower."

Rali's eyebrows shot up. "That's unexpected. Vosper destroyed Aonach Tower to send a message. Those ruins are a permanent symbol of the emperor's triumph. To rebuild them is an act of treason."

"Yes. It's significant. The common people are rising up. Preparing to defend themselves. They know that war is imminent."

"We both know that war is coming, but the dwarves refuse to accept it." Rali sat down, his shoulders hunched. "The treaty talks are stalled. The infighting between the clans is intense."

Tallin shook his head. "That figures. Have *any* of the clan leaders shown a desire to cooperate?"

"Sundergos and Akkeri support the treaty. Utan and Skemtun abstain, and Bolrakei is opposed."

"Bolrakei?" said Tallin, scratching his chin. "That's a surprise. I would not have thought that *Klora-Kanna* would oppose this alliance. Has Bolrakei told you what she wants?"

Rali took a deep breath and told Tallin about Bolrakei's demand for a dragon stone.

Tallin's face darkened with fury. "That *bitch*," he hissed through clenched teeth. Then he spun on his heel to leave.

"Where are you going?" asked Rali.

"I'm taking care of this right now," said Tallin, as he exited the chamber. "Duskeye, wait for me here."

The dragon nodded and yawned. He had already settled down to take a nap.

Rali watched Tallin's retreating figure. Seconds later, Tallin raised his hand and disappeared, casting a concealment spell so he could walk through the caverns unmolested.

"I wonder what that was about?" murmured Rali, who went back inside his chamber and waited. Rali didn't know if confronting Bolrakei was a good idea, but he supposed he'd find out soon enough.

Tallin made his way silently through the vast caverns, taking a less-known path to Bolrakei's suite of rooms. It took him almost an hour to reach her on foot, but walking helped him control his anger. By the time he reached the entrance of her cave, he had calmed down somewhat.

The air shimmered, and Tallin made himself visible again, startling the guards outside.

"Tell Bolrakei that I am here," he said. One of the guards nodded and disappeared into the chamber. The guard returned moments later, his face pale.

"Ah… I apologize, Mr. Tallin, but Lady Bolrakei isn't accepting any visitors at this time."

"I see," said Tallin, raising one eyebrow. "Perhaps you misunderstood me. It wasn't really a request. *Sofna!*" Tallin snapped his fingers, and the guards slumped to the ground, fast asleep.

Tallin walked into the chamber unopposed and saw Bolrakei eating from a giant platter with her bare hands.

She gasped with surprise. "How did you get in here?" she said, her mouth full of food. Droplets of grease dripped from her chin. She wiped her mouth with the back of her sleeve.

Tallin laughed. "I walked in. Did you really think that your pathetic guards could stop me?"

She gulped. "What do you want?"

"You know why I'm here. I know about your request for a living dragon stone. Besides being absurd, it's impossible. A dragon stone cannot be separated from its rider. Did you really think you could stall these talks indefinitely with such an obscene request?"

She made a face. "I'm not stalling. I'm merely... *negotiating* for something I want. There's no harm in that, is there? And who says my request is obscene? A dragon stone *can* be separated from its rider. Elias Dorgumir carries a living dragon stone—an emerald that belonged to his father. The boy will go through his binding ceremony soon. After that, he will have no use for the stone. Why not give it to me?"

Tallin's eyes narrowed at her. He wondered how Bolrakei discovered *that* little piece of information. "While it's true that Elias carries his father's stone, after the boy goes through his binding ceremony, the emerald will be returned to Chua, his father."

"But why?" she asked. "Chua has no use for it. He's done just fine without it for all this time. Why not just give his stone to me?"

Tallin couldn't believe her obstinacy. "Are you mad? Listen to yourself. What possible use could you have for a dragon stone?"

Bolrakei leered. "I'm a *collector,* Tallin. Beautiful stones are the pride of my clan. I promise I will care for the stone and give it a place of honor among my vast collection."

"Dragon stones aren't regular gemstones, Bolrakei," he said, struggling to maintain his patience. "They're living things. They can't be separated indefinitely from their owners, just to sit inside a glass case for your amusement. We're at *war*. And Parthos needs your support to solidify this alliance. Don't you understand that this is an unreasonable request?"

She snorted. "I don't care about your petty war! I don't even understand your desire to help these stupid humans. What have the humans ever done for us? They're nothing to me! Either give me a dragon stone, or I'll continue to block the treaty. It's that simple. The choice is yours."

Tallin walked over to her, hands clenched at his sides. "You greedy *witch*... this insult won't be forgotten."

"What *insult*? I simply know what I want." Bolrakei gave him an innocent shocked look, which dissolved into an evil smile. "And you, Tallin? Have you forgotten where you came from? Why do you fight for them?"

"You presume too much, Bolrakei. You understand nothing about me, or my motivations."

"Bah! You are a fool! Look at yourself. You look *ridiculous*, defending those humans. Wake up, Tallin! You *aren't* human. And you aren't a dwarf. You're a *half-breed*—an abomination!"

Tallin stretched out his hand and grabbed her robe, dragging her out of her chair.

Her eyes opened wide, and she gasped. "W-what are you going to do?"

148

At that moment, five guards burst into the room with their swords drawn. "My lady! Are you all right?" The guards pointed their weapons at Tallin.

Tallin eyed the guards and then looked back at Bolrakei, who looked like she was about to scream. He released her, and she fell to the floor. "It looks like our conversation is over... for now. Don't bother getting up. I'll show myself out."

Tallin turned on his heel and left without another word.

One of the guards approached, offering his hand. "What happened, my lady?" he asked. "Did he try to harm you?"

Bolrakei stood up, attempting to smooth her crumpled gown. "No, no... I'm fine. Nothing happened. But double my guard, just in case," she added.

"The two guards that were stationed outside your chambers are still unconscious, my lady. Shall we notify King Hergung about this?"

"No, that won't be necessary," said Bolrakei, with a malevolent smile. "I'll have my vengeance. Sooner or later, I'm going to destroy that filthy half-breed."

10. FIGHTING SHADOWS

S ela cried, "*Stop!*" as she ran ahead of Thorin and Floki. "Stop!"

Their escape was blocked again, this time by a wall of dirt that had collapsed the surrounding tunnel. The passageway was overgrown with tree roots in numerous areas, which forced them to stop and clear the path.

"We'll have to use our hands," said Sela. "I can't risk another explosion—the walls are too weak here."

They dug furiously to clear the passage. Thorin chopped at the roots with his axe while Floki pulled them out of the way. Sela kept the passageway lit and remained on alert. Eventually, enough dirt had been cleared away for them to crawl through and continue on.

"How long have we been down here?" asked Floki.

"An hour, at least," said Sela. "How far does this tunnel go, Thorin?"

"If I remember correctly, the exit to the tunnel is in that wooded area outside the city," said Thorin. "Not sure exactly where, though. We have at least another league to go."

"We can't afford any more delays," said Sela. "We've been down here too long already."

They were lucky, and the passage remained clear for the remainder of their journey. Floki stumbled a few times, tripping on the uneven ground. Thorin traveled expertly through the tunnel, a testament to the years he spent underground working as a miner.

They finally made it to the end of the passage. Only the left side of the wall had collapsed. After they cleared away the dirt, a circular iron door was plainly visible. Sela closed her eyes and sent a telepathic message to her dragon. "Brinsop, we've arrived at the exit. Can you trace our position using your dragon stone?"

"Easily," said Brinsop. *"I can feel your presence in the distance. But what should I do with this mage? He hasn't moved for an hour—he's frozen in place like a frightened rabbit."*

Sela thought about it for a minute. "Just start walking," she said. "He'll probably follow you."

Sure enough, as soon as Brinsop got up and started making her way toward Sela's location, Islar hopped up and followed, albeit at a distance.

"You were right," said Brinsop. *"He's right behind me like an obedient puppy."*

"I expected as much," said Sela. "He's frightened out of his wits, and he doesn't have much choice except to trust us. Vosper was planning to use him as cannon fodder for one of his spells."

Minutes later, Brinsop stood directly above the

exit door. The door was obscured by blackberry brambles. Brinsop used a massive clawed foot to clear away the brush, exposing the door. She tapped the door with her claws, and the sound echoed below. "*Sela, tell the others to step away.*"

Down below, Sela grabbed Thorin and Floki and pushed them back, away from danger. Brinsop looked over at Islar, who stood trembling several steps away. She waved her paw, and he stepped back a few more paces.

Brinsop grabbed the circular door with her paws. She grunted once, and tore the door out of the ground, sending a huge spray of rocks and soil into the air. The door clattered against a nearby tree, and Islar yelped. Then Brinsop reached into the opening and pulled Sela and the dwarves out of the hole.

"Thank you, Brinsop," said Sela, wiping off her dusty trousers. Then she turned to Islar and introduced herself. "Hello, young man, I'm pleased you made it out of Morholt alive." She reached out her hand in greeting.

Islar reached out warily and shook Sela's hand. "Me too."

"Do you have the dragon stone?" she asked.

Islar nodded, pulling the stone from his pocket. Sela examined the stone, nodding with approval. "This is indeed Hanko's stone. Good job, young man."

Islar blushed. "Thank you," he said. "It wasn't that difficult to get. Vosper leaves the stones unguarded."

"Just hold onto it for now, okay? I have many questions for you," said Sela, "but they'll have to wait. We can't stay here. Empire soldiers are looking for us, and the necromancers aren't far behind."

Thorin looked around, but didn't see the rest of Floki's family. "Floki, where are your wife and children? Did they stay in Morholt?"

Floki hung his head sorrowfully. "I didn't tell you, Thorin... the children are dead. Halda left me. When we fled Jutland last year, we went first to Faerroe. The water is contaminated in that city, and we all fell ill with cholera shortly after we arrived. Our children were sick for months. Halda and I both recovered, but they didn't make it."

"Oh, cousin... I'm so sorry for yer loss."

Floki nodded, and his eyes misted over with tears. He continued quietly. "Halda—she blamed me for the children's deaths. She couldn't forgive me. We went our separate ways last fall. I don't even know where she is now. I've lost everything." Floki put his face in his hands and sobbed.

Thorin patted Floki gently on the back. Islar and Sela stood at a respectful distance, waiting for Floki to compose himself. Sela stepped forward to remind them that they had to go, but she never got the chance. The air shimmered with red light, and a necromancer appeared nearby.

The necromancer hissed. He held a short, hooded figure by the neck.

"Baghra, help us!" Islar gasped. "It's Uldreiyn! One of Vosper's *necros!*"

The necromancer cracked a ghoulish smile. "Islar... how fortunate... to have found you here... with your traitorous friendssss... the emperor will be sssso pleased."

Sela swirled around, facing the necromancer. She raised her hands, already glowing blue. "Stay back, *necro*," she warned.

The necromancer laughed—a bubbling hiss erupting from his blackened mouth. "Ssssela. The leader of the dragon riders... oh, how I have longed for thissss day... to kill you will give me ssssuch exquisite pleasure..."

Sela held her ground. "Get back, all of you," she ordered. Sela's dragon stone began to glow as she prepared for battle. Brinsop growled, rearing up on her hind legs.

"Not so fast! Aren't you the least bit curioussss... to know how we found you?" said Uldreiyn, yanking the hood off his captive. The woman fell to the ground, her face covered with bruises. Thorin and Floki gasped.

It was Halda, Floki's wife. She lifted her head and screamed. The necromancer struck her on the back of the head, and she tumbled face-first into the dirt.

"Recognize her? She was sssso cooperative... she gave us all the information we needed to find you; even how to translate your quaint secret dwarf language." The necromancer laughed again. "We've been intercepting your messages... for a long time."

"H-Halda?" said Floki, in disbelief. "You turned traitor for the emperor? How could you do this to us?"

Halda's hands were tied behind her back, her wrists chafed and bloody from the ropes. Floki stepped forward to help his wife, but Sela jerked him back. She shook her head. "Not yet," she whispered.

Halda spat blood. She stared at Thorin with undisguised hatred. "You! It's *your* fault we were forced to leave Jutland! You showed up on my doorstep with that cursed human child and destroyed our lives! My children would still be alive if it wasn't for you. You signed our death warrants!"

Thorin swallowed hard, but said nothing.

"Sssshut up, *dwarf*," said the necromancer, kicking Halda in the stomach. She writhed in the dirt for a few moments, and then lay still.

Floki tore out of Sela's grip and ran to Halda, tears streaming down his face. "Halda! Halda! Speak to me!"

"Floki, don't!" cried Sela.

The necromancer leered. "A pity... that you've both outlived your usefulnessss... I would have enjoyed... torturing you both at my leissssure... but my emperor has no use... for dwarves."

The necromancer's hand sliced the air in a high arc, and the air crackled with crimson fire. *"Bruni-andlat!"* he shrieked, and Floki gasped, clawing at his throat as red flames shot from his mouth and nose. He was burning from the inside out. Floki's skin blackened as he was burned alive. Halda screamed as the spell consumed her as well.

"No!" said Thorin. But it was already too late. Floki and Halda were dead, their bodies charred beyond recognition.

Uldreiyn smiled, pleased with his handiwork. The necromancer turned to face Sela. "Dragon rider... you will be more challenging prey... Vosper wantssss you captured alive, unfortunately."

Sela raised her glowing hands in defense. "You're welcome to try, *deadrat*. It will take more than a little fire spell to best me."

Thorin drew his axe.

The necromancer looked amused, as if noticing Thorin for the first time. "What do... you plan... to do with that little toothpick, *dwarf*?"

"I plan to defend my lady, dark one," said Thorin, stepping closer.

"Thorin, don't!" Sela warned. "Stay back; this creature can't be harmed with normal weapons. Let me handle this."

Thorin shook his head and stepped closer. "That *thing* ain't a normal man, but this ain't a normal axe, either," he whispered quietly.

The necromancer didn't move. He obviously didn't consider the little dwarf a threat. Thorin raised his axe and swung, aiming for the necromancer's stomach.

The necromancer raised his right hand, casting a simple deflection spell, and was shocked when Thorin's axe struck his arm. Thorin's axe glowed bright pink—a mark of enchanted weaponry.

The stunned necromancer screamed in pain,

grasping his wrist. The necromancer's hand hung limply from a ribbon of skin. Thick, black blood flowed from the wound. Anywhere the necromancer's blood fell, the grass withered and died.

Sela's eyes opened wide. *Of course!* she thought, *Thorin's ax is enchanted, just like his clan amulet.* She reminded herself not to underestimate him again.

Thorin hopped back, easily avoiding a fireball thrown by the enraged necromancer. Uldreiyn howled again, tucking his severed hand into his cloak.

Sela seized the opportunity and struck. "*Landskjalpti!*" she said, and the ground opened up, swallowing the necromancer up to his neck. The necromancer howled.

Sela clenched her fist repeatedly. The earth mimicked her movements, packing itself tighter and tighter around the necromancer's body. Uldreiyn screamed again. The awful sound reverberated through the forest. The undead creature thrashed against the packed dirt, trying to free himself.

"Let's get out of here!" said Sela, and they ran.

"Mistress Sela, I can hear horses in the distance," said Thorin. "The emperor's men are just minutes away."

A short distance away, their trail dropped off into a shallow ravine. Sela pointed. "Let's get in here—it's large enough to fit all of us, and then Islar can cast his spell while I figure out how to get us out of here."

They skidded down the hill and crouched into

the ravine. From the roadside, they were concealed from sight. It wouldn't hide them for long, but long enough to figure out their next move.

"Islar, do you know any protection spells?" said Sela.

Islar nodded. "Yes, quite a few. I know the spell for an elvish protection circle. It's very powerful, but it drains a lot of my energy."

"You learned *elvish* spells in the capital?" asked Sela, shocked.

Islar nodded. "A few. They're part of our training in Morholt. All the master spellcasters learn them."

Sela made a mental note to ask Islar more about the elvish spells later. Right now, they just needed to get out of sight. "Now, Islar: cast the spell," she ordered.

The young spellcaster raised his hands and closed his eyes. "*Grifla-nei-la-rei,*" he said, and the air shimmered around them.

"Okay, it's done," said Islar, panting slightly. "We're safe... for the time being. The spell blocks sound, smell, and sight."

"Impressive," said Sela. "How long can you maintain it?"

Islar's face had already started to perspire. "Ten minutes... *maybe* fifteen if I'm lucky."

"That will have to do," said Sela. "Thorin, can you estimate how many there were, based on the sounds of the horses?"

Thorin paused to listen, with one hand cupping his ear. "More than a dozen. But fewer than twenty.

I can still hear them in the distance. They're comin' this way."

Sela bit her lip. "I want you and Islar to stay here, out of sight. Brinsop and I are going to try and ambush those soldiers."

Thorin shook his head fiercely. "Nay, I'm comin' with ye. What if the other necromancer is with them? Ye shouldn't face that many soldiers alone."

"If the other necromancer is coming, I might have to fight them both," said Sela. "You got lucky with that first one, but he won't fall for the same trick twice. It will take him some time to remove himself from that constriction spell—necromancers aren't very good at countering passive attacks."

"Can't we just fly out of here?" said Thorin.

"Brinsop can't carry all three of us; she's injured. And it's too dangerous to leave either of you here alone. I'll try to draw them away from your location —then I want you to run!"

"*Sela, I can hear them,*" said Brinsop. "*They're seconds away.*"

"Islar, try to maintain the spell as long as you can." Sela mounted Brinsop's back and took flight, rising above the trees. She saw the soldiers immediately.

"There they are," she pointed. There were eighteen men, all on horseback. The other necromancer, Uevareth, floated silently behind the horses.

Brinsop swooped down and landed behind the group, opening her mouth to shoot a river of flame toward the startled soldiers.

"It's the dragon rider!" they screamed. "Look out! Look out!"

Four of the men collapsed immediately, cooked by dragon fire inside their armor. The rest of the men scattered, running for the safety of the trees. The necromancer simply moved aside, unharmed by the dragon's fiery breath.

Sela jumped from Brinsop's back and faced the necromancer. "So... there really are two of you," she said. "I left the other one stuffed underground without a hand."

"I ssssaw what you did to my brother... impressive bit of magic." The necromancer's voice sounded bored. It was flat, without inflection. "But still a futile exercise. He will recover shortly, and I won't... make the same misssstakes."

Sela and the necromancer circled each other.

Uevareth attacked first. *"Hilfaquna!"* he said, striking with a sleep-inducing spell. Sela felt soft tendrils circling her body and grew dizzy.

Brinsop watched the exchange and growled, *"Sela! Stay alert!"*

Sela shook her head and strengthened her wards. She felt the necromancer's spell weaken, then retreat.

"Is that the best you can do?" she taunted. The necromancer hissed. They exchanged fireballs for a few minutes, neither doing any real damage except to the trees around them, which started to burn.

Islar and Thorin peeked over the gulley and watched the battle from a distance. Moments later,

Islar shivered, feeling a cold rush of air and the stink of dead flesh.

"Thorin! I feel something," said Islar. "I think it's the other—"

He didn't have the chance to finish.

Uldreiyn yanked Islar up by his collar, shaking him violently in the air. Islar screamed, staring into the black eyes of the furious necromancer, who was still covered in dirt from Sela's constriction spell. His wrist, now a bloody stump, was tied with a ribbon of cloth.

The injured necromancer flung Islar violently against a nearby tree. There was a loud crack when his skull hit the trunk. Islar slumped to the ground, unconscious. Uldreiyn then turned his attention to Thorin, who scrambled out of the gulley and drew his axe again.

"I'm ready for ye," said Thorin, hopping back and forth on his toes.

"Ssssso, old dwarf..." hissed Uldreiyn. "You bested me once... but you can be sure... it won't happen again."

The necromancer struck, hitting Thorin with a bolt of electricity. Thorin's axe deflected the bolt, but the recoil knocked the dwarf on his back.

The necromancer struck him again and again, and each time Thorin deflected the blow, but his arms began to weaken. After a few minutes, he was gasping for breath. The necromancer was just too powerful.

Eventually, the undead spellcaster stood right

next to Thorin, whose face was streaked with sweat. Nearby, Islar raised his head and groaned. The young spellcaster did not have the strength to rise.

Uldreiyn kicked Thorin's enchanted axe out of his hand, launching the weapon into the gulley. Then he reached down with his good hand and yanked Thorin's protective amulet off his chest. "I'll take this little bauble... as a ssssouvenir..."

Thorin gasped, touching his chest. The amulet had protective powers, and now he was defenseless.

Uldreiyn laughed and gave him an icy smile. "You've been a ssssurprisingly worthy... adversary, *dwarf*. Much more entertaining than I expected."

Then the necromancer struck Thorin for the final time.

Islar regained consciousness just in time to see the necromancer's hand rise for the final blow.

"No!" cried Islar, as he raised a shield to protect Thorin. But it was too late. A red spike entered Thorin's chest, and the dwarf shuddered and collapsed.

"*Vaxa-vina!*" said Islar, and a cluster of roots rose from the ground, wrapping Uldreiyn in a net of tightening vines. The injured necromancer struggled against the spell; Islar knew he had only seconds to act.

Islar ran to Thorin, dragging the unconscious dwarf away from the gulley and toward Sela. "Help! Help!" he cried. "Sela! I need your help!"

In the distance, Sela heard Islar's desperate cries

and sent her dragon to help. "Brinsop! Pick up Islar and Thorin and get them out of here—fly them *anywhere*—just get them away from here!"

"*Done,*" said Brinsop, who was limping badly from her injuries. Before taking off, Brinsop breathed a final stream of fire, and the soldiers fell back.

Brinsop flew over to Islar and scooped up Thorin and the frantic mage.

The dragon only traveled a short distance, landing by a shallow stream. She laid Thorin and Islar on the ground. Thorin did not stir.

Islar shook Thorin's shoulder, and then gently tapped his face. "He's not moving!"

Thorin groaned. "Sela...my lady..." Blood was pouring from his mouth and nose.

"It's not Sela, it's me. Wake up, Thorin," said Islar.

Sela, still defending herself against the necromancer, said a silent prayer.

In the distance, she could still hear Islar's desperate cries for help. *Sweet Baghra, grant me the strength to fight this demon.* She ducked, avoiding another fireball, and then struck the necromancer with a paralyzing spell.

The necromancer hissed and fell to its knees. She knew the effect was only temporary. She took off running in Brinsop's direction, using the dragon stone to help find her location.

"I'm here! I'm here!" said Sela, rushing to Thorin's side.

She slid to her knees and ripped open Thorin's

tunic. Her heart sank as soon as she saw the wound—it was worse than she imagined. Thorin's chest was punctured clean through. His eyes were glazed, his pupils huge.

"Sela... save yourself, and the boy," Thorin said weakly. "I will not survive this wound... we both know it."

"Don't talk like that," said Sela. "Let me try and heal you."

Thorin shook his head. "Nay, me lady... you can't help me. It's dark behind my eyes. Death is near, and Darthnell awaits me."

Sela's eyes filled with tears. "You're a true hero, Thorin. I'll make sure everyone knows about your bravery."

"Aye," he said, with a trembling smile. "Maybe they'll write a saga about me," he said, jokingly. Even facing death, he maintained his joyful spirit.

Thorin stared longingly into Sela's eyes. She grasped his hand tightly in hers. She knew that there was nothing she could do.

"Me lady... it was an honor servin' with you," he said, his voice barely a whisper. He shut his eyes.

Tears flowed down her cheeks as Sela leaned down and gently kissed his lips.

Thorin's eyes fluttered open again. "No kiss was ever so sweet, me lady," he said, smiling faintly. Using the last of his strength, Thorin reached up and touched her cheek. "So lovely..." he whispered, then his hand fell to his side, and he closed his eyes for the last time.

Thorin was gone.

11. THE ELDER WILLOW

Elias and Nydeired arrived at the Elder Willow after sundown. Both were exhausted; they had flown across the Elburgian Mountains and Darkmouth Forest without rest. Despite Nydeired's accelerated speed, it still took them longer than expected.

When they reached the Elder Willow, they found it brightly lit—radiant crystals had been placed among the trees.

Nydeired landed carefully. Tallin had cautioned them about the tree sprites, but his warning was unnecessary. The fairies kept their distance because Chua was waiting for them when they landed.

Chua was lying against Starclaw, his crippled body covered by a brightly patterned quilt. Their damaged eyes were wrapped with strips of cloth. He raised his hands in greeting. "Welcome, my son. We have been expecting you."

Elias felt a lump rise in his throat. He coughed and took a few moments to compose himself. His voice was surprisingly calm when he responded, "Thank you... father."

Bowls of nuts, berries, and mushrooms were laid out for them. "Are either of you hungry? Please help yourselves to our humble food."

Elias shook his head, and then remembered that Chua and Starclaw were both blind. "No... no, thank you."

Elias looked up, awed at the size of the Elder Willow. The tree was enormous; the trunk was easily the size of a small house. Then he noticed the little-winged creatures within the leaves.

"Are those the tree sprites?" he asked. "Tallin warned me about them."

"You needn't worry about them while I am present. They won't harm you—they're merely curious."

As if on cue, one of the tree sprites fluttered down to Elias and landed on his shoulder. It was a tiny female. Her hair was white and tangled, matted with dirt and pieces of grass. She wore a ragged square of cloth as a dress. The sprite leaned in close, sniffing Elias' neck. Then she reached out and poked the tip of his nose with her tiny foot. Elias laughed, which startled the little creature. The sprite flew away, landing on a nearby branch, where she continued to stare.

"So, my son," said Chua. "Why have you come here?"

"I wanted to meet you. Plus, it was time to return your dragon stone. I've had it long enough," he said. "Nydeired wanted to meet his mother, too."

Starclaw rose up, sniffing the air delicately for the scent of her hatchling. Nydeired crawled over to her, dragging himself on his belly. Although he was more than twice as large as his mother, Nydeired lowered his head to the ground so that his body was prostrate before the older female.

Nydeired stopped short of actually touching Starclaw. He remained face down, waiting for Starclaw to address him first.

Instead of speaking, Starclaw reached out with her single good wing and placed it around Nydeired's enormous neck. Nydeired purred in response, and his rasping voice blended with his mother's to create a warm sound that echoed softly throughout the clearing.

"You were expecting us," said Elias.

"Yes. I've known for a long time that you were coming. We have both been waiting for this day. Nydeired is Starclaw's only living hatchling, and you are my only son."

"Tallin told me you're the oracle of the east. Is that true?"

"Your friend is correct. The gods have blessed me with the gift of prophecy. The visions began when I was a young man, shortly after I went through my changing time."

"Sometimes I have visions, too. Dreams, mostly. I'll see events that are going to happen, or have happened, even though I'm not there. It's difficult for me to tell sometimes what's real and what's a dream."

Chua nodded slowly. "You may have inherited the gift from me, or perhaps from your mother, Ionela."

"She's dead, you know," said Elias. "Sisren killed

her in the desert."

"I know, son," said Chua, sighing softly. His mind was clearly on a trip into the past. "The truth is, your mother died over fifteen years ago, right after you were born. Once she chose to become a necromancer, she lost her soul to darkness."

Elias settled onto the damp grass, tucking his tunic around his knees. "Can you tell me anything about her, before she became evil?"

Chua sighed again. "Your mother was clever, beautiful, and extraordinarily powerful. She became a Master Spellcaster at a very young age. She was a teacher at Aonach Tower when we met and fell in love. I was already joined with Starclaw at the time, and Ionela was a popular instructor at the school. She was never matched with a dragon, but she spoke fluent dragon tongue. The ability to talk to dragons is a rare gift, even among powerful mageborns. We were married just before the Dragon Wars broke out."

"What happened after that?"

"Aonach Tower was captured by empire troops. The spellcasters surrendered peacefully. It was still early, and no one understood the depth of Vosper's madness. Months passed, and all of us were transported to Morholt as prisoners of the emperor. Even then, no one was too alarmed. At that point, Vosper was still treating us well.

"During my incarceration, I experienced several visions, and they became more violent as time went on. I knew what was going to happen. The gravity of the situation became clear to me, but none of the others accepted the truth. It wasn't long before Vosper started killing spellcasters, dragons, dwarves, and anyone else that refused fealty to him."

"Why didn't anyone believe you?" asked Elias.

"People believe what they want to believe. No one wants to hear bad news, and my news wasn't just bad—it was horrific. Everyone just hoped that things would improve. But they didn't. In fact, things got worse. Vosper attacked Mount Velik, and the war escalated. Vosper destroyed all the dwarf cities above ground, and thousands of people were killed. The empire was eventually driven back, but the dwarves were forced into the mountain. Their kingdom never fully recovered."

"What about the prisoners? What did Vosper do to you?"

"Nothing, at first. But then he started killing us off... one by one. Any survivors swore a blood oath to the emperor. They had no choice. It was either obedience or death. I refused to take the oath, so Vosper took away my dragon stone and locked me in his dungeons. But he didn't kill me—because he had special plans for your mother. Vosper wanted another necromancer. He already had two: Uldreiyn and Uevareth, who were twin brothers. But Vosper wanted a more powerful necromancer, and he chose Ionela. He knew he could manipulate her because she was pregnant, and also because of me. Vosper promised to let us all live if she took the *Necromancer's Oath*."

Elias shook his head in disbelief—it seemed like such a waste of a promising life. "Couldn't she see what Vosper was doing?"

"She was headstrong and refused to listen to my warnings. After a while, she stopped talking to me altogether. In the end, it didn't matter. She desperately wanted to save us both, so she clung to the only hope she had. Do you know what happened next?"

"Yes," said Elias quietly. "Vosper tortured you and Starclaw as soon as I was born. Then he sent us all to die on the Orvasse River."

Chua nodded. "Your grandmother saved us all. She was a hero. She was the one who found us floating down the Orvasse, and she was the one who nursed us back to health. Without her help, all of us would have died. "

"But how did my grandmother find us? Did she have help?"

"Carina got help from the Shadow Grid—and Sisren. Your grandmother had many powerful friends."

That surprised Elias. "I know Sisren. She was my bodyguard—sort of—during the siege of Parthos. Sisren was the one who actually killed... Ionela." Sisren had cut the necromancer's neck with an enchanted knife, beheading the creature. Elias still couldn't manage to call Ionela his "mother," because she wasn't. Nothing like that came to mind. His grandmother had raised him.

"Sisren is a powerful mage in her own right, and much older than she looks. I suspect she has a touch of elvish blood. She may have been instrumental in our rescue, but I can't be sure. I was in such poor health during that time. It took months for me to recover, and my memories of that time are foggy."

Elias reached up and touched the dragon stone around his neck, as he had done countless times. "I've had your stone for a long time. Can I ask—how do you communicate with Starclaw without it? Do you speak dragon tongue?"

This time, Starclaw answered. "*Youngling, having the dragon stone only makes communication easier. Chua and I have lived in darkness and silence for years. We communicated using our stones at first, but as our link grew stronger, we found that we had no need for it.*"

"But how is that possible?" asked Elias.

"Elias, every dragon rider has some level of telepathic ability. Some more than others. When a rider goes through his binding ceremony, the joining creates a permanent telepathic link between rider and dragon. The link is always active, because the magic of the dragon stone keeps it that way. But, as you know, there are other ways to communicate with dragons. You communicate with Nydeired because you have my stone, and the dragon stone of a parent can be transferred to a child and vice versa. The magic you get from the stone is limited, because I'm still alive, but the stone can be useful to you nonetheless."

Elias looked down at the gem, which was glowing faintly. "It's saved my life more times than I can count. Sometimes the spells that come from the stone are ones that I've never heard of. It's difficult to control."

"I'll admit there were times when I intervened," said Chua. "I could sense that you were in danger, and I directed a spell through the stone to protect you."

Elias nodded. "I thought so, although at the beginning I wasn't sure. There were times when the stone drained my strength. When Hanko attacked me in Miklagard, I fainted. I had to take the stone off my neck. Tallin was the one who eventually saved me."

"There are some risks. The energy for the spells must always come from you, and I knew you were an inexperienced spellcaster. I just prayed you would be able to maintain the spell long enough to save yourself."

Elias removed the stone from around his neck and reached out. "Here, take it. I've brought it back for you."

Chua waved his hand. "No, no, Elias. Keep it for now. You need it to communicate with Nydeired. You can return it to me when you complete your binding ceremony."

"But that could be months from now. Sela will be performing the ceremony, and she's at Mount Velik with King Rali right now."

Chua looked up at the sky. "No, she's not. Sela will be coming here."

Elias gave a flabbergasted gasp. "Sela is coming all the way here? To the Elder Willow? But why?"

Chua took a deep breath, and then he said quietly, "I have foreseen it. Sela has been attacked by necromancers. She is coming here... because she is dying."

12. THE ATTACK

T horin was gone. Sela was stricken. "I don't want to leave his body here, out in the open," she said. She didn't want to leave his body for the necromancers to find, and they didn't have time to bury it.

"I'll cover him up with branches," said Islar, "and hide the body in the woods, so someone can come back and retrieve it later. I'll cast a spell of misdirect. That should keep the animals away, at least."

Sela nodded, still in a state of shock. It was the best they could do for now, and they knew it. Islar hastily dragged the body into the underbrush.

"*We need to leave now,*" said Brinsop. "*The necromancers will be here at any moment.*"

"No," said Sela. "I'm not leaving yet. Those *deadrats* need to pay for what they've done."

"But you can't fight them *both!*" said Islar. "They're too powerful."

"Wait here, Islar," said Sela, ignoring his warning. "I'll send Brinsop back to pick you up. She'll transport you to safety." Then she mounted Brinsop's saddle and flew away.

Islar walked over to the nearby creek. The water was stagnant and brackish. He reached down and swirled his hand into the water. When he brought his hand back up, a leech had attached itself to his palm.

"I know what to do!" he cried. "Wait, wait—I have an idea!"

But it was already too late. Sela had left to fight the necromancers once again.

Sela and Brinsop flew over a small copse of trees and found the necromancers almost immediately, and they were back in the fight.

Uldreiyn looked up at her with mild surprise. "You have returned." The necromancer had re-attached his severed hand. The wound was still visible, and a ring of crusted dirt and clotted blood circled his wrist. "I thought you would run."

Uevareth had almost recovered from Sela's paralyzing spell. He kneeled near his brother, coughing and wheezing while he struggled to stand.

"I'm not a coward," Sela snarled. She circled the two necromancers while Brinsop kept the remaining soldiers at bay. "You'll pay for what you did today."

"I seriously... doubt it," said Uldreiyn, reaching out with his good hand. "*Villieldr-binda!*" he said, and a fiery orb shot out from his palm. Sela sidestepped the attack, but lost her footing.

She stumbled, hitting the ground with one knee. The orb landed harmlessly in the dirt behind her. Before she rose back up, she filled her hands with sand. She regained her balance and lunged forward, sending two fistfuls of sand into the eyes of the necromancers. They howled with rage, blinded by the simple trick.

"*Hringr-Incêndio!*   *Hringr-Incêndio!*"   they screamed, shooting fireballs in every direction.

Sela avoided them easily—the necromancers couldn't see well enough to aim. She dashed behind them and kicked Uevareth in the small of his back, sending him sprawling to the ground.

Uldreiyn reached out and jerked his brother back to his feet. They squinted, trying to focus. Oily black tears ran from their eyes and mixed with the sand, making them look even more ghoulish than usual.

"*Dreyma-lita-purs-krellr!*" said Uldreiyn, and an apparition materialized before Sela. It was a green monstrosity, looking somewhat like a cross between an orc and a giant lizard.

"An *illusion?* Really?" said Sela. "Is this supposed to frighten me?"

"No... not really," said Uldreiyn, as the apparition struck Sela full force in the chest.

She staggered to the ground; the wind knocked out of her. Her mouth opened and closed like a fish while she struggled to breathe. She touched her side and knew immediately that several of her ribs were broken.

"Surprised?" said Uevareth, leering. "It's... not an illusion, really, but a bound ssssspirit. The ssssspell doesn't last very long, unfortunately, but certainly long enough... to kill you."

The specter writhed and spun, trying to free itself. As it struggled to escape the necromancer's control, the spirit-creature became more and more infuriated.

"Kill her, and I shall release you!" Uldreiyn cried.

The creature screamed with rage, then reached down and grabbed Sela by the leg, lifting her off the ground. Sela tried to kick herself free, but the creature's grip was like iron.

"*Nagl-meizi!*" said Sela, twisting in the air. Her body spun like a tiny hurricane, and the creature released her. "*Nagl-meizi!*" she said again. This time, she twirled her wrists, and the air filled with choking dust, spinning upward.

This only seemed to make the creature angrier, and it reached out blindly to attack Sela again.

It swung and missed, but Uldreiyn had maneuvered himself behind her, and the necromancer grabbed her by the back of the neck and squeezed. She twisted her body, trying to throw the thing off, but the necromancer's strength was too much for her.

Sela cried out as the necromancer's nails bit deeply into her flesh. There was a loud crack, and then the necromancer let go. Sela crumpled to the ground.

"*Sela!*" cried Brinsop in anguish. Trembling with fury, the dragon inhaled, sending a river of fire at the soldiers. The few that remained were experienced fighters—they kept their distance, but continued to engage the dragon in combat. Brinsop's legs and wings were covered with dozens of shallow cuts.

"Get the dragon!" ordered Uldreiyn, and the

spirit-creature obeyed, running over to attack Brinsop before she could come to Sela's aid. Brinsop spat a river of flame at the creature, and it stopped advancing, but it blocked her path.

The necromancers lifted Sela up by the hair and began slowly burning her flesh. They were laughing hideously, toying with her, as a cat toys with a mouse.

She tried to scream, but could not. Unable to cry out, Sela sent a desperate telepathic message to Brinsop, *"Go find Islar! He can help!"*

Brinsop left the fight and took flight, looking for the young mage.

Brinsop found Islar where Sela had left him, waiting by the creek. She pointed at her saddle, indicating that Islar should get on. Islar swallowed hard. "I don't know how to ride a dragon."

Brinsop pointed again, more insistently.

"Uh, wait... dragon... you can *understand* me, right?" he asked.

Brinsop nodded sharply. She could understand human speech, although she knew that Islar would be unable to understand her responses.

"Look, Vosper uses *leeches* to torture his necromancers. I've seen him do it. They're terrified of them. A necromancer's blood is enchanted, and once the leech attaches, it continues to suck blood until it explodes. The necromancers can't remove them on their own—there's something about the leech that makes it impossible. The creek over there is full of them! This might give us a chance."

Brinsop nodded again, understanding the plan. "*Hurry!*" she growled.

Islar seemed to understand the dragon's urgency. "Just hold on—I'm going to collect some." He dipped a leather waterskin into the creek, and scooped the leeches inside. Islar stood back up and raised the waterskin in the air proudly. "Got them!"

"*Good!*" growled Brinsop. She went over and grabbed the startled mage, who yelped. Brinsop placed him on the saddle and took off. Islar grasped the reins and struggled to hold on. Within seconds, they were back at the fight.

The spirit-creature was gone, released by the necromancers. The remaining soldiers had formed a semi-circle around the fight. Sela's crumpled body lay on the ground, surrounded by a puddle of blood. Her body was covered with hideous burns. Even from a distance, Islar could see she was in serious trouble.

One of the necromancers looked up into the sky and saw Islar riding in on Brinsop. Uldreiyn and Uevareth abandoned their play. Sela didn't stir.

"Look! It'ssss the traitor. Who would have thought... that he dared to return?" said Uldreiyn.

"Thank you... for ssssparing us the trouble... of having to go look for you," said Uevareth, his raspy voice bubbling with laughter. The two necromancers raised their arms to attack. Brinsop flew in close, and before they had time to react, Islar squeezed the water skin. Dozens of leeches sprayed out, hitting them on their face and arms.

The necromancers screamed, clawing at their faces. The thirsty parasites attached themselves immediately and began sucking their enchanted blood. The necromancers writhed in pain, twisting in circles.

"It worked!" said Islar. The necromancers were incapacitated.

Brinsop shot a river of flame at the remaining soldiers, who fled in all directions.

On the ground, Sela groaned. Islar reached down and lifted her in his arms. *At least she's alive,* he thought.

Brinsop reached out with one clawed foot, striking down the necromancers. They tumbled to the ground, convulsing.

The engorged leeches were now the size of oranges. Gaping holes had opened up on the necromancers' chalk-white skin. Then, one by one, the leeches began to pop, exploding their foul contents onto the grass.

Islar jumped back, avoiding the stinking gore. The necromancers gurgled and started foaming at the mouth.

For good measure, Brinsop sent another river of flame into the forest. The trees and shrubs burned like matchsticks, filling the area with smoke. Brinsop grunted and jerked her head.

"Right! Let's get out of here," said Islar, flinging Sela's limp body over the saddle. Islar hopped on the dragon's back, and Brinsop took off into the sky once more.

Islar held Sela's body, which was slick with blood and sweat. The burns on her neck, face, and torso were severe. Her face was puffy and unrecognizable. Brinsop also had many injuries—the worst of which was a serious cut to her wing.

"Brinsop, I know you can understand me. Sela's badly hurt. I don't know what to do... I don't have any training as a healer," he said desperately. "I can try to stabilize her somewhat, but we need to get her some real help, and fast. Otherwise, she's going to die."

In the distance, he could still hear the necromancers' horrifying screams; he would remember the sound as long as he lived. He held Sela tighter and closed his eyes, thankful to be alive.

Brinsop grunted, pumping her wings faster as she flew south. She didn't bother to speak—she knew that Islar wouldn't understand her anyway.

Brinsop knew exactly where she had to go.

13. CLAN FIGHTS

Rali prepared for the clan meeting wearing his formal attire, including his crown. They all expected him to sit through another yelling match, but the atmosphere of this meeting was sure to be different because of Tallin's presence.

Tallin had so far refused all of the king's official requests and only capitulated when Hergung forced the issue. Hergung issued a formal order for Tallin to attend tonight's banquet.

Tallin accepted the invitation only after Rali pleaded with him to attend. Now he waited outside Rali's chambers to accompany the young king to the meeting.

Rali came out, dressed in full regalia. He wore his father's crown, a velvet cape, and ornate leather armor, dyed in the official colors of his realm, orange and blue.

"Well... how do I look?" he asked.

Tallin snorted. "Uncomfortable."

Rali chuckled. "I've gotten used to wearing light tunics in the desert. This clothing is cumbersome and heavy." He clipped an ornate brooch to his lapel and sheathed his sword.

"The clans expect to see a king, so I suppose you must look the part."

Rali sighed. "I just hope that the clans will come to an agreement soon. I'm still not sure how things would go, but we need this treaty. Parthos *needs* an ally in this war."

Tallin only grunted at him and turned away. He walked over to Duskeye, who was sleeping. He patted him on the shoulder and Duskeye opened his good eye. Rali watched the rider and dragon communicate silently for a few moments, and then Tallin turned to leave. "Ready, your highness?"

Rali smiled thinly. "We may as well get this over with."

Aor, Rali's private guard, left his post at the chamber entrance and followed silently behind the king.

They walked in silence until they reached the main hall, where the other clan leaders were waiting.

Rali took his seat near the head of the table on Hergung's right side. A space had been reserved for Tallin on the left. The clan leaders all greeted Tallin and Rali warmly, save Bolrakei, who ignored them both.

King Hergung stood and spoke. "We are pleased to have two esteemed guests this evening. May the banquet begin!"

Hergung clapped his hands, and servants appeared, holding huge platters of food and placing them in strategic places on the table. Roast goose, fried fish, giant plates of sautéed mushrooms, and a whole roast pig, glistening with fat, were just a few of the entrees.

Hergung took the first cut from the roast pig and offered it to King Rali, as was customary for visiting royalty.

"Thank you, your highness," said Rali, accepting the thick cut of ham.

Hergung cut a piece for himself and then nodded his head, indicating that everyone else had permission to eat.

The attendees served themselves, except Tallin. His plate remained empty. He refused offers of wine or mead from the servants.

"Tallin, my friend, please, enjoy the food," said Hergung. "This banquet is for you."

"Thank you, but I prefer to eat with my dragon, your highness," said Tallin.

"Nonsense! Eat! Eat! There is enough food here for fifty men," said Hergung.

"No, thank you," said Tallin, refusing again.

"Well then, why not invite Duskeye to eat with us?" said Hergung.

Tallin focused his cold eyes on the king. "Duskeye is a dragon, not a man. He has no desire to attend *banquets.* He prefers solitude, as do I," said Tallin, indirectly referring to the fact that it was Hergung's order that had forced him to attend the banquet.

Tallin's behavior did not go unnoticed. It was an insult to refuse food from the king. Silence settled over the table, and the other leaders set down their forks.

Bolrakei sneered, seeing an opportunity to start a fight. "Who is this person? A dragon rider, or a king? How dare you insult our hospitality!"

"No insult is intended, Bolrakei," said Tallin coldly. He locked eyes with Rali for a moment. "I am here to support my king. My ways are not your ways."

"Your *king*?" said Bolrakei. "Tell us, which king do you serve? Your *human* king, or your *dwarf* king? No man can have two masters."

Tallin knew that Bolrakei was baiting him. "My allegiances are none of your concern, Bolrakei. Your petty squabbles are merely a distraction, and undermine the peace we should be forging between our two races."

"Fah!" she scoffed. "Now you're a diplomat? Your insolence is astounding!"

"It is never too late to make peace," said Tallin. "Your protests do nothing to ensure the safety and security of this mountain. An alliance would help Parthos and Mount Velik. You don't seem to understand that fact."

Bolrakei gave a furious shriek. "How dare you lecture me! I am a clan leader, and I will not tolerate this disrespect!" She shook her fist in Tallin's direction.

Tallin remained seated. "My intent is not to lecture, only to observe," he said calmly.

"Tallin is dedicated to the security of Parthos," said Rali, "but he cares deeply for his dwarf kin, as well. These talks have been derailed repeatedly by Bolrakei, who seems only to care about herself."

"That's preposterous!" she said.

"Bolrakei should focus on the needs of her people, rather than her own greed," said Tallin. "It's time that everyone knows the truth of her refusal to cooperate. I'm talking about blackmail."

Bolrakei's eyes grew wide. "What do you mean by that? I have no idea what he's talking about!"

A collective gasp went up from the table. Hergung paused, his face grim. "These are serious accusations, Tallin."

Tallin faced Hergung, his face expressionless. "Lady Bolrakei has vowed to block all treaty negotiations until she is given a *living* dragon stone. She specifically requested the emerald dragon stone carried by Elias Dorgumir."

Another gasp went through the room. Bolrakei's face went pale. "That is a barefaced lie!" she screamed. "How dare you accuse me of this crime!"

Tallin ignored Bolrakei's outburst and continued speaking calmly. "It is true. She admitted it to me, and to Thorin. King Rali also knows the truth."

King Hergung turned to Bolrakei. She was shaking with rage. "Lady Bolrakei, these are grave accusations."

"These are lies!" she cried. "All lies! This interloper—Tallin—he has no proof of anything. How could anyone possibly believe him? He's not even one of us! He's a *half-breed!*"

A few of the other men at the table shook their heads with disapproval but said nothing. Tallin didn't flinch at the insult. Hergung frowned. "King Rali, do you have any proof of these accusations?"

"No, your highness," said Rali. "But if you search Bolrakei's chambers, I believe you'll find a collection of dragon stones, albeit damaged ones."

"Lies! All lies! I can't believe I'm hearing this!" she screamed, pounding her fist on the table.

Hergung pushed himself up on his hands and looked down at her. The room fell silent.

Bolrakei raised her chin defiantly. "I refuse to dignify this *preposterous* accusation with an answer. I am the clan leader of *Klora-Kanna*. What is the word of this *halfling* and this *human* against mine?"

"I would like to believe you, Bolrakei," said Hergung quietly, "but it's no secret that you collect rare gems. And what is rarer than a living dragon stone?"

"B-but, my lord, I would never..." Bolrakei said, but she didn't get the chance to finish.

Tallin interrupted her by holding up his hand. "Wait! I'm receiving a message from Sela," he said, staring off into the distance. Rali, sitting across from Tallin, felt the pull of the spell as he was caught up in the telepathy.

Tallin heard Sela's plea. Her voice was very weak. *"Tallin... don't speak... just listen... we were ambushed... Thorin and Floki are dead... Vosper took the oath; he is one of the undead... I am gravely wounded... we go... to the Elder Willow..."*

Sela's communication cut off abruptly. Tallin sat frozen for a moment.

"What news, dragon rider? How goes Sela's mission at Ironport?" asked Hergung.

Tallin turned a stricken face to him. "Badly, your

highness... Thorin and Floki are dead."

Hergung's mouth dropped open. Thorin was Hergung's dear friend and favorite cousin.

"There's more. Sela is gravely injured. She and Brinsop are flying to the Elder Willow in hopes that Elias and Chua will be able to save her."

"Elias? The mageborn boy?" asked Hergung. "What can he do?"

"Elias is a gifted healer," said Tallin. "And Chua is a powerful spellcaster in his own right. But that's not the worst of it. Vosper has taken the *Necromancer's Oath*."

Nervous murmurs rose from the table.

Rali, clearly shaken, stood up. "King Hergung, in light of this news, I'm going to excuse myself and Tallin from this banquet. I must confer with Tallin in private and decide our next course of action."

The king looked shaken, but he said, "Of course. I understand. I, too, must prepare a memorial for my cousin, Thorin. He was like a brother to me. This is a sad day for us all."

Rali and Tallin rose from the table and exited the great hall, with Aor following closely behind. Bolrakei crossed her arms and sat down.

As they walked back to their chambers, a great horn sounded through the caverns.

"What was that?" asked Rali.

"The *Mourning Horn*," said Tallin. "It signals to the clans that someone in the royal family has died."

"Thorin was dwarvish *royalty?*" asked Rali. "I

189

never would have guessed."

Tallin nodded. "Thorin's family is *technically* royalty, although far removed. He wasn't really the regal type. They're most likely making more of a fuss about it because Hergung really liked Thorin personally. They weren't just cousins; they were also close friends. I'm sure Hergung feels his loss in more ways than one. No one can take Thorin's place."

Rali shook his head sadly. "Thorin's death is a serious blow, not just to the dwarves, but to everyone. He was really helpful to my mother and I. Now that he's gone, I don't think we're going to make any more headway with these talks. Hergung needs time to grieve, and my mother's message concerns me deeply. I am going to the Elder Willow," said Rali. "I want you to stay here and continue the negotiations any way you can."

Tallin hesitated, then nodded. "All right. Perhaps after you leave, the clans will consider negotiating with me. I may be a halfling, but I was raised here, and many of the dwarves still consider me one of them." Then he added, "Sela's strong. She's going to make it."

Rali swallowed hard. He was trying not to think about his mother's condition. "Please notify Miklagard about everything that's happened. The High Council should know."

"Agreed. I'll see if I can contact someone there telepathically. I might get lucky and catch Sisren outside the shield. I'll send a bird messenger, too, just in case."

Rali turned and addressed his guard. "Aor, ready my belongings. We're leaving for the Elder Willow tonight. Book us a passage down the Orvasse River on the fastest barge you can find. Once we get far enough south, we'll finish the rest of the journey on horseback. I'm sure Hergung will lend us a few of his horses."

"As you command, my lord," said Aor, who turned and immediately began packing their belongings for the journey.

Tallin quickly composed a message to Miklagard. He decided to address the letter directly to Sisren. Tallin read the note aloud to Rali, who nodded his approval.

Sisren: A treaty between Parthos and the dwarves is not forthcoming. Sela and Thorin were attacked by Vosper's necromancers. Thorin is dead. Sela is seriously injured. Rali is leaving for the Elder Willow tonight. Vosper has taken the Necromancer's Oath. Notify Komu and the rest of the council. War is imminent.

~Tallin.

"*Gloggr-vel,*" said Tallin, placing a minor glamour on the scroll. The runes slowly faded and disappeared. Once he was satisfied that the spell was working properly, he rolled up the tiny parchment and stepped outside the chamber.

Duskeye slumbered quietly near the exit. Tallin went up to his companion and tapped him on the nose. "Duskeye, I need you to fly me outside the mountain. I need to call a bird messenger; plus, I'm starting to feel claustrophobic. We've had some terrible news and I need to get out of here for a few hours."

Duskeye stretched lazily. *"A claustrophobic dwarf? Wonders never cease."*

"Funny," said Tallin, cracking a slight smile. "It's been a long time since I've spent so much time underground. I've gotten rather used to living outdoors. I have to admit that I prefer it."

"You and me both," said Duskeye. *"Hop on, let's get some fresh air."*

Tallin climbed on Duskeye's back. Within minutes, they were flying high above the dwarf caverns. Duskeye's sapphire-blue scales shimmered against the reflected light coming through the mountain's crater. They exited through the caldera.

Tallin closed his eyes and inhaled deeply. "The air's thin up here. Let's go down a bit."

They flew downward for a while, and then Duskeye landed in a nearby forested area. The trees were sparse, but there was wildlife there. Tallin whistled, and within minutes a dozen birds responded to his call.

Tallin chose a beautiful male eagle, strapping the little scroll to the bird's enormous clawed foot. After listening to Tallin's brief instructions, the eagle flew north, disappearing on the horizon.

"The message should arrive at Miklagard in three or four days. I'll try to contact Sisren telepathically, but if she's within the city walls, I won't be able to reach her."

"*What now?*" said Duskeye.

"Now... we wait." Tallin sighed deeply. "War is upon us, Duskeye. The oracles have predicted dire consequences."

"*Are you thinking about Chua's foretelling?*"

"Yes. It's discouraging to think that all this preparation and planning might not matter at all. Perhaps we waited too long to act, and Vosper is already too powerful. Was Sisren right? Did we waste too many years hiding in the desert, our heads buried in the sand?"

"*Tallin, how many times have we faced death? The emperor hasn't been able to kill us yet. I don't worry about oracles, and neither should you.*"

Tallin managed a wan smile. "You're right. There's no sense in worrying. I just wish I knew how this was all going to end."

14. THE DARK EMPEROR

T he air in Morholt's dungeons was stagnant, thick with the odor of sewage and rotting garbage. The city's sewer system ran directly beneath the castle. The emperor never bothered to do anything about the smell, because he knew that it made the prisoners more uncomfortable.

Vosper had been forced to use the dungeons for the last few days. The stench was intolerable, but the dungeons went on for leagues under the city, and there were always rooms available.

He needed absolute privacy for the *Necromancer's Oath*. While the spell was being cast, his physical body would be vulnerable to attack. He chose a small room deep in the catacombs under his castle for the final step. He had lied to his advisors, saying that he would be traveling through the city.

Outside the door, his two most trusted guards stood watch. Two weeks ago, the emperor and three of his most powerful spellcasters entered this room, and Vosper had sealed the door behind them.

Days later, the spellcasters lay dead, their desiccated bodies arranged in a circular pattern on the floor. The spell had sucked every ounce of life from the mages. Their bodies looked like dried-up raisins. And in the center of the room, surrounded by corpses, the undead emperor slumbered while all his vital organs died within him.

On the evening of the fourteenth day, Vosper awoke, his body forever altered. He rose from the floor and stretched. It was the last time he would ever enjoy the pleasure of sleep.

Vosper stared at his hands. His skin was now chalk-white. He walked to the door and tapped on it six times.

His guards opened the door and gasped. All the color drained from their faces. "M-my lord?" said one of the soldiers. The other guard stood still and silent.

Vosper hadn't revealed the true reason for coming down here to anyone—he had simply ordered his guards to remain at the door until he signaled them to open it.

The emperor exited the room silently, shutting the door behind him and then sealing the room permanently with a spell. The bodies of the dead spellcasters would remain there forever, unburied.

"Yes... it is I," said Vosper, his voice rasping, like the sound of old leaves. "You are dismissed." He waved the men off, ignoring their shocked expressions.

The emperor walked toward the throne room and quickly realized that walking was painful. He mouthed a quick spell and his feet lifted from the ground. It was more comfortable to levitate. In fact, touching anything with his hands or feet was uncomfortable.

On his way back, he passed dozens of shocked onlookers. Servants dropped plates. Soldiers stepped
back, afraid. Vosper heard their frightened whis-
pers, and he ignored them all. The news spread
through the palace, and it was just as well. It saved
him the trouble of having to make a formal an-
nouncement—that he was now the emperor for all
eternity.

On his way back to the throne room, Vosper caught his reflection in an ornate mirror. The
face looking back at him was unrecognizable. He
touched his cheek. All his wrinkles had disappeared; his milky skin was as hard and smooth as
a polished stone. His eyes, once tired and hooded
with age, were alert. They were also completely
black; no pupil was visible. He opened his mouth,
revealing a gray tongue and sharpened red teeth.
The overall shape of his face was the same, but his
features had been transformed.

A short while later, Vosper reached his throne
room. Uldreiyn and Uevareth, his necromancers,
floated silently in their favorite corner. They both
looked over and observed Vosper without emotion.
They had returned from their battle at Ironport just
days ago.

Uldreiyn and Uevareth still bore the scars of
their encounter with Sela and Islar. Their white
skin was mottled with healing sores. The wounds
would heal eventually, but scars would remain. Vosper didn't particularly care about their injuries, but
he considered the necromancers his personal prop-

erty, and an attack on them was an affront.

"When the time comes, I'll make sure that traitor Islar... and that infernal dragon rider ssssuffer the most horrific deathssss... imaginable," said Vosper.

Uevareth turned to face the emperor. "My lord. You have become like ussss."

"Yessss," said Vosper. "My skin... it itches like it is crawling with insectssss. I hunger... but have no appetite for food."

"The itching... shall not cease. Instead, you sssshall grow accustomed to the sensation," said Uevareth. "The hunger is normal... we feed off the life force of otherssss... when you first cross over, the feeling is agonizing, but this, too, shall pass, as you learn to feed off those around you."

Vosper nodded. He felt tired and incredibly hungry. The emperor floated over to the window and looked down. The city seemed darker somehow, as though he was staring through a dirty screen.

Without turning around, he issued his command: "Go fetch my generals."

Uldreiyn and Uevareth left silently. They would return shortly with his military commanders. No one ever questioned his orders, and even less so when the necromancers were involved.

Vosper backed away from the window and tried sitting in his old throne, an ornate seat made from beaten silver and rare wood. He sat for a few seconds and then decided that the sensation was too uncomfortable. Now he knew why necromancers preferred to levitate upright. He decided to have the chair removed from the room. It was doubtful he would use it again.

Vosper heard a cough from the other side of the throne room. He looked over, seeing the guard as if for the first time.

"How long have you been standing there?" said Vosper, floating over to the man.

"S-sire—I have been here since you entered the room." The soldier was young, stocky, and muscled. As Vosper approached him, the man began trembling violently.

Vosper examined him impassively for a minute and then reached out with one white hand, grabbing the man's chin. The emperor felt a surge of energy as the soldier's life force was drained into him. The soldier's knees buckled and he screamed.

I've never felt so powerful! Vosper thought, continuing to feed. Seconds later, the soldier convulsed and collapsed unconscious. Vosper decided to stop before he killed him. He left the soldier lying on the ground and went back to the window to wait.

The sun moved across the horizon slowly—it was the only way that Vosper could tell that time was passing. Otherwise, it seemed to stand still. The seconds felt like minutes, and the minutes like hours.

Eventually, Uldreiyn and Uevareth returned with three other men in tow. They were Vosper's generals, all dressed in their finest clothing for their audience with the emperor.

The men entered the room, and their mouths

dropped open. Their faces were frozen masks of horror.

"What took so long for you... to respond to my ssssummons?" said Vosper.

There was a pause, and one of the generals responded haltingly. "Your Highness, we chose to dress formally for this meeting. I apologize for the delay."

"In the future, Ajit, do not bother changing your mode of dresssss... those things do not... concern me anymore."

"As you wish, your highness," he responded. The infantry general, Ajit, was in his late fifties, with muscular arms and thinning brown hair. Dozens of medals glittered on his breastplate, each one earned in battle.

"Ajit, give me... a complete report on my troopssss," said Vosper.

The general cleared his throat and looked down at his feet, unable to meet Vosper's dead-eyed stare. "Sire, we have ten thousand regular infantry in various stages of training. About nine thousand are currently fit for battle. Of those, approximately four thousand are trained as horsemen."

"And the ressst?"

"The others are either too old or too young. Many are untrained farmers, more skilled with a scythe than a sword."

"I see," said Vosper. "Place the untrained men on the front lines. They shall act... as human shieldssss for the rest." He turned to the second general, a tall, younger man with rusty-blond hair.

Vosper licked his lips before speaking again. As his gray tongue swept across his lip, a faint sound like sandpaper was heard.

"Carelo... you lead my archerssss. How many... are ready for battle?"

"My lord—my archers are ready to serve," said Carelo. "There are over a thousand, all well trained."

"I need at least five hundred more," said Vosper.

The man swallowed hard. "By when, your highness?"

"By the next... full moon," said Vosper.

"B-but sire! It's impossible—that's only fifteen days away!" sputtered the young general.

Vosper's eyes narrowed dangerously, and the young man squirmed under the emperor's stare. "You dare... question my orders?"

"N-no, sire—please forgive me," said Carelo. "I spoke out of place. I'll have the archers ready for you by the next full moon."

"Good," said Vosper. "Prepare... my armies for battle. We will sssstrike... Mount Velik at the next full moon."

All the generals stared, wide-eyed. The third commander, who had remained silent until now, finally spoke. "Mount Velik? We aren't ready for a protracted war with the dwarves! We haven't enough men!"

Vosper growled, deep in his throat, and floated over to the man. "Flajut... you have alwayssss...been my most trusted commander. And now you question me?"

The man trembled, his face reflecting a deep inner struggle. Flajut was the eldest of the three—a hardened veteran who had survived many battles. Seconds stretched into minutes, and still the old man did not respond.

"Answer me!" hissed the emperor.

Finally, it seemed that his internal battle was over. Flajut raised his chin, defiant. "I always thought that using necromancers was a mistake, and I told you so. They're dangerous and unpredictable. But I respected your decision, because you were my emperor. But now—you've *become* one! You aren't my king—you're nothing but a corpse! An abomination! Kill me if you must, but I refuse to take orders from a filthy *deadrat!*"

Vosper sighed. "Flajut... although it pains me to lose such a valuable military leader... I cannot abide ssssuch disloyalty."

Flajut clenched his teeth. Unlike the others, he did not look away, and his gaze did not falter. The old man stared directly into Vosper's eyes, meeting the dead emperor's chilling glare.

Vosper reached out, brushing Flajut's chest with his index finger. The touch was gentle, and nothing happened at first. But as the seconds passed, Flajut's breathing became labored. Vosper smiled, savoring the life force as it drained from the old man's body. Minutes later, Flajut collapsed to the floor, dead.

Ajit and Carelo looked on, their faces stricken with fear. They said nothing.

Vosper looked up, his face flushed from the rush of power. "The two of you... are now in control of all my armies. Divide up Flajut's duties... as you wish. You are both... dismisssssed." Then he waved them off. The two remaining commanders left the throne room, shaken, but alive.

Vosper turned to his necromancers, floating silently nearby. "Uldreiyn and Uevareth... I want you to monitor them both. I cannot risk... any sss-subversion... If you see anything suspicious, report back to me immediately."

"As you command... my lord," said the necromancers in unison. They left the throne room to follow the generals.

Vosper looked impassively upon the corpse of his former general. He felt nothing. Nothing except a numb and deathlike serenity. The only desire he had was the desperate desire to feed.

He would have to work on that. Even in his newly-altered state, he knew that having goals was important. A man had to have goals, didn't he? The emperor floated back to his window and stared out into the distance. The time for war was almost here.

At the entrance to the throne room, horrified servants looked on, whispering among themselves.

General Flajut's dead body lay crumpled on the floor. It was an atrocity to leave a body unburied, laying in the open. But the emperor, now an immortal, cared little for human conventions.

The servants ran off, whispering the horror that they had witnessed. And the gossip spread like wildfire through the city.

15. SAVING SELA

Elias had been at the Elder Willow for several days when Brinsop finally arrived, carrying Islar and Sela. The dragon's chin was streaked with blood-speckled foam, a testament to her grueling journey. Brinsop landed hard, her chest heaving. Crippled with exhaustion, she collapsed to the ground.

Islar was holding Sela's body, which was only partially covered by the remnants of her charred tunic. Islar's face was white from the strain and lack of sleep.

Sela's condition was grave. The skin on her face and arms was blackened in several places, and her shoulder was grossly swollen.

Islar struggled to climb from the saddle, grunting as he dragged his body from the position he had held for days. He eventually gave up and fell, tumbling onto the grass. Sela fell on top of Islar, and neither moved. Elias rushed over, lifting Sela's limp body off the exhausted young mage.

"Are you all right?" said Elias.

"I'm fine," said Islar breathlessly. "Tend to Sela—I don't even know if she's still breathing."

Elias checked Sela's pulse and was relieved when he felt a faint heartbeat. "She's alive—but just barely." Elias carried her body to the center of the clearing and laid her on top of a clean blanket. Then he carefully began to remove her tattered clothing. In some areas, dried blood had hardened, making the clothing stick to her wounds.

Elias removed all the burnt clothing and set it aside. None of it was salvageable, not even her boots. Everything was caked with dried blood. Even worse, the clothes had a rancid smell.

"Nydeired, can you burn these for me? They have the stench of necromancer on them."

"*Gladly*," said Nydeired, thankful for something to do. A splinter of fire erupted from the dragon's lips, and the clothes burned instantly. Seconds later, only a pile of clean ash remained.

"Thanks," said Elias.

Islar blushed and looked away, unused to seeing an unclothed female. Elias, on the other hand, had years of experience as an apprentice healer. He had been present at countless births, helping his grandmother bring new children into the world. He thanked the goddess again for his grandmother's invaluable training.

First, he had to see how severely she was injured. To do that, he had to remove all the dirt and blood. Elias filled a bowl with clean water and washed Sela's body carefully, trying not to aggravate her wounds. As he bathed her, he gently searched for broken bones.

Some of the injuries were obvious. Her right shoulder was dislocated; it was swollen to the size of a melon. Her left eye was sealed shut, the socket crushed.

Her left cheekbone was shattered. Multiple ribs broken, wrist broken, skull fractured—but worst of all were the burns. In some places, the skin was so damaged that Elias was unsure if any living tissue remained underneath. He'd never seen burns this severe—on someone who was still alive, anyway.

Using his arms, Chua dragged himself over to Elias. "What do you think, son?" Chua asked. "Can you save her?"

"Honestly? I don't know," said Elias. "I'll need your help."

"*Take whatever strength you need from us,*" said Starclaw. "*Use Chua's dragon stone. It will allow you to draw some power from both of us.*"

Elias nodded and closed his eyes, resting his hands on Sela's body. Her skin was clammy. "*Curatio,*" said Elias. The spell began to work, draining his energy. "*Curatio,*" he said again. Underneath his glowing palms, Elias felt Sela's bones knitting back together. Her damaged skin fell away, shedding like the skin of a snake, revealing bright pink skin underneath. Elias knew that the scars would be awful in some places, but that couldn't be helped.

He moved his hands over to her damaged left eye. The shattered optical bones knit back together, but Elias knew that the eye was lost. "I can't save her sight in this eye—it has been damaged beyond repair."

Elias began to sweat. It was just too much at once

—he couldn't maintain the spell. Even with considerable assistance from the others, he knew that his energy would soon falter. He felt himself weakening. He wasn't sure if he had done enough.

Just then, Sela groaned: an excellent sign. Elias smiled—she would survive. He stopped the spell and slumped down. He would have to repair the rest of the injuries after his strength had returned.

Chua and Starclaw exhaled and sat back. They also needed to gather their strength after the healing.

"Elias, how do you feel?" said Chua.

"Drained, but happy," said Elias. "I'll dress her remaining wounds. I wish I had the energy to fix that terrible shoulder, but it will have to wait. The worst of her injuries are healed. She'll survive."

Brinsop, who had been waiting anxiously nearby, crawled over and nudged Elias with her snout. *"Thank you, Elias. I am in your debt."* The relief in the dragon's voice was palpable.

"Sela would have done the same for me." Elias got up and went inside the Elder Willow. Moments later, he emerged with a fresh tunic.

Elias lifted Sela up gently and slipped the clean tunic over her head. It was a man's size, but it would suffice for the time being. Sela remained unconscious, but her breathing and heart rate had stabilized.

"Islar, are you strong enough to help me carry her? I don't want to leave her here. It's warmer and safer for her underground."

Islar nodded. Together, they carefully carried Sela into the chamber underneath the tree. They placed her on a bed of clean straw, and Elias covered her with a thin blanket.

"There, that's better," said Elias, smiling at his handiwork. Years ago, he didn't fully appreciate his talent as a healer. Now he found it to be very rewarding. Out of all the training and spells he had learned over the past year, it was his work as a healer that satisfied him the most.

"She'll be comfortable here," said Elias.

Just then, Islar's stomach growled, and he blushed. "Sorry," he said, embarrassed.

Islar was approximately the same age as Elias, but the differences between them were vast. Islar was self-conscious and socially awkward. Elias patted him on the shoulder and asked, "Islar, are you hungry?"

Islar's face brightened immediately. "Starving! I was afraid to ask."

"Don't be shy, we're all friends here," said Elias. "Follow me. There's plenty of food; the tree sprites gather it for us. No meat, I'm afraid, but plenty of fruit, nuts, and vegetables. I'm a fairly proficient small-game hunter; I can probably catch us a rabbit or a duck, but we'll have to cook it away from the grove. The sprites don't like the smell of cooked animal flesh, and they're dangerous when they're displeased."

"Anything is fine, really. I'm so hungry right now that I won't be picky."

Elias laughed. "I've been there, believe me."

They exited the tree, and Elias showed Islar to the food: a collection of brightly colored bowls, all filled with hearty wild foods. Islar grabbed handfuls of the nuts and berries, stuffing his mouth full. After eating his fill, he lay down on the soft grass and promptly went to sleep, snoring gently.

Elias returned to the clearing, and Brinsop approached him.

"How is Sela?" she asked.

"Alive. But she's going to be in a lot of pain when she wakes up. I could prepare a sedative to make her more comfortable, but I'm pretty sure she'll refuse it."

"You're right," said Brinsop. *"Sela doesn't like anything that alters her mind."*

"She may awaken tonight. I may be strong enough to heal the rest of her injuries by this evening. Even so, she'll need a lot of time to recover."

"I'll excuse myself and join Sela below. I prefer to be by her side when she regains consciousness."

"I understand," said Elias. Brinsop disappeared underground, squeezing herself into the narrow chamber.

Elias walked over and sat down next to his father. Chua and Starclaw sat quietly. Elias touched Chua's shoulder gently. "I am here, Father."

"I know," said Chua. "I always feel your presence, and the presence of the stone."

"That was the most difficult healing I've ever done," said Elias. "I wasn't certain that she would survive. Her condition is still serious, but I'm sure she'll recover."

"You have a powerful gift," said Chua. "Your grandmother trained you well."

"When I was younger, I never really appreciated the skill it took to be a healer. I thought that all spellcasters could do it."

"No," said Chua. "Skilled healers are rare, even among the most gifted of us. Healing spells themselves are often deceptively simple, but the ability to heal major injuries cannot be taught. It's intuitive, as much as anything else."

"I wonder why that is," said Elias.

"It's relatively easy to heal wounds on the surface. Any spellcaster can do that. Cuts and bruises are obvious. It's the *hidden* injuries that are difficult —internal bleeding, shattered bones, poisons; these are all invisible to the naked eye. Most cannot heal beyond what they perceive. But you see beyond the surface. A true healer can sense the depth and breadth of a person's injuries—this is why you can heal wounds that others cannot."

It makes sense, Elias thought. "When I place my hands on someone, it's almost as if their body becomes transparent. I can 'see' everything that's wrong, at least in my mind."

"It's your true calling, Elias," said Chua.

"I love being a healer. It's exhausting but very rewarding. But what I don't understand is this—if being a healer is my *true calling*, then what about the prophecy? Everyone expects me to be a warrior.

How am I supposed to defeat the emperor? I can't imagine going to Morholt, much less facing Vosper in battle."

"You must follow your destiny, Elias. Nothing more; nothing less. Your destiny is somehow tied to the emperor. You are instrumental in this war, but no one knows exactly what role you shall play in the outcome. You are a healer. I am certain that if this power has been given to you, it is for a reason."

"You're a living oracle," said Elias. "Can't you tell me what to do?"

"No, my son. Even I cannot know for sure if Vosper will prevail or fail utterly. That is the way of things."

Elias sighed. "Perhaps it's better that I don't know the answer. I might get too confident if I knew Vosper would be defeated, and I might give up entirely if I knew I didn't have a chance."

Chua smiled. "That's a sensible attitude."

Elias was about to respond when he felt a familiar itch on the back of his neck. Seconds later, he felt the echo of Tallin's voice in his mind. A second consciousness, weaker, but still present, also joined the communication. It was Rali, listening in with his limited magical skills.

"Elias: Rali is leaving Mount Velik; he's coming to the Elder Willow. He and Aor will arrive within the next few days by horseback. Did Sela survive?"

"Yes," said Elias, struggling to maintain the spell in his weakened condition. "She is alive and resting."

"*Excellent,*" said Tallin. He sensed Elias' fatigue and ended the spell abruptly. "*Talk to you shortly,*" he said, and Elias felt Tallin's consciousness drop away.

"Whew! That was tiring," said Elias, rubbing his throbbing temples. Although Tallin spent some time practicing telepathic spells with Elias, he knew that it would never be easy for him. It just wasn't one of his innate skills.

"Telepathy is an inborn gift, Elias, just like healing. The skill is difficult for humans."

"Why is that?" asked Elias.

"The strength of the telepath is generally dependent on the spellcaster's race. Elves are natural telepaths. They communicate easily with their minds—not just with other races, but with animals, as well. Mageborn dwarves typically have telepathic powers, as well. Strong human telepaths are rare. The most powerful human telepaths invariably have some elvish blood, and the same holds true for the dwarves, although they are loath to admit it."

"When Thorin and I were traveling together, he talked about the dwarves and their prejudices. Tallin doesn't really talk about it, but the dwarves mistreated him when he was growing up, just because he's a halfling. It seems really unfair, considering he risked his life so many times to defend them."

"People are set in their ways," said Chua. "Old bigotries die hard. The dwarves aren't immortal, but they are a long-lived race, and change comes very slowly for them."

"The elves seem even worse in some ways, but it's difficult to tell. Three of them came to Parthos: Amandila, Fëanor, and Carnesîr. They were all dragon riders, like us."

"What did you think of the elves, when you met them?"

Elias shrugged. "They're beautiful and mysterious, but so manipulative. I have no idea why they even came to the desert."

"Elves are unlike any of the other races. The elves are neither evil nor good. Instead, they are largely indifferent to the mortal races. They do dislike the orcs, however."

"When I first met the elves, I couldn't control myself. I was entranced."

"Elves are creatures of magic, and normal mortals cannot resist their charms. If trained properly, mageborns can cast defensive wards to combat the effect of elvish glamour. Even so, their allure remains strong."

"Are all elves able to use magic?"

Chua nodded. "Yes. Unlike humans or dwarves, elves are born with magical abilities. Like us, their magical powers vary in intensity. Some are more gifted than others. They also have acute senses and can see and hear better than any mortal."

"Tallin *hates* them," said Elias. He remembered the heated arguments between Tallin and the elves.

Chua chuckled softly. "Perhaps 'hate' is too strong a word. I recall that Tallin has an unpleasant personal history with the elves, especially Carnesîr.

Their mutual animosity started long before the Dragon Wars. I do not know the origin of their hostility. Carnesîr is unique because he is rumored to be a spirit conjurer. It's a dark gift for an elf to possess. Elves cannot perform *necromantic* spells, but calling spirits is another thing entirely. Not *all* spirits are unclean. It's just not something that an elf would readily admit."

"A spirit conjurer?" said Elias. "Spirits are *real?*"

"Oh, yes," said Chua. "Very much so. How do you think a necromancer is created? *The Necromancer's Oath* is one of the darkest spells in existence; a necromancer cannot be created unless a living spirit is ripped from the body of three willing victims."

Elias cringed. It sounded horrible.

"It's even *worse* than it sounds. The souls of the sacrificed enter the black heart of the necromancer, and there they remain—trapped for all eternity, or until the necromancer is destroyed."

Elias shivered. "Who would willingly submit to such an awful fate?"

"Mortals will do almost anything when their loved ones are threatened. Vosper has ways of convincing people, and none of his methods are noble. The emperor will do anything to secure his position, even killing innocent people. No one is safe."

Despite himself, a yawn interrupted Elias' response. "Sorry," he said.

"That's enough for tonight," Chua said, motioning that he should lie down. "Go get some sleep.

You'll need your strength to finish the healing."

Elias yawned again. "I suppose you're right."

Elias went down to check on Sela, who was sleeping. Brinsop lay close by, also sound asleep. Islar lay curled up in a nearby corner, snoring softly.

Sela's dislocated shoulder looked even worse than before. Elias touched the grossly swollen joint, and she groaned softly. There was still so much to do. Unfortunately, it would have to wait until tomorrow. He comforted himself with the knowledge that Sela would survive.

A few minutes later, Elias came back up to the grove and settled down next to Nydeired, who was waiting for him at the edge of the clearing. Nydeired was too large to enter the Elder Willow, so he and Elias slept together outside. Elias crawled on top of Nydeired's curled tail and covered himself with a wool blanket.

The first night, the tree sprites had buzzed around them constantly, not allowing them to sleep. Eventually, though, they lost interest. Now the sprites ignored them, and Elias was able to sleep peacefully under the stars.

"*I've enjoyed my time here,*" said Nydeired. "*Spending time with Starclaw has been very enlightening. She is very wise.*"

"I feel more comfortable here than I've felt anywhere in a long time," said Elias. "It's weird, but it feels like home."

"*I like it, too. The woods are vast, and there's much to explore. I would like to try some hunting tomorrow.*

How is Sela?"

Elias sighed. "I won't know the extent of the damage for a while. She's lost sight in one eye, and her shoulder is in bad shape. The burns were the worst of it. I've healed lots of regular burns, but hers were caused by a necromancer's flame. The scars will remain on her face and body forever. She'll never look the same again."

"At least she's alive," said Nydeired. *"You saved her."*

"I know," said Elias. "When Chua told me that Sela was dying, I panicked at first. But when I actually saw her, all my fear melted away. I knew exactly what I had to do. Healing just comes naturally. For the first time in my life, I know what I want to do. I don't want to fight—I want to be a healer."

"But what about the prophecy?" asked Nydeired.

Elias shrugged. "I'm not sure what's going to happen, but I'm going to follow Chua's advice. I'll just trust my instincts. Sometimes the best way to defeat your fears is simply to have faith in yourself." Elias smiled and closed his eyes, and was soon fast asleep.

The next day, Elias woke up early, feeling more refreshed. He went to Sela's side and was able to heal the rest of her wounds. She did not stir and remained unconscious that day and the next. On the fourth day, she regained consciousness briefly. She drank water but did not eat.

Elias followed the same routine for the next few days. He and Nydeired awoke at dawn. After Elias checked on Sela, they went to a nearby stream to drink and wash. Nydeired dipped his tail in the water and splashed Elias playfully.

Elias howled, arching his back as the cold water hit his shoulders.

Elias splashed back, and they were so engrossed in their play that they didn't even notice Rali and Aor's arrival on horseback.

"Hey, you two!" said Elias, waving. The tree sprites buzzed dangerously around these new intruders, and Elias made a swift gesture in the air to ward them off.

"Thanks," said Rali. "The buzzing sound from those little creatures was giving me a headache."

"It's a defensive mechanism," said Elias. "The sprites guard this place. Chua taught me a spell to keep them at bay. As long as you're not doing any harm to the grove, they'll leave you alone."

"How's my mother?" asked Rali, worry in his voice.

Elias quickly described Sela's current condition. Rali gave a deep sigh of relief. Rali then told Elias the sad news of Thorin and Floki's death.

Elias' eyes misted over with tears. "I didn't know. This saddens me greatly. He was a good friend. What happened in Ironport?"

"It was a *trap*," said Rali. "Vosper knew about everything, including Islar's desertion and betrayal.

The emperor *allowed* Islar to leave Morholt, hoping that he would lead him to Sela, or you. Without Thorin's intervention, Sela and Islar would be dead. Thorin died a hero."

"Were they able to give Thorin a proper burial, at least?"

"Yes," said Rali. "King Hergung sent out a search party and was able to retrieve the bodies. Hergung honored Thorin with a royal funeral."

"That's good," said Elias, but it didn't make him feel any better. "I wish I'd had the chance to say goodbye."

Rali put his hand comfortingly on Elias' shoulder. Elias looked up and saw sympathy in Rali's eyes. Elias recalled the first time he met the young king —it was over a year ago in Miklagard, where he had assumed that Rali was merely an apprentice. Since then, everything had changed. Rali had been crowned king, and his youthful appearance had disappeared. He had matured into a compassionate, shrewd leader.

The young men locked eyes, and a silent understanding passed between them. Rali and Elias had enormous responsibilities thrust upon them at a young age, and both had been forced to grow up very quickly. How things had changed for both of them.

Islar and Chua appeared. Brief introductions were made, and Rali began questioning Islar. "Tell me everything you remember. Even minor details are important, so don't leave anything out."

Islar recounted the events slowly, from the day that he and Floki escaped Morholt, to the ambush inside Ironport, and finally, the battle outside the city.

"I knew I wasn't strong enough to battle one necromancer on my own, much less two of them. But I remembered that they're afraid of leeches. I found some in a nearby creek and threw the leeches on the necromancers. They stopped attacking—the effect was immediate."

"How did you know it would work?" asked Rali suspiciously.

"To be honest, I didn't. It was just a hunch. After the necromancers collapsed, I just grabbed Sela and jumped on Brinsop's back. I held on for dear life, and a few days later, we ended up here."

"While I was still at Mount Velik, Tallin received a brief telepathic message from Sela," said Rali. "Did she regain consciousness during the journey?"

"A few times, but only briefly," said Islar. "She was in a lot of pain. The first time she attempted tele-pathic communication, she failed. I tried to help her as much as I could, but I'm not a strong tele-path."

"Neither is Sela," said Rali. "I'm surprised that she was able to contact anyone at all."

"Me too, considering the severity of her injuries," said Islar. "It must have been pure will. I've never seen a spellcaster so fearless. Sela faced those two necromancers alone and still managed to survive. I doubt I would have been able to do the same."

Rali looked away, overcome by emotion. "If you'll excuse me, I'd like to see my mother."

"Of course," said Elias, directing him to the opening. "Just follow the narrow path inside the tree. It will take you to a lighted chamber. Sela is resting inside."

"Thank you." Rali produced a finger-flame to light his way and disappeared underground. A few minutes later, Rali returned to the clearing, visibly shaken.

"She's still unconscious," said Rali. "Honestly, I'm glad I didn't see her when she first arrived. She's covered from head to toe with scars. Seeing my mother like this is bad enough."

"The scars are bad, I know, but she will recover," said Elias. "And they will fade, eventually. Even the worst ones."

"Is there anything else you can do for her?" asked Rali.

Elias sighed. "No, not really. I have done as much as I can for her. Her body needs time to heal itself. She has a long convalescence ahead of her."

"She won't be able to help us against Vosper then," said Rali. It wasn't really a question. It was a statement.

"No. She's not in any shape to fight. Not anytime soon. She's lucky to be alive."

"What are we going to do?" asked Rali. "How are we going to have a chance against Vosper without Sela?"

Chua spoke up for the first time. "You're her son.

You could take her place."

"What do you mean?" said Rali. "I'm not a dragon rider. How could I take her place?"

"You are mageborn," said Chua. "Granted, your powers aren't as strong as your mother's, but you could still do it. The same way Elias carries my dragon stone and communicates with Nydeired, you could carry Sela's stone and communicate with Brinsop."

"He's right," said Elias. "It won't be a true pairing, but if Brinsop agrees, you could act as her temporary rider. It could work."

"No, no..." said Rali, shaking his head. "I'm only a second-degree mage. What good would I be in battle?"

"We all started out without any experience," said Elias. "You've had years of magical training at Miklagard, and lots of practice using your powers."

"But I have no training as a dragon rider," said Rali.

"Start now," said Chua. "There are two dragon riders right in front of you. We could train you."

Rali still looked unconvinced, but he wasn't protesting as loudly as before.

"At least consider it," said Elias.

"Maybe you're right," said Rali. "We need all the help we can get. We can't afford to lose any of the dragon riders."

Suddenly, there was a flash in the sky. It was Sisren, riding Charlight!

"Hello, everyone! I'm glad you feel that way, because I've brought another dragon rider with me," she said, materializing suddenly after dropping her concealment spell.

Elias couldn't believe it. Sisren had arrived on Charlight's back. Charlight—the dragon who had betrayed her own kind. And there, seated behind Sisren, was Hanko.

The *traitor.*

16. THE COUNTERATTACK

Back in Parthos, the elves grew restless. Though Rali's guards were always respectful, none of the elves could tolerate the current situation any longer. Taking orders from Rali's honor guard was galling. The three elves gathered on the palace rooftop after sunset to discuss their plans.

"We're wasting our time in this place," said Fëanor, the youngest of the three. "It's time for us to leave."

"I agree," said Amandila. "The orc attack last year was a failure. Vosper isn't going to attempt another attack on this city—at least not yet. I agree with Fëanor. We must leave Parthos and go east."

Carnesîr's jaw clenched. He wasn't ready to admit he was wrong. "It's possible that the orcs will attack again from the north, or the Balborites from the west."

"Not bloody likely," snorted Fëanor derisively. "The orcs were decimated in last year's attack, and King Nar hasn't shown his ugly green face in months. As for the Balborites, why would they send an assassin here now? All the riders are gone, and so is their child-king, Rali. The Balborites don't care about conquering cities. Their glory is killing spe-

223

cific targets. They could care less about Parthos, or Morholt, or any other mortal city, for that matter."

"Are you questioning my authority?" said Carnesîr.

"No, I'm not questioning your authority," said Fëanor hotly. "I'm questioning your *judgment!*"

"You're nothing but an insolent youngling!" said Carnesîr, his jaw clenched. He and Fëanor started to face off.

Amandila stepped forward and placed herself between them. "Please! Stop this bickering. There's an easy solution to all of this. There are three of us. Together we're strong enough for a scrying circle. We can stop guessing: let's find out what's really happening across the continent."

Fëanor nodded. "It's a good idea."

"No," said Carnesîr, shaking his head. "It's too risky. A scrying spell like that will weaken us for several days."

"Can you think of a better solution?" said Amandila.

Carnesîr frowned. He could tell he wasn't going to win this argument. "Fine," he said. "Prepare yourselves; we will smoke-scry at midnight. I will gather the necessary herbs." Scrying with smoke was extremely demanding on the operator, but it provided the most accurate visions. This was especially true if one wanted to observe people who didn't want to be watched.

Just before midnight, everyone but the three elves and their dragons were ordered off the palace rooftop. Fëanor gathered several bolts of firewood and placed them in a star pattern on the floor. Carnesîr then laced the wood with herbs that would intensify the spell's effectiveness.

"*Incêndio!*" said Carnesîr, and the wood burst into flames. The elves sat down cross-legged in a circle around the fire. Their dragons took their places behind them; they would all participate in the conjuring. Once the fire started producing enough smoke, Carnesîr recited the incantation that would reveal what they wanted to see. "*Stjarna-heimtail-draumr.*"

The column of smoke grew higher, and hazy images materialized. At first, the faces were blurry —unrecognizable. Slowly, the images sharpened. It was Morholt. Hundreds of soldiers worked frantically outside the city walls, stacking supplies and weapons. The scene changed, and now the soldiers stood at the bank of the Orvasse River, loading barges with supplies.

"Vosper's troops are mobilizing for war," said Fëanor. "If they're moving up the Orvasse River, then their target is either Mount Velik or Miklagard."

The vision changed again. This time, they could see the throne room of the emperor's palace. Vosper's body was turned away from them. He was speaking to his guards. The men nodded occasionally, but otherwise said nothing. Vosper raised his arm, and his sleeve fell away, revealing the emperor's black fingernails and pallid skin.

"Look at his hands!" Amandila gasped. "He did it!

He took the oath! He's a *necromancer!*"

The elves continued to watch, horrified. Then, slowly, Vosper turned his head, looking behind him. Vosper stared, as if he knew someone was watching.

"Carnesîr... look at his expression—is it possible that he can see us?" Fëanor said.

"Impossible," said Carnesîr. "This spell is elvish—my incantation was perfect. He can't see us."

But just then, Vosper raised one glowing finger and mouthed a silent curse. Carnesîr's face blanched. "No! End the spell! End the spell!" he shouted, but it was too late.

The fire exploded, sending fragments of rock and burning wood in a million directions. None of the elves were able to raise shields in time and were struck senseless by the force of the blast. The stunned elves lay prostrate on the ground.

Fëanor propped himself up on his elbows and shook his head. "By the gods... you were wrong *again*, Carnesîr."

Carnesîr also tried to rise, but stumbled, falling back down to one knee. He ignored Fëanor's remark. "Check on Amandila. She's unconscious."

Nagendra had turned Amandila over and was shaking her softly. A bleeding gash ran down the elf's right cheek. Fëanor crawled over to Amandila and tapped her cheek lightly. "Amandila—are you all right? Wake up."

The female elf groaned and sat up. She had a dazed expression in her eyes. "What happened?"

"It appears that the emperor *could* see us," Fëanor

said with a sneer. "Vosper turned our own spell against us."

"But how is that possible? How could the emperor sense our presence?" asked Amandila.

"I don't know," said Carnesîr. "He shouldn't have been able to. Mortals can't sense elvish scrying spells. He shouldn't have been able to counterattack at such a vast distance."

"Vosper *isn't* mortal. Not anymore," said Fëanor through clenched teeth.

"What does this mean?" said Amandila.

"It means that Vosper is the strongest necromancer in a millennium," said Fëanor. "We must notify our queen."

"Vosper's troops are preparing for battle," said Amandila. "They'll probably attack Mount Velik. Their barges will arrive in Ironport in a matter of days."

"I know," said Carnesîr. "We'll leave Parthos and go to Mount Velik to aid in the dwarves' defense, as we did during the Dragon Wars."

"What about the other dragon riders? Tallin, Sela, and the rest?" said Amandila.

"They'll find out soon enough," said Carnesîr. The elf's extreme dislike for Tallin prevented him from even saying the rider's name. "Let them discover the information on their own."

Carnesîr contacted the elf queen, Xiiltharra, with the news of Vosper's condition and the impending attack on Mount Velik. After the queen's initial surprise, she agreed that Carnesîr and the others should go to Mount Velik. When it was over, Carnesîr inhaled deeply, leaning on a nearby wall. Carnesîr caught Fëanor staring at him, and he straightened up immediately, smoothing his tunic.

Fëanor ignored Carnesîr's orders and contacted Mount Velik. After a while, he found Tallin.

"Tallin, I have an urgent message for Hergung," said Fëanor.

Tallin stiffened, feeling the touch of the elf's alien mind. *"Fëanor?"*

"Yes, it is I. Vosper has taken the Necromancer's Oath. He's now one of the undead," said Fëanor. "He's loading barges with supplies and men. His armies could arrive on your doorstep any day. Tell Hergung to prepare for war."

Tallin accepted the information calmly. "Thank you. Is that all you wanted to say?"

"Yes," said Fëanor, slightly taken aback by Tallin's politeness. "Let Hergung know that Carnesîr, Amandila, and I will be coming to your mountain by dragonflight. We'll arrive before the next full moon."

"I'll tell Hergung to expect you," he said, abruptly ending their communication.

After their messages had been sent, the elves gathered again. "We should wait a day before leaving," said Carnesîr, "so we can gather our strength for the long flight. Vosper's attack took a lot out of us."

"Speak for yourself, Carnesîr. I'm strong enough to travel now," said Fëanor. "We've wasted too much time here already. I say that we leave for

Mount Velik immediately."

Carnesîr frowned. "What about you, Amandila?"

The female elf was silent for a moment. She seemed uncomfortable with the growing animosity between the two and didn't want to be the one in the middle. "I'm sorry, Carnesîr. I agree with Fëanor. We should not wait."

"I see," said Carnesîr. "It appears that I'm outvoted again. If you want to leave tonight, we shall leave tonight. But don't complain when you don't have the energy to continue. I'll ready my things." With that, Carnesîr left the rooftop and returned to his quarters within the castle.

As soon as he reached the room, he locked the door behind him and collapsed on the bed. He had taken the brunt of Vosper's counterspell, and the attack left him shaky and nauseated. It had been eons since he'd been caught off-guard like this.

Carnesîr closed his eyes and immediately felt his dinner rise up in his throat. He barely made it off the bed in time to vomit in a nearby chamber pot. He continued to heave until there was nothing left in his stomach. Then he fell back on the bed.

He didn't want to alarm the others, so he waited in his chambers until he felt well enough to stand without feeling dizzy. He knew he would have to fabricate an excuse for the delay.

Carnesîr felt an overwhelming sense of dread. This was the most dangerous threat they had ever faced, and he knew it. He couldn't help thinking: *How in the world did Vosper ever get so powerful?*

17. HANKO'S RETURN

R ali shook his head. "Sisren, how could you bring this traitor here, to this sacred place?" he said. "This man can't be trusted!"

Hanko shrank back, his eyes rimmed by dark shadows. The disgraced rider looked as though he'd aged twenty years.

Sisren raised her hands. "Rali, relax. I didn't have any choice. Charlight agreed to transport me here, and Hanko wants to make amends."

"Amends?" said Rali. "You can't be serious. He's nothing but a *traitor*. Is he going to bring back Riona or Stormshard? He tried to murder Elias!"

"I *know* that," said Sisren. "But the fact is we need his help. We could use the skills of another dragon rider, even if it's him."

"How can we be sure he won't cross us again?" said Elias. "I can't be looking over my shoulder every five minutes."

Islar stepped forward. "Maybe I can help. I have Hanko's dragon stone. Sela asked me to smuggle it out of Morholt." Islar reached into his pocket and drew out the stone, carefully wrapped in brown paper and tied with a hemp cord. "I'm sorry I didn't mention it earlier. I was so tired and hungry I forgot about it."

Sisren accepted the stone from Islar's outstretched palm. She unwrapped the paper carefully, and the ruddy stone began to glow.

Hanko's eyes grew wide. "I knew it! I felt it was here! Oh, thank the goddess!" He reached out desperately for the stone.

Sisren yanked it away from his reach. "Not so fast, Hanko. I may have allowed you to come here, but you're still my prisoner."

Hanko fell to his knees. He clasped his hands together and begged. "Please, Sisren, have mercy!" he cried. "Please give me back my stone! I've been so long without it. It's been torture!"

Rali faced Hanko, his eyes filled with disgust. "Get up, you fool. What do you know of torture? Look at Chua. Look at Starclaw. This is what happened to riders who were captured during the war, Hanko. My mother was almost killed because of traitors like you."

Hanko hung his head in shame. He couldn't meet Rali's eyes. Finally, Hanko spoke, his voice barely above a whisper. "I'm sorry," he said. "What can I say?"

Sisren wrapped Hanko's stone back up and tucked it in her pocket. "I don't think you deserve to get this back. Perhaps later, after you've proven your loyalty."

Hanko cried out, reaching for the stone again. It was excruciating to know the stone was so close and still out of his reach. "Please, Sisren. Reconsider! I promise—I won't..." he said, but Sisren interrupted him, putting a finger up to her lips.

"Shush," she said, as though she was chastising an unruly child. "That's enough, Hanko. I'm not giving you the stone, and that's the end of it. Please don't ask me again, because the answer will be the same."

Hanko's lower lip trembled. He rose up from his knees and walked away from the group. He joined Charlight at the edge of the clearing, where she sat alone. The dragon nuzzled Hanko's neck.

"Sisren, how are we going to control him?" said Rali. "What's to stop him from betraying us again?"

"Well, thanks to Islar, we have his dragon stone, so Vosper no longer has any way to manipulate him. That's a plus," said Sisren. "And Hanko agreed to accept a runestone implant. Komu put it in his chest as a condition of his release."

Elias' mouth dropped open. "A runestone? You mean, like the ones that the Balborite assassins have implanted in their chests?"

Sisren nodded. "Yes. And only I know the words that trigger the runestone. If I suspect any foul play, I'll activate the spell."

"What will happen to him?" asked Elias.

"It's not a black runestone, so the spell won't kill him. But it *will* incapacitate him," said Sisren. "He's effectively under my control, at least for now."

"What about Charlight?" said Rali. "How can we be sure *she* won't escape?"

Sisren shrugged. "She hasn't thus far. Throughout this whole mess, she's stayed deeply loyal to Hanko. Our evidence against her was lacking, so at one point, the High Council offered to let her leave. She refused, choosing instead to remain at Hanko's side."

Elias watched the interaction between the dragons. Starclaw and Nydeired turned their bodies away from Charlight. It was subtle, but they were snubbing the young female dragon and her rider. Charlight hung her head in shame. Hanko, accustomed to his treatment as an outcast, simply sat down and stared into space.

There was a moment of silence and then Elias felt a familiar itch on the back of his neck. A foreign mind touched his own—it was Amandila, the female elf.

"*Elias?*" she asked, her voice wary.

Elias had only spoken to her once, and only briefly, right after the elves had arrived at Parthos. Elias accepted the communication but strengthened his wards, just in case. He didn't have any reason to suspect Amandila of anything, but it was better to be cautious. She was an elf, after all.

"I apologize, but I must make this brief," she said. "Carnesîr didn't want us to contact you, but I felt that it was necessary. Vosper plans to attack Mount Velik. The emperor's troops are moving down the Orvasse on barges loaded with supplies. The first troops will arrive in Ironport within two days."

"Are you certain?" said Elias.

"Yes," said Amandila. "I saw them with my own eyes. We did a group smoke-scry, and the visions were very clear."

Elias was impressed. The elvish spell must have been powerful indeed.

"Fëanor contacted the dwarves. Hopefully, it gave them enough warning. We're leaving for Mount Velik tonight."

"Is that all?" asked Elias.

There was a pause. "No... I probably shouldn't be telling you this, but something happened while we were scrying. We found Vosper. You probably already know, but he's taken the oath. He's a necromancer. But that's not all. He could see us, Elias! He could see us watching him during the scry. Then he attacked us using our own spell—he sent an ancient curse through the smoke. It disrupted the spell and drained our powers. There was no permanent damage, but I've never experienced anything like it. A mortal spellcaster probably would have been killed. Be warned."

"Thank you for this," said Elias. *"I shall notify the others."* They ended their communication, and Elias exhaled deeply. He gathered his strength and then relayed the message to the others.

"So, what should we do?" said Rali.

"If what the elves said is true, then Vosper's strength has increased a hundredfold," said Sisren. "The emperor is our primary target, and he's still in Morholt. We need to go to the capital city."

"It is as I have foreseen," said Chua quietly. "Vosper must be stopped, or all the mortal races of Durn will fall like dominoes before his armies. This is our last stand. I never thought I would see this day."

"Sisren should lead us," said Elias. "She has the most experience."

"No," said Sisren. "It is neither my place nor my desire to lead us into war. The prophets chose Elias for a reason. He should lead."

"But I'm not even a true dragon rider," said Elias. "I haven't had my binding ceremony yet."

"I suggest we solve that problem immediately," said Chua. "It is customary to wait until the dragon is a little older, but these are special circumstances. Sela should be the one performing your binding ceremony, but her condition prevents it. Therefore, as the senior dragon rider and Master Spellcaster present, the honor falls to me. I shall bind you to Nydeired, my son."

"Chua... are you sure you're strong enough?" asked Sisren. "It's a challenging spell, even for... a healthy spellcaster." She chose her words carefully, but the implication was clear. No one thought Chua was strong enough.

"I can do it," said Chua. "I'll perform the spell tomorrow at sunrise. In the meantime, please make yourselves comfortable and enjoy my hospitality. I must admit that I've never had this many visitors at once, and it's been a bit tiring for me. I will retire to my chamber to meditate and prepare for tomorrow. Good day." With that, Starclaw gently picked up Chua and carried him back inside the Elder Willow, where he could rest.

Rali followed Chua inside the tree, choosing to return to his injured mother's side. Sela's condition had not improved. Sisren walked away from the group to join Hanko and Charlight. She started talking to Hanko in hushed tones. Elias watched their exchange. Hanko seemed to hang on Sisren's every word. She placed her hand on his shoulder, and Hanko smiled faintly—the first time Elias had seen any cheer from him.

"Nydeired, look at them," said Elias. "Hanko and Sisren are so friendly with one another. They despised each other before. I wonder what happened between them, and why Sisren really chose to bring him here."

"*Nothing's changed,*" said Nydeired. "*They still hate each other. I can sense it. But Sisren has Hanko's dragon stone, and he'll do anything to get it back. He'll do whatever she asks, if he believes it will get him the stone back any quicker.*"

Elias nodded. "You're probably right. Sisren has a dragon rider under her direct control, something she's always wanted. Be careful around them, Nydeired. Those two bear watching."

The next morning, Elias awoke at sunrise in his familiar position, tucked inside the crook of Nydeired's tail. His eyelids fluttered open, and he stared across the clearing. He caught Hanko watching him with hollow eyes. The other rider met Elias' eyes for a moment before looking away.

Elias got up, and he and Nydeired walked over to

the nearby creek to relieve themselves and wash.

"*Are you nervous?*" asked Nydeired. His black eyes glittered with excitement.

"No, not really," said Elias. "I thought I would be, but I'm not. I'm not nervous or afraid. I've never felt so ready for anything in my life."

"*Me too,*" said Nydeired.

Hanko approached him from behind. Elias saw him out of the corner of one eye and tensed.

Nydeired growled, low in his throat. The dragon knew that Hanko had tried to kill his rider just a short time ago, and he wasn't about to give him another chance. Elias put his hand up reassuringly. "I'll be okay, Nydeired. What do you want, Hanko?"

"Can I speak to you privately for a moment?" he asked.

Elias shrugged. "Sure."

Hanko paused, looking down at the ground. He struggled to find the right words. "I know it doesn't erase the past, but I wanted to apologize... for what I did. I was so desperate during that time, but there's no excuse for it. I don't expect you to forgive me, but I just wanted to tell you how I felt. That's all... I guess." His voice broke at the end, and he fell silent. Hanko's shoulders were hunched. He ran his fingers through his thinning hair and sighed. He was a broken man.

Elias bit his lip. He hadn't expected this. After everything that happened, he was unsure how to respond. Hanko was still unable to meet his eyes. Then Elias remembered the look on Frogar's face when he had confronted the old man.

It was the same look.

The sadness... the humiliation... the regret. Deep down, Elias felt that the gods were testing him. Not his bravery or strength, but his ability to feel sympathy and compassion for others.

If I can pardon Frogar for his role in my grandmother's death, then I can do the same for Hanko, he thought.

"I don't agree with what you did," said Elias. "And I still believe that you should be punished for your actions. But I believe in my heart that people can change. So I forgive you."

Hanko's chin trembled. "Thank you... I hoped that you would understand."

Elias said nothing else. Instead, he left the creek with Nydeired. He knew that Hanko would stay behind while trying to recover his composure. Elias looked back over his shoulder.

Hanko was kneeling by the creek. Even from a distance, Elias could see Hanko's shoulders, shaking with sobs.

"Why did you do that, Elias? Aren't you still angry?" said Nydeired.

"No, I guess I'm not," said Elias. To his surprise, it was the truth. "It's more exhausting to sustain one's anger than to release it. Even if I wanted to stay angry, I couldn't. I have to think about what's best for our cause. There are too few of us, and we can't afford to quarrel among ourselves. I care too much about the dragon riders. If we're going to have a chance against Vosper, we have to fight as a united front. I believe that with all my heart."

"*I understand,*" said Nydeired. It was amazing how much Elias had changed. The once-frightened boy had become a man.

They walked back to the clearing, where Chua was waiting for them. Chua had exchanged his plain, undyed tunic for an ornate robe, specifically for this occasion. A chalk circle had been drawn into the grass and Chua sat in its center, his body propped up against a stone. Starclaw waited nearby, just outside the circle.

Sisren and Islar arrived and stood off to the side. They would keep a respectful distance during the ceremony. Hanko and Charlight did not appear, choosing to stay away.

"Elias, do you have my dragon stone?" said Chua.

"Yes. I always carry it with me," he replied.

"Return it to me now, so that we may begin." Elias reached into his pocket. He withdrew the stone that he had carried faithfully for over a year.

Elias placed the stone into Chua's outstretched hand. He jumped slightly, feeling a bolt of electricity as the transfer was made.

Chua breathed deeply, savoring the familiar sensation. He rubbed the stone with his thumb.

Chua opened the neck of his tunic and placed the flat side of the stone against his chest. Then he said a short spell under his breath, and two ribbons of skin rose up and encircled the stone, gripping the stone back in place. Chua had reset his implant. There was some blood, but Chua wiped it away with his sleeve.

The stone glowed brightly—a beautiful, fiery green. Starclaw's stone was glowing, too. Chua and Starclaw could communicate telepathically again.

Elias smiled. This is how it *should* be. His father's stone had saved his life many times, and although part of him was sorry to part with it, he was glad that it was back with its rightful owner. After today, he knew that he wouldn't need to borrow anyone's dragon stone again, as he would soon be the rightful owner of his own.

"Please kneel," said Chua, and Elias obeyed. "Nydeired, come forward. I must touch both of you to cast the enchantment." The white dragon complied, craning his enormous neck. He stepped inside the circle and gently nuzzled Chua's arm to let him know he was ready. Chua placed his left hand on the dragon's snout and his right hand on Elias' forehead.

"Are you ready?" asked Chua. "This is your last chance to change your mind. Once the ceremony begins, it will be impossible to stop."

"I am ready," Nydeired replied.

"I am too," said Elias. The excitement was almost too much for him. He tried to control his tension by clenching his fists.

Chua began the incantation. *"It is the destiny of these two beings to be joined forever. By Kuros, the father god, by Golka, the goddess of war, and by Baghra, the mother goddess, I sanctify this union between Nydeired and Elias."* Chua's voice echoed as if coming from far away.

The effect was almost immediate. Elias shuddered; his limbs felt like they were on fire.

Nydeired was gasping, struggling to breathe.

Chua's voice grew louder. "*Tilkall-sveipa-lidr,*" he cried.

There was an explosion of light, so bright that Elias couldn't see. Elias reached out blindly with one hand and touched Nydeired's trembling flank. The diamond on Nydeired's throat glowed so brightly that it was impossible to stare at it directly. It was like a miniature sun.

"Elias, it is time! Reach out and accept your half of the dragon stone," said Chua.

Elias obeyed, touching the glowing diamond. It felt blistering hot to the touch. Instantly, Elias felt the touch of Nydeired's mind. They could sense each other's thoughts, feelings, and emotions.

"*It's working!*" shouted Elias joyfully.

There was a loud "pop!" and half of Nydeired's dragon stone dropped into Elias' palm. He looked at the glowing diamond with wonder.

"It is done," said Chua, who collapsed on the grass.

"Father!" said Elias, rushing to his side. Elias lifted Chua up, and the old man coughed slightly and stirred.

"I'm fine, son," said Chua weakly. "Just tired. I need a few minutes to recover. Stop worrying about me and go enjoy your new dragon-friend."

Elias nodded and set Chua down in a comfortable position. Then he walked over to Nydeired and touched his friend's enormous jaw. Elias closed his eyes. "Can you hear me?" he asked silently.

"*Yes,*" the dragon answered. "*More clearly than ever.*"

Elias smiled. It was better than he had imagined. Nydeired's red tongue shot out and licked Elias' cheek, and he giggled, wiping his face with a corner of his tunic.

Sisren walked over and shook his hand. "Congratulations. How do you feel?"

"Great," said Elias. "I feel great!"

"Do you want to wear your stone as an implant?" asked Chua. "It's a bit painful at first."

"Yes," Elias nodded. "Can you show me how to do it?"

Chua nodded, reciting the spell that was required to create the implant. Elias held the stone to his bare chest and spoke the enchantment quietly. As it happened with Chua, Elias' skin rose up to grasp the edges of the dragon stone. It was painful, but the throbbing subsided quickly.

"Don't try to heal your skin with magic, or the stone will fall out. Let the wound scab over. The implant must heal naturally," Chua advised.

"Thank you," said Elias. He touched the stone carefully, wiping away the blood that had dripped on the surface.

"Go spend some private time with Nydeired," said Sisren. "Practice communicating, because we're leaving for Morholt tonight."

◆ ◆ ◆

Four days later, Carnesîr, Fëanor, and Amandila arrived at Mount Velik, casting concealment spells to disguise their approach. Thousands of empire soldiers had already made camp outside the mountain; the dwarves were under siege. The supply train from the river to the enemy camp ran for many leagues. Hundreds of wagons and carts transported supplies from the river to the soldiers.

At the base of the mountain, a battering ram had been set up, and it repeatedly slammed against the iron doors that were the entrance to the dwarf kingdom. Although the doors were exceptionally well made, they would not hold out indefinitely.

After sending a quick message to announce their arrival, the three elves and their dragons flew up the mountain and into the caldera.

The dwarf city was nearly empty. "What's going on here? Where is everyone?" said Fëanor.

A few men and women rushed by, ignoring the elves completely. Carnesîr grabbed a passing dwarf by the collar. "You! Tell me! Where is everyone?"

The man yelped. "We're under attack! Our people are in hiding!" The frantic dwarf tried to squirm out of Carnesîr's grip, but the elf held fast.

"Where is Hergung?" he asked.

"King Hergung is dead! Our king is dead!" the dwarf shrieked. "He was attacked in the night, and now we're doomed! The end of days—as the *Kynn*

Oracle has foreseen! Now let me go! I must return to my family!" The terrified dwarf twisted out of Carnesîr's grip and ran in the opposite direction.

"Hergung is *dead?*" said Amandila.

"I know where Hergung's royal suites are located," said Carnesîr. "Let's get to the bottom of this. Follow me." The dragons stayed behind, waiting patiently in the nearly abandoned city.

The elves walked up a corridor, which led to a steep stairwell. Even taking the steps two at a time, it still took a long time to reach the king's chambers.

When they arrived, they were stopped momentarily by the guards stationed outside the door. "Halt! No one may enter."

"You shall let us pass," said Carnesîr, waving one finger in the air. The guards' faces took on a dazed expression. The men stepped aside and let the elves enter.

The smell hit them immediately. There was no mistaking the odor; it was the stench of rotting flesh. Carnesîr covered his nose and looked at the others; this was a terrible sign.

Hergung lay on his ornate bed surrounded by his personal physicians.

Tallin stood silently nearby. As the elves approached the bed, they were surprised to see Hergung's eyes open. He lay gasping, barely able to breathe. The king was still alive, but just barely.

Hergung lifted one arm weakly, motioning for the elves to come closer. His physicians and attendants stepped aside, and Carnesîr went to the king's bedside. Hergung's face shone with sweat and his skin had a greenish pallor.

"What happened, your highness?" Carnesîr asked.

Hergung didn't respond. Instead, he tapped the bedspread. Carnesîr lifted the covers and gasped. An infection had ravaged his body. Hergung's legs were ghastly. Swollen and disfigured, they drained pus from countless lesions.

One of the physicians was bold enough to touch Carnesîr's sleeve. "No one knows what happened," the man said quietly. "Yesterday morning, Hergung awoke in terrible pain. He hasn't been able to walk or even lift himself from the bed since then. At first, we thought we could control the infection, but despite our best efforts, it has spread. It's taking all our skill just to keep him alive. We don't know what caused it."

"I do," said Tallin. He held up a glass knife. The deadly blade was smeared with blue liquid.

Carnesîr drew a sharp intake of breath. "The Balborites have been here."

"Yes, but the doctors don't believe me. They think this is a natural illness. I've been arguing with them for hours," Tallin said, placing the deadly knife on the bed.

"It's over then," said Carnesîr. "If Hergung has *kudu oil* in his bloodstream, we won't be able to save him. I can make his passing more comfortable, but that is all."

"It's not kudu oil," said Tallin. "Otherwise, he'd

be dead already. The knife was merely a clue, or a warning, but this sickness is something else."

"I'm open to suggestions," said Carnesîr. "What do you think it is?"

"I've seen rashes like this in the desert. It's *Orandi fungus.*" Tallin poked Hergung's leg with his index finger, and the king groaned. "Look here—see those purple sores? That's the fungus. It's been introduced directly into his bloodstream. The physicians insist I'm wrong."

"You *are* wrong!" said one of the physicians, a stubby little man with a face like a turnip. "The whole idea is ludicrous. There's never been a recorded case of *Orandi fungus* at Mount Velik. How could Hergung possibly have been infected? He hasn't been anywhere near the desert in years!"

Carnesîr examined Hergung's legs. If it was *Orandi fungus,* he'd never seen a case this severe. The sores looked similar, but it was difficult to be sure. The infection was very far advanced.

Carnesîr hated to admit it, but Tallin was probably right. "I agree with you, Tallin. This attack was a warning. The assassin chose to send a message— punishment for Hergung's alliance with the desert."

"The assassin must have snuck into Hergung's chambers," said Tallin. "It would be easy. Just a nick in the skin and a few fungal spores in the wound would be enough. Dark magic was used to make the infection worse."

Carnesîr grunted. "Do you have any experience curing this disease?"

Tallin nodded. "I cured a few cases while I was living in the Death Sands. Nomads, mostly. But I've never seen an infection this severe, or spread this quickly. It's everywhere. It's probably in his lungs by now."

Carnesîr turned to Fëanor and Amandila. "Go down to the city and calm the dwarves. Use tranquility charms if you have to. There's black magic afoot here; I can feel it. The unrest is too great. Watch yourselves—it's possible that the Balborite assassin is still here, hiding somewhere within the mountain."

The two elves nodded and left the chamber, making their way back down to the main city.

Carnesîr pointed at the physicians and the rest of Hergung's attendants. "All the rest of you—get out. Except you, Tallin. You stay."

The physicians sputtered and protested loudly. "Under whose authority? You can't force us to leave!"

"I don't have time for this," said Carnesîr, waving one hand. *"Hilyoni!"* Instantly, their spines stiffened and they turned to face the door. Forced to obey, the furious physicians walked stiffly out of the room, single file.

"That's a neat trick," said Tallin.

"It's an elvish spell," said Carnesîr. "I'm a believer in expedience. Let's get started. We're going to be stuck here a while."

Neither Carnesîr nor Tallin were experienced healers, but they went to work. Tallin was correct—

it was a fungal infection. "*Orandi fungus* is rare outside the desert, and unheard of in dwarves. We have no natural immunity to it."

They used all their combined magical skills to stabilize the king. Hours passed as they worked together in silence. By the following morning, Hergung's fever broke. The king slept peacefully, no longer in excruciating pain.

"He's sedated. The worst is over. He will survive," said Carnesîr.

"Yes, but it's a shame he's going to lose that limb," said Tallin.

Despite their best efforts, Hergung's right leg would have to be amputated above the knee. The leg had been without circulation for too long. It had blackened during the night, and they had been unable to reverse the damage. "Still—it's good. He'll live." Tallin sat down, exhausted from his efforts.

"Call the rest of Hergung's physicians back. They'll need to remove that leg today," said Carnesîr.

Tallin bit back a retort. Carnesîr was so used to giving orders. But Tallin decided that he was too tired to argue. "I'll let them know."

Carnesîr nodded and left the chamber. He went down the long stairwell and into the main city. The hubbub had quieted down somewhat. Although a few dwarves still looked distressed, the populace had returned to their regular routines.

Carnesîr found Amandila first, working to calm a group of women and children. The elf said a few words of encouragement and then whispered an elvish tranquility spell under her breath. The dwarf women sighed and their faces took on dreamy expressions. The women dispersed slowly.

Carnesîr waited until all the women had left and then said, "How goes it?"

Amandila yawned and rubbed her eyes. Although elves are known for their stamina, she hadn't slept for several days. "The hysteria wasn't natural—it had a magical origin, a malicious bit of dark magic. But under the circumstances, it didn't take much to stoke a panic. The mountain is under siege and Hergung was on his deathbed. The dwarves would have panicked anyway. It took all my strength just to restore some order to this place."

"Where is Fëanor?" asked Tallin, as he was coming down the stairs.

"A few of the other clan leaders were seriously ill," said Amandila. "Fëanor went to help them. The dwarves' own mage-priests tried to heal them, with varying results."

"Did they survive?" said Tallin.

"Sundergos and Akkeri are both dead. Skemtun will survive. Utan and Bolrakei are fine. Neither of them was attacked," said Amandila.

Tallin's jaw clenched. "Sundergos and Akkeri supported an alliance with Parthos. The other leaders opposed the treaty."

"Then that's the reason they're dead," said Carnesîr. "The assassin targeted them specifically. This probably means that Vosper knows exactly what's been happening during your treaty talks. The dwarves have a traitor in their ranks."

It's Bolrakei! thought Tallin, remembering how she had sworn to block treaty negotiations until she got what she wanted.

"Do you suspect anyone, Tallin?" asked Amandila.

Tallin paused. He decided to keep his suspicions to himself. "No. I can't think of anyone offhand," he lied. "Mount Velik is under attack, and Hergung needs time to recover. I suggest that Carnesîr takes over temporary stewardship of the city. Under the circumstances, I don't anticipate any objections from the dwarves."

Carnesîr looked startled for a moment, surprised at Tallin's suggestion. "Are you sure?"

"Yes," said Tallin. "Hergung is still unconscious, and Sundergos is dead. The other clan leaders don't have any military training or experience. You offered support to the dwarves during the last two wars, and you're familiar with their methodology and training."

Carnesîr smiled, pleased to be in a position of authority again. "I will begin organizing the troops for battle. What will you do, Tallin?"

"I'm going to check on Skemtun, Utan, and Bolrakei. If the assassin is still here, it's possible that the others will be targeted." With that, Tallin turned and left, making a beeline for Bolrakei's chambers. *He couldn't believe he hadn't realized it before. Bolrakei was the one feeding the emperor informa-*

tion—that's how Vosper knew precisely when to strike.

When he reached the entrance to Bolrakei's chambers, it was unguarded. He stepped inside unopposed. The air felt stagnant, heavy with perfume and the smell of something else: an odor that was familiar but that Tallin couldn't identify. He walked carefully into the main room, and then he saw it—a trail of blood going into the next chamber. The hair on the back of his neck stood up.

"*Hud-leyna,*" he whispered hastily, saying the concealment spell under his breath. The air shimmered and Tallin disappeared, hidden by the spell. He continued to move forward, staying close to the wall.

The next room was dark, but Tallin could see well enough to make out the bodies of Bolrakei's two guards, crumpled in a heap in the corner. Their blank eyes stared up at the ceiling. Both of the men were dead.

The trail of blood continued down a narrow flight of stairs, and Tallin moved forward in silence through Bolrakei's labyrinthine chambers. The stairwell opened up to a maze of rooms, halls, and even more staircases. He entered another enormous room, which was awash in crystal light. The light was so bright that it looked like midday. The walls held countless glowing crystals, and the mosaic of light was breathtakingly beautiful. Tallin started to understand Bolrakei's obsession with gemstones.

The next room was a small oratory, and Tallin found a larger pool of blood in the center of the room. Then he heard a groan. He looked around but saw nothing except empty chairs and a small podium. The person groaned again. Where was the sound coming from?

Tallin refrained from calling out in case it was a trap. Then he felt it. A drop of blood landed on his cheek. He looked up and was utterly unprepared for what he saw.

It was Fëanor, wrapped like a mummy and nailed to the ceiling. A giant hook, which was used to move supplies, had been lodged into the center of his chest. Bright red blood dripped from the horrible wound. If Fëanor had been mortal, he would have been dead already. As it was, he would bleed to death slowly.

Fëanor was stuck so high up, that Tallin knew he wouldn't be able to reach him, so he sent out a frantic telepathic message to Carnesîr and Amandila.

The resonance of their shock hit Tallin like a blow. He relayed Fëanor's location and ended the communication before either could respond. He knew he had to keep moving. He continued following the blood trail, which became fainter and fainter as he advanced.

Eventually, the blood disappeared, and Tallin was forced to guess where to go next. He paused and listened. Then he heard it—a faint crying in the distance. Tallin thanked the gods for his excellent hearing and walked cautiously toward the sound, still maintaining his concealment spell and being careful that his footfalls were as silent as possible.

The crying grew louder, even though it looked as though he had reached the end of the hall. The only thing in front of him was a stone wall, but the sound was louder than ever.

And then Tallin heard a woman's voice and his blood ran cold. He could never forget *that* voice.

Memories flooded back. She had taunted him over a year ago in Parthos, laughing viciously over the bodies of innocents she had slaughtered. This was the master assassin that had gleefully killed King Mitca.

She and Tallin had fought on the palace ramparts. She was the deadliest opponent he had ever faced. Tallin won the battle, but she had escaped. Now she was here, killing indiscriminately, without remorse, without pity, and without regret.

It was Skera-Kina.

18. MORHOLT

As they had discussed, Rali borrowed his mother's stone and took her place as Brinsop's temporary rider. Sela was recovering slowly, but steadily, though her body was still very delicate.

Aor insisted on accompanying his king, and the faithful guard took his place behind Rali on Brinsop's saddle. Aor was very heavy, and Brinsop seemed to struggle a bit with the extra weight, but she didn't complain.

Hanko and Sisren rode Charlight, and Nydeired carried Elias and Islar, whose knowledge of the castle was deemed invaluable.

Six spellcasters. Three dragons. This small group was the world's best hope of defeating the emperor, an immortal mad with power.

Elias embraced his father before leaving. "Thank you for everything, Father."

Chua smiled at him gently. "Godspeed, my son. May Baghra guide you on your journey."

"Thank you," said Elias. They both knew that this might be the last time they saw each other.

Nydeired said his goodbyes to Starclaw, as well.

"Be careful, my hatchling, my thoughts are with you," said Starclaw, nuzzling her enormous off-

spring.

Nydeired cooed softly.

"You'll take care of Sela for me, won't you?" said Rali.

"As if she were my own daughter," said Chua. "Don't worry. I promise Sela will be well cared for. Concentrate on the task at hand. You'll need all your wits about you in order to defeat Vosper."

"Ready?" asked Sisren. "We should leave before it gets too late."

"Yes," Elias replied. "I'm ready." Although this was the most dangerous threat that he had ever faced, Elias felt calm. Chua was right—no matter what happened, he felt that this journey was his destiny.

They took off into the night sky, ascending quickly into the darkness.

Islar fidgeted in his seat behind Elias. The former palace mage was shivering.

"Islar, what's wrong? Are you cold? I have an extra cloak in my saddlebag if you need it."

"No, I'm not cold," said Islar. "I'm *scared*. I don't want to return to Morholt. It was difficult enough trying to escape the first time."

"I understand your fears," said Elias, "but we need you. No one else knows the layout of the castle."

"If I get caught, the emperor will kill me. And it won't be an easy death. I've seen what he does to traitors."

Elias felt the other mage's gaze on him. "Stop thinking about it," he said. "We're not going on this mission to lose."

Islar shifted in the saddle. "Aren't you the least bit afraid?"

Elias glanced over his shoulder at the others. "Not anymore. I've learned a lot since I left Persil, and I feel like a completely different person. There were times in the past when I felt scared. But if this is my destiny, I'm not going to shrink from it."

"Vosper is a madman," Islar said quietly. "He'll do anything to destroy the dragon riders. Aren't you the *least* bit worried?"

Elias shrugged. "Worrying doesn't solve anything. I learned that from Thorin. He was my friend, and he was always so calm and positive about everything. We were in so many close scrapes together, and I don't remember him ever being overly troubled about anything. In the end, he died a hero. He gave his life to save someone else. I can't think of a greater sacrifice than that. If that's the way I have to die, then so be it. At least I know I would have died trying to defend the people and country that I love."

"I wish I had your courage," said Islar.

Elias scoffed a little. "Give yourself some credit. You escaped Morholt without help from family or friends, faced off against two necromancers—and survived! And you saved Sela's life. That's pretty impressive if you ask me."

Islar smiled. "I guess I did pretty good, didn't I?"

"Yes, you acted with bravery and honor, which is more than I can say for some people." Elias glanced at Hanko and was going to mention something about his cowardice, but decided to let it go. "I'm proud to have you fighting by my side."

Islar's eyes shone with tears. "Thanks. No one's ever said anything to me like that, especially during my mage training. I was constantly punished for my mistakes, and praise was rare. I promise I'll do my best."

"I would expect nothing less," said Elias.

They continued in silence, following behind the others until they reached Ravenwood.

Sisren contacted Elias telepathically. "We're right at the forest's edge. The sun will rise soon. Now would be a good time to stop and rest."

"Agreed," said Elias, and the group swooped down into a wooded area. Ravenwood was precisely as he remembered, dark and mysterious. He recalled his travels with Thorin through this ancient forest.

The pale, predawn light filtered through the trees, casting irregular shadows on the ground. In the distance, they heard the sound of animals fighting. First, a growl and then howling, followed by a whimper.

"I'll go scout the immediate area," said Sisren. "Don't attempt to build a fire until I return." She left, moving silently through the trees.

"I feel like something is watching us," said Hanko. "It's making my skin crawl." He reached into his pocket and pulled out a yellow light crystal. *"Liuhath!"* he said, and the crystal glowed brightly.

"You have nothing to fear," said Elias "Ravenwood is safe, as long as you're watchful. The animals here are nocturnal, so they'll settle down as soon as the sun rises."

Hanko gave him an odd look. "How do you know so much about this place?"

"Thorin and I traveled through this forest while we were trying to escape Vosper's bounty hunters. Sisren tracked us and eventually captured us near the northern border. That's how Thorin and I ended up in Miklagard." Elias said it without anger or an accusing tone, but Hanko flinched slightly when Elias mentioned Miklagard. Elias knew that Hanko remembered the attack in the catacombs when he tried to kill him. Hanko nearly succeeded, except Tallin intervened at the last minute.

Hanko turned away, his face filled with shame. The last thing he wanted was to be reminded of his betrayal.

Sisren returned a few minutes later. "The area is clear. I suggest we rest here a few hours and then continue on. We shouldn't stay in one place for very long. It's too risky."

"We should formulate a plan before we reach Morholt," said Rali. "How are we going to enter the city unnoticed? Vosper has bounties on all our heads."

"Morholt is a fortress," said Sisren. "Unless we want to go through the sewers, there's only one way in and out of the city: the front gate. The dragons could stay outside the city, and we could disguise ourselves. I'm fairly certain we could sneak in that way."

"*I will not leave Elias' side,*" said Nydeired. "*We cannot hope to defeat Vosper unless all of us stay together.*"

Sisren shot the white dragon an irritated look. "Well, what do you suggest? Fly into the city using a concealment spell? In case you didn't notice, you're absolutely *huge.* The noise from your wings will give us away. Concealment spells don't hide shadows, sounds, or smells."

"Actually, I know a protection spell that masks all those things," said Islar. "I learned it during my training. It's harder to maintain than other concealment spells because it's elvish."

"Elvish spells were part of your training in Morholt?" asked Rali disbelievingly.

Islar nodded. "I only know a few. Vosper's personal grimoire included elvish and dwarvish spells."

Sisren let out an exasperated sigh. "Alright, let's see your concealment spell."

"Okay," said Islar. "I can't hold it very long. *Griflanei-la-rei!*" he said, and promptly disappeared from view.

Charlight sniffed the air delicately. "*He's gone,*" she said. "*I can't smell him at all. It's as if he truly disappeared.*"

"There's no sound and no shadow, either," said Elias. "Impressive."

The air shimmered again, and Islar reappeared, breathing heavily. "Did it work?"

"Like a charm," said Rali. "Could you teach it to

us?"

"Sure," said Islar. "But, like I said, it's exhausting to maintain. In fact, *all* elvish spells are exhausting. I practiced this one for months, and I can scarcely hold it for fifteen minutes. It's even harder if you're trying to conceal an additional person. I can't imagine trying to conceal a dragon, especially one as large as Nydeired. It would be too difficult for me."

Elias sighed. "That's our main problem—hiding the dragons. The spell probably won't work. None of us are strong enough to maintain an elvish concealment spell around anything that large."

"The majority of Vosper's troops have moved to Mount Velik to support the siege of the mountain. He won't be expecting a direct attack on the city," said Rali.

"Are you advocating that we just fly into Morholt in broad daylight and attack?" said Sisren.

"No, I'm not," said Elias, "but Rali makes a good point. Vosper is a necromancer now. His powers are weaker during the day. Instead of trying to enter the city under cover of darkness, we should strike when Vosper is at his weakest."

Sisren threw up her hands in a frustrated gesture. "I can't believe what I'm hearing! What you're proposing is insane. We can't attack during the day. They'll see us coming."

"It's a suicide mission," Hanko agreed.

"I agree with Elias," said Islar. "Necromancers are weakest when the sun is the highest in the sky, at noon. That would be the best time to strike. We can't wait until nightfall. After the sun sets, Vosper becomes almost invincible. Not to mention that we still have two other necromancers to deal with."

"How do we kill them?" said Hanko, kicking a stump absently with his foot.

"The only sure way to slay a necromancer is decapitation, dismemberment, or complete immolation," said Sisren. "Even after decapitation, it's best to burn the body. Necromancers can survive grievous wounds."

"You killed Ionela by removing her head," said Hanko. "If all of us worked together, couldn't we do the same to Vosper? Surely our combined powers are enough to defeat him."

"Don't be so sure about that," Elias warned. "Ionela wasn't actually *trying* to kill me. She wanted to capture me alive. That's the only reason I was able to get close to her. I cast a spell that paralyzed her, and Sisren cut her neck with an enchanted dagger. It took both of us working together, and even then, it was a close call." Elias' hand drifted instinctively to his belt, where he had tucked the precious dagger before leaving.

Sisren crossed her arms over her chest and leaned up against a nearby tree. "Elias and I got lucky in the desert," she said. "Ionela almost killed us both. Her power was beyond belief, and you can bet that Vosper is even stronger. The emperor won't be pulling any punches with us."

A gust of icy air swept through the trees, and several of them shivered against the cold. The trees bent in the wind, and dark clouds became visible in the morning sky. A fine mist started to fall, and Elias drew a heavy cloak out of his rucksack. The others followed suit, putting on warmer clothing as the skies darkened even further. The sunrise would not bring any warmth today.

"We have to catch him during the day," said Elias, "while he's separated from the other two necromancers. Otherwise, we won't stand a chance. Vosper is our primary target. We shouldn't risk engaging Uldreiyn and Uevareth unless absolutely necessary."

"Perhaps we can create a diversion and draw them out of the castle," said Islar. "Sometimes Vosper sends his necromancers down to the market to snoop on his merchants. If we could instigate a fight or an explosion, then we might be able to coax Uldreiyn and Uevareth into the city and out of the palace."

"It's worth a try," said Elias. "My grandmother's spellbook contains a number of illusions. They're easy to perform. The illusions won't fool a trained spellcaster, but they're convincing enough for the common folk. I could conjure a raging bull, a pack of rabid dogs, or anything else that would cause widespread panic. It only has to last for a short while."

"It's settled then," said Sisren. "We'll attack Morholt at midday and try to isolate the emperor. It's not much of a strategy."

"It'll work," said Elias. "It has to."

"I hope you're right," said Sisren. "Because this is

our only chance."

19. SKERA-KINA

Tallin heard two voices behind the wall: both female.

"Please don't hit me again," came a whimpered plea. "I've done everything you've asked!"

Tallin recognized the voice. It was Bolrakei, begging for her life.

He heard a vicious slap, and then a harsh voice say, "You worthless, puling, wretched *dwarf*. The boy was supposed to come here, not go to the Elder Willow! It was *your* job to lure him to Mount Velik. Twice he's eluded us. Now he's beyond our reach. Even Rali is gone. Where are my targets? What's left? A bunch of dwarves and a few miserable elves! There's no one here even worth killing! This trip was a complete waste of my time."

Tallin knew that Skera-Kina would kill Bolrakei if he didn't hurry. He ran his fingers along the surface of the wall, desperately trying to find an entrance to the room, but there was nothing—no switch, no markings to indicate an opening. *How do I get in?*

"I tried my best, I swear it!" said Bolrakei. Another slap. Bolrakei wailed.

"You've made a giant mess of everything. I should have killed you months ago," said Skera-Kina.

"Please don't kill me!" Bolrakei screamed. "I

promise I won't warn them. I swear it!"

Tallin stepped back, checking the floor for something—*anything*—that would indicate a secret entrance. In the corner of the room, he finally found a broken tile with a loop of copper wire underneath it. He pulled the cord, and the wall rolled away, revealing a tiny room that had obviously been designed for torture.

A chain and pulley system dangled from the ceiling, with weights attached at the bottom. There was a stretching bed, where a victim could be pulled apart. A series of barbed whips hung on the wall, ranging in thickness from fine wire all the way to heavy cable.

Fleetingly, he wondered how many of Bolrakei's enemies had met the same fate as Fëanor, or worse. It *really* gave him second thoughts about rescuing her at all.

In the center of the room, Bolrakei sat tied to a chair, her face swollen and covered with blood. Her mouth hung open, and bloody drool ran from her lower lip. Several of her teeth were missing. She was still alive, but unconscious.

Tallin didn't step inside. He dropped his concealment spell.

The only sound was Bolrakei's labored breathing. "I know you're here, Skera-Kina. Show yourself!" he barked.

The air shimmered, and she materialized behind Bolrakei's chair. "So, you found me. That's a shame; I was saving you for last. All these others have been such *tedious* kills. Killing these stupid dwarves has been no more difficult than pulling a carrot out of the dirt. Even the elf was relatively easy to subdue. Elves are such vain creatures, you know. He didn't even turn around—he was too busy looking at himself in the mirror."

"Surrender now, Skera-Kina. You can't hope to defeat me here."

The sound of her throaty laughter filled the room. "Surrender? You can't be serious. I *never* yield. There is only victory—or death." She licked her lips. "I do enjoy a challenge."

He stepped back and drew his sword, flashing her a wicked smile. "I was hoping you'd say that."

Skera-Kina placed her foot on the back of Bolrakei's chair, near the small of her back. "Catch this!" she said gleefully, kicking the unconscious dwarf in Tallin's direction. Despite Bolrakei's substantial bulk, Skera-Kina managed to launch her high into the air, and Tallin was forced to either catch Bolrakei or step aside and let her come crashing to the floor. It was a smart play—if Tallin caught her, then he would be vulnerable long enough for Skera-Kina to strike.

Unfortunately for Bolrakei, he didn't like her enough to catch her, but he could slow her fall. *"Rhond-risa!"* he said, while stepping out of the way. A shield came up, and Bolrakei bounced off it and then fell to the floor. She hit the ground, still tied to the chair, and groaned.

"Nice job," she said, pulling two weapons off the

wall of the torture room. She held a barbed whip in one hand and a spiked mace in the other. "Let's see how well you fight without help from that overgrown lizard of yours."

Tallin ignored the taunt and maintained his guard.

Skera-Kina advanced slowly. She stepped over Bolrakei's unconscious body as if it was a piece of trash.

Without looking down, Skera-Kina stomped Bolrakei's leg. There was a loud crack as her femur shattered. Bolrakei's whole body shuddered, but she did not wake up. Skera-Kina chuckled. "Mmmm... I never get tired of hearing that sound."

Tallin clenched his fist and swung, aiming for the assassin's chin while simultaneously lashing out with his right foot. Skera-Kina hopped back, easily avoiding the attack.

"Nice try, dwarf," she said, raising her mace. She brought it down in a high arc, aiming for Tallin's neck. He blocked the blow with his sword. With her other hand, she swung the whip at his legs. Tallin jumped back, but not before one of the wires struck his left leg, tearing open his pants and the back of his calf.

"First blood is mine," she said.

Tallin felt the warm liquid running down his leg and into his boot. *"Hekklaa!"* he said. There was a loud boom, and Skera-Kina was thrown backward. She crashed into the wall with a thud, and then sprawled onto the floor. She shot back up, her face livid.

"I'm sure *that* didn't feel good," said Tallin. He smiled at her and was rewarded with a furious glare.

"Laugh while you can, *halfling*. You won't defeat me this time. I've removed my runestone. You've lost your advantage."

Tallin knew she was telling the truth. The black energy that he felt last time they fought was gone. "You underestimate me, *blood-dog*. I don't need a runestone to defeat you. First blood may be yours, but the last blood will be mine."

"I doubt it. Let's dispense with trivialities, shall we?" said Skera-Kina, dropping her weapons. "*Binvigi!*" she said, and something hit Tallin with the force of a battering ram, sending him lurching backward.

His injured leg buckled, and Skera-Kina struck again. "*Binvigi!*"

This time, Tallin was ready with a counterspell. He crossed his arms over his chest. "*Traustt!*" he said, and the attack spell dissipated in a shimmer. "Is that the best you can do?"

Skera-Kina growled and threw a hail of fireballs in Tallin's direction. He raised a shield and deflected them all. Tallin returned the attack, and she jumped out of the way.

Skera-Kina paused, rubbing her fingers together. "You've been a worthy adversary, *dwarf*. But as much as I've enjoyed playing with you, I think it's time to end this. Do you want to know how I subdued Hanko and stole his dragon stone?"

Tallin's jaw clenched. "Not particularly, no."

"Our priests learned something. A dragon stone becomes a physical part of the rider, almost like another body part. That's why you riders become such blubbering fools when your stones are removed."

"You're not telling me anything new," said Tallin. "Aren't you tired of listening to your own voice?"

Skera-Kina drew a small knife from her belt. The knife looked ordinary enough, with a simple wooden handle, except the blade was a brilliant blue. "Do you recognize this?"

"*Another* poisoned blade? You Balborites are getting lazier and lazier. Are you going to use *kudu oil* for everything?"

"No—it's not poison. This knife is different. It's a sapphire blade," said Skera-Kina, lunging for Tallin. Her first swing missed.

"You can't harm me with a tiny knife like that. Even if it's enchanted," said Tallin, mockingly. Expecting another magical attack, Tallin raised a shield, accidentally leaving his left leg exposed.

Skera-Kina buried the blade deep into Tallin's thigh. Agony ripped through him, so fierce and sudden that he lost control of his body. He convulsed and fell to one knee. Skera-Kina grabbed his shoulder and shoved him down to the floor.

She sat on his chest while twisting the knife deeper and deeper into his leg.

"Didn't expect that, did you?" she hissed gleefully. "A dragon stone is a living gem... and it won't tolerate the existence of another stone inside the body."

Tallin had no voice to speak. He could barely breathe. He had no strength to pull out the blade. The room spun; his body felt trapped inside a barrel rolling downhill.

"Do you feel it? Your dragon stone is attacking the sapphire blade with all its strength; too bad the knife's stuck in your thigh. As long as it's inside your body, you're powerless. Have you ever felt such pain in your life?"

Tallin could feel his consciousness fading. Skera-Kina reached down and tore the implant from Tallin's chest. Tallin howled in agony as the stone left his body for only the second time in his life. Skera-Kina raised her hand in triumph, shouting her victory. "I have your dragon stone!"

Her triumph was short-lived.

Carnesîr ran into the narrow room and hit Skera-Kina full-force, a crushing blow to the spine that sent her flying through the air. Tallin heard her muffled scream when her body hit the opposite wall.

Carnesîr battered Skera-Kina against the wall again and again, until a loud crunching noise rang out. Her body dropped to the floor, her spine broken. Tallin's dragon stone fell from her hand and slid across the floor.

Carnesîr kneeled next to Tallin and whipped the blade out of his thigh with a flick of his wrist. The effect was immediate, and Tallin felt strength rush back into his limbs. Carnesîr didn't seem surprised by his condition.

"Thank you, Carnesîr," he said, between gasps.

"Glad to help," said Carnesîr. The elf walked over to Skera-Kina and kicked her body with his foot. Skera-Kina didn't move. Her body was twisted in a crumpled heap, and blood ran from her ears, mouth, and nose. "Is this wretched creature the one who caused all the trouble here today?"

"Yes," said Tallin. "She's a Balborite assassin named Skera-Kina. I've fought her before. She's the one who killed King Mitca."

Carnesîr's brows furrowed as he studied her face. "She looks... familiar."

Gritting his teeth against the pain, Tallin dragged himself to his feet. "How is Fëanor?"

"He'll live," said Carnesîr. "But he's in bad shape. I thought you were in a worse situation."

Tallin couldn't argue with that. He went and recovered his dragon stone from the floor.

Amandila rushed into the room. "Please come quick! I can't stop the bleeding. Fëanor needs your help."

Carnesîr and Tallin returned to the oratory, where Fëanor lay on the ground, covered in blood. The giant hook in his chest had been removed, but the wound was awful, and he'd lost a great deal of blood. They all worked together to close the wound, and eventually, Fëanor opened his eyes.

"What happened?" he said weakly.

"You were attacked by a Balborite assassin," said Tallin. "If you had been a mortal man, you would already be dead."

Fëanor groaned weakly. "I got hit from behind. I don't remember anything after that."

Tallin nodded. "The assassin was torturing Bolrakei when I found them. Bolrakei is still alive, but I'm certain she's got a broken leg and a few other broken bones."

"Let's go take care of her then," said Carnesîr, walking back into the corridor. When they returned to the torture room, they found Bolrakei exactly where they had left her: bleeding on the floor, still tied to the broken chair.

Skera-Kina was gone.

20. VENGEANCE

E lias, Islar, and Nydeired arrived in Morholt before the others. It was an hour before dawn and rosy twilight illuminated the sky. When they finally emerged into the pale light, they saw that the land outside the city was blighted and scorched.

"Look at that," said Nydeired. *"What happened to the land? There isn't any grass. Where are all the trees?"*

"It's deliberate," said Islar "Shortly after rising to power, Vosper sowed the land with salt to prevent the growth of anything that could hide approaching enemies. All the city's food has to be carted in. The ground is dead. Nothing grows in this soil. It's been like this for years."

Outside the city, there was a succession of shattered walls and barricades. Over the years, people had stolen bricks for use in other projects, but there were some walls that no one dared touch.

"Land over there," said Islar, pointing to a high wall behind the city. "That's the *Wall of Tears.*"

Nydeired landed and crouched, hiding his body behind the wall as best he could.

"The others should be here shortly," said Elias. "Are you sure this place is safe?"

"It's the safest place outside the city that I know of," said Islar. "No one comes here. Everyone is too afraid. They say it's haunted."

Broken chains and cracked bits of gray rock lay scattered on the ground. Elias reached out and touched the wall. Unlike the others, this wall was undamaged—none of the bricks had been removed. "Why do they call it the *'Wall of Tears'*?"

"Because hundreds of dragons died here. See the color of the bricks? That's not paint. It's dried blood."

Elias jerked his hand back. He quickly wiped his hand on his tunic. Elias scanned the ground again, and his eyes widened with horror. The chains... the broken pieces of gray stone... it all made sense.

Islar noticed Elias' horrified expression. "I know what you're thinking. They're dragon stones. I know that they shatter and lose their color when the dragon dies. No one touches them, because it's believed that the stones bring bad luck. There's even stories that the dragons' spirits come here at night to mourn their dead riders. That's why they call it the *Wall of Tears*."

Elias felt a deep sorrow wash over him. The thought of all the dead dragons and their riders was heartbreaking. He wondered if their spirits were trapped here, on this barren hill. "I would never have believed it, but my father told me that spirits are real. Have you ever seen one?"

Islar shook his head. "No. Not personally. But during my training, some of the older mages used to talk about it. Spirit conjuring is an uncommon gift. I've never met a human mage who could do it."

"It's an evil thing to trap a spirit," said Elias.

"Yes, it is. It's said that necromancers can conjure because they are essentially trapped spirits themselves. The spellcaster forces the spirit to do his bidding. Spirits are almost impossible to control, because of their rage."

"Why risk it, if it's so dangerous?" asked Elias.

Islar shrugged. "Some spellcasters see it as a challenge. Controlling a spirit is exciting, I guess. Quite often, the spirit turns on the spellcaster and kills him. With the necromancers, though—they're already dead, so conjuring spirits doesn't frighten them."

"Are all spirits evil?" said Elias.

Islar seemed to think for a moment. "No, I don't think so. Sometimes they appear spontaneously. During my training, we learned about a spellcaster that lost his wife and children in a fire. Overcome with grief, he called their spirits back to this world. The spirits didn't harm, but he wasn't a true conjurer, and he descended into madness. He took his own life shortly after that. No matter what the circumstances, spirit magic is always dangerous."

Elias saw a shimmer of light as Charlight and Brinsop landed nearby. The others dropped their concealment spells and dismounted.

Sisren walked over to the wall and touched it. "I know this place. It's been years since I've been here, but some things never leave you." She hung her head. "Many of my friends died here in this godforsaken place."

Everyone grew quiet for a few moments, remembering exactly where they were.

Rali cleared his throat to get everyone's attention. "Is everyone ready? The sun's going to rise in about thirty minutes."

Everyone nodded their heads.

"Rali's powers aren't strong enough to maintain a concealment spell, so he and Aor will go through the front gate," said Sisren. "I'll accompany them, just in case. Hanko can ride Charlight over the city walls, and Elias and Nydeired can do the same."

"What about Aor?" said Rali. "He's so huge, and his tattoos will give him away."

They all looked at the long line of people entering the city, visible in the distance. The line snaked across the plain below them, men and women of all sorts, including peddlers and beggars.

"Disguise him as a cripple," said Islar. "Dress him in a heavy cloak and give him a walking stick. The tattoos can be covered up with soot. No one will look twice at a filthy beggar in Morholt. The capital is full of them."

Aor donned a borrowed cloak and stuffed the back with straw, creating a false hump. Then he covered his visible tattoos with a mixture of ashes, dirt, and water. Sisren found a dead branch nearby for his walking stick. He hunched his back as if it were deformed and twisted his face into a mask of dumb confusion. He looked at lot less imposing after that.

"Just one more thing. Sisren, it's time you returned Hanko's dragon stone," said Elias.

Hanko's mouth dropped open with surprise. No one had spoken to him much, and he'd kept to himself as much as possible. But now he looked at Elias with pleading eyes.

Rali threw Hanko a distrustful glance. "Elias, are you sure about this? He's still our prisoner."

"We can't hope to defeat the emperor unless all of us work together as a team," said Elias. "Hanko is stronger with his dragon stone, so, logically, he should have it. He's already here. There's no point in restricting his powers now."

Sisren's mouth tightened. "I don't trust him! Once he has his stone, what's stopping him from leaving? He's supposed to return to Miklagard for his trial. Don't give it to him. It's too risky."

Elias sighed. How could he explain something even *he* didn't understand? "If we lose this battle, Hanko's trial will be the least of our worries. Hanko attacked me because he was terrified of losing Charlight. Now that Nydeired and I are bound together, I understand the fear he must have felt." Then he added, "I have a gut feeling about this."

"But he's a traitor!" said Sisren.

Elias held up his hand. "I'm not excusing his crimes. But we need to concentrate on what's happening right now, *today*. My father told me that the fate of the entire kingdom hinges on this mission. If we fail, Vosper will destroy this land, and all the remaining dragons will die. Hanko is smart enough to realize that the success of this mission is imperative to everyone's survival, *including* his own."

"Fine," Sisren sighed, finally relenting. "I don't agree with this, Elias. But you're in charge of this mission. If you want him to have it, then *you* give it to him." She handed Elias the stone, wrapped in paper.

Elias unwrapped the stone and looked at Hanko, who for a second looked as though he would burst into tears. "Here," he said. "Take it."

Hanko grabbed the stone from Elias' palm, then kissed it. He placed the stone against his scarred chest and set the implant. His skin rose up to grasp the edges of the dragon stone, and it was done. Hanko closed his eyes and inhaled deeply, savoring the feeling.

"It's been so long... thank you, Elias," he said. Then he went over to Charlight, who was cooing softly with pleasure. They could finally communicate telepathically again.

"It's settled then," said Elias. "Sisren, Aor, and Rali will enter through the front gate. Hanko, Islar, and I will fly over the city. I'm strong enough to conceal Nydeired and Brinsop for a few minutes, as long as we can find a safe place to hide once we get over the walls."

"No place in Morholt is really *safe*," said Islar. "But the aqueduct system may be a solution. The water runs through concrete channels and passes into covered catch-basins throughout the city. There's a large one right outside Vosper's palace. On hot days, we used to play inside them as children." He shrugged. "The city workers hated us for it, and they would chase us out when they caught us, but we never stopped doing it. The basins are big enough to conceal us, but only temporarily."

"But won't it be full of water?" asked Rali.

Islar shook his head. "This time of year, the basins are only a quarter full, so the water doesn't even reach your waist. But if by chance they're full... well, I hope you know how to swim."

"It's a good plan," said Sisren. "It's been years since I've been inside this city, but I can't think of any place safer that would be large enough to hide Nydeired."

Rali looked up at the sky. "The sun's rising. We need to get moving."

They walked toward the front gate with Aor trailing behind them, faking a pronounced limp. Soon, they were in line with the other travelers and merchants entering the city. The line outside the gates was already long, so they jumped right in.

Elias watched until they reached the gate and disappeared inside the city. "Let's go," he said, casting the elvish concealment spell that Islar had taught him. The drain on his power was intense and immediate. "You're right, Islar. Elvish spells are exhausting."

Elias gritted his teeth and slowly expanded the spell to cover Nydeired, and then Brinsop.

"Are you strong enough to do this?" asked Brinsop. *"We have a fair distance to fly in order to reach the city."*

"Yes," said Elias. "But we'll need to hurry. I can

only hold this spell for a few minutes. Stay near us; fly as close to Nydeired as you can."

Brinsop nodded and they all took off into the sky. Hanko and Charlight had already left, also hidden by a concealment spell.

Within minutes, Elias and Nydeired were over the city. Morholt was an architectural wonder. There were stone temples, a large theater, and public baths. The center of the city had hanging gardens and an enormous fountain.

"This place is beautiful," said Elias.

"You should have seen it fifteen years ago," said Islar. "It was even nicer before. The emperor has let the city deteriorate. All he really cares about is his military."

"Islar, where is the aqueduct basis? We need to land soon. I'm losing control of this spell."

"There. That's it!" said Islar, pointing in the distance. It was a concrete structure with terra-cotta pipes extending outward from every direction.

Nearby, Vosper's palace made an imposing sight, with its high walls, black brick, and heavy iron doors.

Nydeired and Brinsop landed on the roof, and Islar jumped down and opened the large service door.

"Hurry!" said Elias. "I feel like I'm going to pass out!"

They crawled inside, with Nydeired barely able to squeeze his huge body through the entrance. The basin was almost empty. The water only reached their knees. As soon as the door was shut, Elias released the spell and slumped against the wall.

"*Baghra's garters!* That was difficult! Toward the end, I thought I was going to faint. I still feel lightheaded."

Sisren, Aor, and Rali arrived about forty minutes later, also sneaking inside the basin, which then became very crowded.

"Did you have any trouble at the gate?" said Elias.

"No," said Sisren. "There were only a few armed guards. Other than a few taunts in Aor's direction, they let us pass without incident."

"I was a bit worried that the necromancers would be out there," said Elias.

"Vosper doesn't use his necromancers for regular guard duty," said Islar. "They're probably inside the palace with him."

"Where's Hanko and Charlight?" said Rali. "Shouldn't they be here by now?"

"Yes, they should," said Sisren.

Everyone paused and looked around uneasily.

"They left before I did," said Elias. "Maybe something's happened to them."

"Or maybe Hanko's deserted us, like the *traitor* and *coward* that he is," said Rali.

"Let's not jump to conclusions," said Elias, but he was getting worried.

"We can't stay here and wait for him," said Sisren. "If we're going to strike, it has to be now."

Elias nodded. Sisren was right. They couldn't wait. "We can land on the castle rooftop and take it from there. Islar, how many soldiers guard the bulwarks?"

Islar bit his lip. "I think it's *usually* five or six. Sometimes as many as ten, if there's some foreign dignitary visiting."

"There are plenty of us. We can incapacitate them easily," said Rali.

"Don't be so sure," said Sisren. "Vosper's soldiers are well trained. Be prepared for a fight. We must defeat them before they can sound the alarm. The last thing we need is for the emperor to be alerted to our presence. We can't afford to lose the advantage of surprise."

"As soon as we land, drop your concealment spells and stop the guards," said Elias. "Don't use any magic that would call attention to us. Ready, everyone?"

"Not really," said Islar, who looked very pale.

Elias patted the young spellcaster's shoulder. "Just stay close to me and Nydeired. I promise I'll do everything I can to keep you safe."

Islar nodded, too shaky to respond.

They sloshed through the water and exited the basin. Sisren and Elias cast concealment spells, and they were back up to the roof of the basin. The riders mounted, and Nydeired and Brinsop landed on the palace rooftop within seconds.

Elias pulled the enchanted crossbow that Frogar had given him out of his saddlebags. The gemstones on the stock were glowing. He could feel the weapon's power skittering across his skin.

There were eight guardsmen patrolling the rooftop, spread at irregular intervals. The men radiated boredom, chatting and smoking.

Elias pointed at one holding a war horn hanging by a leather cord around his neck. "That one first," he whispered. "Get close to him, and I'll drop the spell."

The dragons landed almost without a sound. Nydeired crawled slowly to the guard, and Elias hopped from the saddle to the ground. Aor and Islar followed. The air shimmered, and the dragons and their riders materialized in front of the surprised guards.

"It's a dragon rider!" screamed the guard, who rushed to blow his horn. Elias aimed the crossbow and fired, knocking the horn out of the guard's mouth. It went skidding along the cobblestones and over the side of the wall.

Then Aor grabbed the man by the neck, lifting him off the ground. The guard gurgled and twisted in the air. Aor held fast, and seconds later, the guard lost consciousness. Aor flung the man to the ground.

Nydeired's tail swung out, knocking three other guards off their feet. The men fell, screaming as Nydeired brought his massive tail down on them again and again.

Sisren drew her knives and faced off with a guard. The man lunged, swinging his sword. Sisren avoided the attack by crouching down. She sprang back up, blocking the man's wrist with one knife. She plunged the other knife deep under the man's ribs.

He collapsed, blood coming from his mouth.

Rali drew his short sword while circling another guard. Before he could swing, Aor came up behind the man and cracked his neck with a single move.

Sisren, Elias, and Brinsop made short work of the remaining soldiers. When they finished, five guards were unconscious and three lay dead.

Brinsop had suffered a stab wound to her right leg. Elias healed it quickly. "It's only a surface wound. Nothing's damaged underneath."

"*Thank you, Elias,*" she said.

Sisren went to Elias and touched the crossbow. She hadn't stopped staring at it since he'd drawn it out of his saddlebags.

"Where did you obtain this weapon?" she asked. "It's so beautiful."

"An old man gave it to me," said Elias. "Kind of an apology gift, actually. He told me it was elvish. I haven't had much time to use it."

"It *is* elvish," said Sisren. "I haven't seen a weapon like this in years. Those inlaid gemstones aren't just for show. They're a power conduit; the gems collect energy and store it. Keep that weapon close, Elias. You might need it."

He slung the crossbow over his shoulder. "I can tell you the story later. Right now we are seriously in danger and need to get out of sight." He turned to Islar. "Where's the exit in this place?"

Islar pointed to a covered doorway. "That's the rooftop access door. It goes down into the atrium. Vosper doesn't post many guards up here. He doesn't feel the need since he has two necromancers at his beck and call. From there, it's only a short distance to Vosper's throne room."

"Everyone, be on the lookout," Sisren warned, turning to Elias. "I'm a more experienced fighter than you are, Elias. I'll go out in front. Can you conceal us?"

Elias nodded. "I can for a short while, but I'm not sure how long I'll be able to maintain a concealment spell while we're on the move." He was still feeling drained from the aftereffects of the previous spell that concealed their flight into the city. Only he and Sisren were strong enough to camouflage them. Rali's powers weren't strong enough to hold a concealment spell.

They proceeded through the doorway into a large open space. The atrium was filled with stained glass and rich ornamental wood carvings, as well as a fair amount of dust. It was obvious that the room hadn't been used in a long time. Now that Vosper was a necromancer, he probably didn't feel the need to entertain visiting dignitaries anymore.

They continued walking toward the throne room. The hallways were conspicuously empty.

"Where is everyone?" whispered Sisren.

Islar gulped. "I don't know. It's making me nervous. There should be at least *someone* around. The palace is usually crawling with servants."

They got closer to the throne room and still didn't see anyone: no servants and no guards.

Then they heard a piercing scream. "Please have

mercy!" a man cried out.

Everyone froze. It was Hanko's voice.

A rasping voice floated out to the hallway. "I know you're all here... outssssside. Why don't you come in and enjoy... my hospitality?"

"He knows we're here!" Islar whispered furiously.

Elias put his finger to his lips. "Remain calm and stay behind me. If this goes south, I want you all to run. I'm going in alone. It's time for me to face him."

Sisren shook her head furiously at him. "Don't be an *idiot*," she snapped. "We're coming in with you. You can't possibly defeat him on your own."

Elias rolled his eyes at her but didn't argue any further. There wasn't any point.

They all drew their weapons and stepped inside the throne room, with Elias leading the way. Vosper was facing the window, and his two necromancers were floating nearby.

Hanko and Charlight were chained up in a corner. Charlight's muzzle had been wrapped with steel cable to prevent her from breathing fire. The wire was wound so tightly around her mouth that blood streamed down her neck. Even worse, her wings had been shattered. They hung limply at her sides, broken in a dozen places.

Hanko had been stripped to the waist and flogged. His arms and legs were covered in welts. He sagged in his chains, weakened by blood loss. His dragon stone had been ripped from his chest again and lay on the floor near his feet.

Vosper turned to face Elias, and the other two

necromancers moved into place behind him.

"Sssso... we finally meet," said the emperor. "You're... *younger* than I expected."

"And you're *deader* than I expected," said Elias.

Vosper's black eyes narrowed. "Do you ssssee your friend Hanko? My necromancers brought him down from the sky... in an instant. The fool wasn't strong enough to maintain his concealment spell. You dragon ridersss shouldn't attempt elvish enchantments. The magic is really beyond your... capabilities."

Elias raised the crossbow and pointed it directly at Vosper's face. "Speak for yourself, *deadrat*. I don't think you'll find me an easy target."

Vosper looked back at his necromancers. "Kill them. But not the boy... or the white dragon. Thosssse two... are for me."

Uldreiyn and Uevareth shot from their positions behind the emperor, their gray mouths gnawing with ghastly anticipation.

The necromancers passed right by Elias and engaged the others.

Uevareth reached out to grab Rali's throat. Aor blocked the necromancer with his forearm. Aor's tattoos glowed faintly, their power activating against the necromancer's magic. The guard grunted and his knees buckled slightly, but he remained standing. Aor flung the necromancer away from him and gestured for Rali to get behind him.

Sisren faced off against Uldreiyn, who struck her with a paralyzing spell. Unable to counterattack in time, she froze, crying out in pain.

Elias heard Sisren scream behind him. He swiftly turned and swung his crossbow in her direction. He aimed for Uldreiyn's neck and let his arrow fly. The arrow flashed through the air, trailing bright ribbons of power. The enchanted metal head sank into the undead creature's neck and promptly exploded, leaving a fist-sized hole in its wake.

Uldreiyn staggered back, holding his neck. Black blood pumped from his jugular, spilling between his fingers. The necromancer looked... *perplexed* rather than angry. He obviously hadn't been expecting any mortal weapon to harm him.

Sisren snarled and kicked the creature hard in its chest. She was stronger than she looked, because he *flew* backwards with such force that he hit the opposite wall.

The necromancer slithered to the floor like a stringless marionette. He was still moving—amazingly—but he was only twitching on the ground. Sluggish blood continued to pour from its neck.

Elias eyed the fallen creature warily. Even with that ghastly wound in its neck, he wasn't sure the necromancer would *stay* down. Killing something *undead* took a lot more work than killing something with a heartbeat.

Elias turned to face the emperor again. Vosper hadn't moved. He was still standing frozen in the same spot, staring at him with eerie calm.

"Release Hanko and Charlight," Elias demanded. "You're outnumbered."

Vosper laughed as if it was the most ridiculous thing he'd ever heard. *"Outnumbered?* Even with the help of that hulking dragon, I'm ten times... more powerful than you. Do you really... believe yoursss-self a match for me, boy?"

"Let them go!" said Elias, not dropping his weapon. He wondered if he could take his eyes off Vosper long enough to reload his crossbow. Nydeired stepped forward, growling defensively.

On the other side of the room, Hanko raised his head. Even in his dazed condition, he understood what was happening. Elias was trying to save him.

Vosper laughed again: a hissing, bubbling sound that chilled Elias' blood. Then the emperor raised a glowing hand and lashed out. *"Forn-hatt!"* he cried. A sound like a thousand firecrackers filled the chamber. The noise was deafening.

Elias covered his ears with his hands, but it was no use. He could feel the awful sound all the way down to his bones. Nydeired howled as the noise intensified, threatening to burst his eardrums. The noise got louder and louder, and the others fell to their knees.

Of them all, only Aor remained standing, his protective tattoos blocking the worst of the spell. His eyes were popping out and he had a horrible grimace on his face. He was obviously in pain, but he managed to maneuver his body over Rali's. The young king writhed on the floor in agony.

"Sound familiar?" said Vosper. "It's the *Sprite's Shriek*. It won't kill you, but your pain will increase until you're unconscious, and then I'll be able to play with you at my leisure."

The necromancers seemed unaffected. Uldreiyn was still laying on the floor, but Uevareth floated over to Sisren and absently plunged a knife into her chest. She clutched her chest with a soundless scream, her mouth opening as she struggled to breathe.

Elias searched his memory for *anything* that would work as a counterspell. He finally remembered one from his grandmother's spellbook.

"Forn-vel!" he said, and a protective bubble enveloped them, muffling the awful noise. Elias extended the protective barrier around everyone but Hanko and Charlight, who were chained on the other side of the room. Elias could still hear the awful sound, but it wasn't loud enough to harm them.

Vosper tapped on the barrier with his finger, which wobbled like a soap bubble under his touch. "You expect to sssstop me... with this little protection spell?" The emperor's voice sounded muffled, as though he was speaking through cotton.

Aor propped Sisren up so she could breathe. The knife stuck out of the middle of her chest. The wound bled sluggishly, and Sisren's face was deathly pale.

"She's going to die if we don't get her out of here," said Rali.

"I know," said Elias, "but it's taking all my concentration just to maintain this shield. It will protect us for the time being, but once I drop the barrier, Vosper will attack again."

Although the energy shield was not weak, it was only a defensive spell. Nydeired's dragon stone pulsed brightly as he shared his strength with Elias. The spell was draining them both.

The necromancers circled like wolves around a wounded animal. They didn't seem bothered at all. On the contrary, they seemed entertained by the whole situation. Every once in a while, Vosper reached out and touched the barrier with his hands.

"What are we going to do?" said Islar. "We're trapped in here."

"Vosper is going to wait until you tire, Elias," whispered Rali. "Even with Nydeired's help, you can't hold this spell forever. And Vosper has all the time in the world."

"Maybe I won't have to," said Elias quietly. "Look at Hanko and Charlight."

With Vosper occupied, Hanko had managed to free himself and reach the dragon stone lying at his feet. Hanko wasn't paying attention to them. He wasn't even paying attention to Vosper. He was paying attention to Charlight.

He crawled over to Charlight and released her chains. The shackles dropped to the floor, and Charlight's body collapsed. Her shattered wings sprawled in every direction, and her head hit the floor. Her eyes were fixed and staring at nothing.

Hanko tore frantically at the wires around her mouth and nose, but it was too late.

Charlight was dead.

Hanko cradled her head in his lap and *screamed.* "No... no! Charlight, wake up! Please come back to me!"

Even through the protective barrier, Elias and the others could hear Hanko's grief-stricken cries. Vosper turned around and raised an eyebrow, somehow looking bored and watchful at the same time. He called Uevareth to his side. "Finish him," he ordered. "He's lossst his... usefulness."

Uevareth floated over and calmly raised one hand to strike a death blow. Hanko grabbed the necromancer's wrist. Vosper cocked his head to one side.

Hanko, driven mad with fury and despair, rose up and struck, mouthing a vicious spell under his breath.

An explosion erupted from the necromancer's chest, blowing a hole in it the size of a man's fist. Foul black ichor splattered everywhere, spraying Hanko's face. Uevareth buckled to the ground, thrashing in agony as black blood poured from the gaping wound.

Elias gasped. "How is this possible? When did Hanko get this strong?"

"He always has been..." said Sisren weakly. "He's hidden his *true* powers for years. I've always known he was stronger than he let on. He's... a spirit conjurer."

Uevareth was writhing on the ground. Hanko turned to face the emperor. His eyes were wild, his breathing ragged, the fury that emanated off of him palpable. "You've taken the only thing that mattered to me," he whispered. "Now, you're going to pay."

"Your powerssss... are no match for mine, dragon rider," said Vosper.

"You're wrong," said Hanko. "Did you know that I'm a conjurer? A fairly competent one, too—except that I haven't used those powers in years. It's a rare gift in human spellcasters. I was afraid to conjure; I thought it would kill me. But I'm not afraid of *anything* anymore. Charlight is gone. I have no reason to live, and for that... you're going to die."

"Bah! I can conjure sssspirits... more easily than you," said Vosper. The emperor didn't look afraid, but he wasn't laughing anymore, either.

"Yes, but there's a difference. You conjure spirits and trap them against their will. I do not," said Hanko.

"That's impossible," said Vosper.

"It *is* possible," Hanko hissed. His own red blood was smeared on his teeth. "How many dragons have you killed? How many spellcasters have you murdered? Hundreds? Thousands? I'm going to give them a chance for vengeance. And I won't have to trap them—they'll come willingly."

"You couldn't," said Vosper, who managed to look slightly alarmed. "You won't be able to control them. The sssspell will... kill you. It will... kill all of you."

Hanko stared at the emperor with glassy, dull

eyes. "Exactly. Now you understand. You have stolen the most important thing from me—my dragon. What more do I have to live for?"

Vosper's eyes widened. "You... can't be sssserious! This cannot... occur! Not this! Not after all my careful planning!"

"Your *planning?*" Hanko was trembling with unspent rage. "Have I ruined your *plans*, emperor?" he raised his hands. "You wicked, evil bastard—I'm going to ruin a lot more than just your *plans!*"

Instead of the normal blue light that appeared during spellcasting, Hanko's palms turned black. "*Dreyma-lita-purs-krellr!*" he screamed, and the room grew icy, as cold as death.

A deep, thunderous sound filled the chamber, echoing off the walls. When the sound stopped, everyone froze.

It was a ghoulish scene—Hanko's face and chest were smeared with the blood of the dead necromancer, and he was swaying and moaning and staring out into the distance with dead eyes.

The blackness in Hanko's palms expanded, and a dark, swirling maw opened in the center of the room. And they came—the spirits of the dead riders and their dragons. First there were only a few, and then there were dozens, and eventually the throne room was full of them—a throng of shimmering figures, glowing all the colors of dragonkin.

Elias' heart pounded as he looked at the lifeless shades materializing in front of him. There were so many, he could not even count them all. "Hanko...

stop! Don't do this! You won't be able to control them all!"

Hanko ignored him and addressed the emperor, who was now floating back towards the exit. "See? I don't have to *control* them," said Hanko, his body slick with blood and sweat. "All I had to do is *call* them, and they'll do the rest."

A great roar rose from the spirits, and they descended on the emperor and the two fallen necromancers. Uevareth and Uldreiyn screeched as the frantic horde tore them to pieces. Pieces of their bodies flew outwards in a ghastly shower of gore. A few minutes later, there was nothing left of him except a black smear on the cobblestones.

The apparitions turned on the emperor. They moved towards him slowly, inexorably. Vosper raised his hands, muttering frantic spells, but his strength failed him and his shield wavered and sputtered. The shades crowded around him, battering his shield.

Despite his power, Vosper was overwhelmed by their sheer numbers. The shield collapsed, and the spirits pounded him relentlessly. The furious throng ripped Vosper's arms from their sockets and tossed them across the room. When he finally fell, they trampled his body until it was unrecognizable.

Elias turned away from the gory scene.

Hanko, unable to maintain the spell any longer, fell to the floor, unconscious.

"Don't drop your shield, Elias!" warned Islar. "The spirits will kill us all!"

"No," said Elias. "They won't." He ended the protection spell and paused. The spirits closed in around them. Islar screamed. But Elias remained calm, and spoke softly. He knew that not all sprits were evil. "I am Elias Dorgumir. I am a healer and a friend."

One of the spirits, a beautiful female with glowing blue eyes, reached out to touch him. Elias didn't quail as her cold fingers ran down his cheek. Her face looked so familiar, and Elias struggled to remember where he had seen her. The spirit-woman pointed at Hanko.

"You must save him," said the woman. "That is your destiny. Only he can open the gates and show us the way home."

"Elias, you must heal Hanko," whispered Islar frantically. "He's the only one who can reopen the portal to send them back. If he doesn't, the spirits will be *trapped* here, and they'll destroy us all!"

Elias walked slowly over to Hanko, who was lying unconscious on the ground in a pool of his own blood. A pack of shades floated after him, dully curious. He could feel their cold presence, but they kept their distance from him.

Elias kneeled down and put his hand on Hanko's chest: his heartbeat was very faint and his skin was cold.

"*Curatio*," said Elias, and healing magic flowed from him, curing Hanko's injuries. The cuts on his back and arms sealed up, and color returned to his cheeks. The scar from the dragon stone on his chest remained inflamed, but Elias was able to stop the bleeding.

"Hanko? Can you hear me? Wake up," said Elias gently.

Hanko's eyes fluttered open, and he groaned. "No..." he said, as his eyes filled with tears. "Why did you heal me, Elias? I don't want to live anymore. I can't go on without Charlight. *Please*, just let me die," he whispered.

"We need your help," said Elias. "The spirits need to go home."

Elias lifted Hanko up, gently supporting his back. Hanko was sobbing, his whole body shaking.

"Please, Hanko. Won't you help us?" said Elias quietly.

Hanko's body shuddered, then he took a deep breath and nodded. "I know you tried to help me. I'll do it for you," he whispered. Even after everything that had happened, there was still something inside him that made him want him to live. "*Dreyma-lita-purs-stodva*," he said softly, and the black portal opened again.

The spirits left silently, one by one, filing out of the room and back into the darkness of the after-world.

One spirit lagged behind—the woman who had touched Elias' cheek. She floated over to Elias and spoke one final time. "Thank you for saving me, my son."

Elias looked up, stunned. "Mother?"

"Yes, I am Ionela. You released me... from a prison

inside the body of that necromancer. You freed me, and I was able to move on to the next life. I love you, and I'm so proud of you. Farewell, my son."

Then she walked away and into the portal, which sealed up and disappeared.

Elias was speechless, trembling with emotion. His mother had recognized him! She had known him, had talked to him. He had been too numb with the shock of everything that was happening, but now his emotions overwhelmed him.

Islar's voice shook him out of his reverie. "Elias, Sisren needs your help. She's dying."

Elias nodded, wiping the tears from his cheeks. He was healing a lot of people too quickly for his body to keep up, but he knew he had a job to do. An important job.

"Lift her up," he ordered, and Aor lifted Sisren gently so that she was in a seated position.

Amazingly, she was still conscious. She certainly was a *lot* stronger than she appeared.

Elias looked into her glazed eyes. "Sisren, listen to me. I'm going to take out the knife. It's going to hurt more coming out than it did going in. But I need you to stay awake, okay? I'll have a better chance of saving you if you remain conscious. Do you understand?"

She uttered a bubbling gasp. A line of bloody spittle dripped from her lip. "Just do it and be done with it," she rasped.

Elias grasped the handle of the knife with both hands and pulled it out in one swift movement. Sisren cried out as the knife tore her flesh anew.

Blood shot up from her chest like a fountain. Elias put his palms on her chest, crossed over the wound. "*Curatio*," he said, and the tendrils of his healing spell entered her body, closing the severed veins and sealing up the horrible wound.

When he was finished, he sat back on his heels and exhaled. He hadn't felt this drained in a long time.

Sisren watched him with dulled eyes, and smiled feebly. "Thank you," she said weakly. "I didn't know if I was going to make it this time." Her breathing was labored, but steady. She would recover.

Rali was leaning against the wall, his face pale and covered with sweat. "I can't believe it," he said. "We did it. We actually defeated Vosper."

"With Hanko's help," said Elias.

They all looked at Hanko. He had crawled back to Charlight's body and was crying softly into her neck.

"I guess I was wrong about him," said Rali. "I was certain he would betray us, and you were the one who vouched for him. If Hanko hadn't been here, all of us would have died."

Elias looked over at Hanko. He looked so broken, so dejected and crushed. Elias felt pity swell in his heart. "Maybe. We'll never know for sure. None of us could have done this alone. We defeated the emperor because we fought together."

Elias walked over to Nydeired and put his hand around his neck, thankful for his dragon's strength and friendship. Nydeired purred and nuzzled him gently. *"How do you feel, Elias?"*

"I'm glad it's over," he said. "Let's go home."

21. ENDINGS

A year had passed since Vosper's defeat, and rebuilding was underway. As the sole surviving heir of the Five Kings, Rali assumed leadership of the capital and its troops. *The Nine* came to Morholt and took their place as Rali's personal guards, as they had done at Parthos.

Sisren returned to Miklagard with Hanko, who went on trial for treason. Elias declined to testify against him, and the charges were eventually dismissed for lack of evidence. After a period of deep depression, Hanko began teaching in Miklagard, training students in the art of spirit conjuring. He eventually attained the rank of Master Spellcaster and helped Galti and Holf finish their training. The young dragon riders then went back to Parthos to help patrol the city.

The siege of Mount Velik ended as abruptly as it began, and the empire soldiers returned to the capital after the emperor's death. Rali accepted the soldiers back into their regular positions but dismissed all of Vosper's old commanders.

The dwarves fared the worst. After the assassin's attack, Hergung was seriously injured and two clan leaders were dead. Bolrakei was removed from office.

After losing his leg, Hergung became a recluse, overcome by fear and anxiety. With more than half their leadership gone, the dwarf clans fell into disarray and eventually into civil war. Two splinter factions were formed, one that supported King Hergung, and another that opposed him. The rebel faction was led by Utan, the surviving leader of the *Vardmiter* clan, which had for centuries been treated like pariahs by the other clans.

Tallin and Duskeye remained among the dwarves for most of the year, trying to broker peace between the two factions, but even they could not salvage the situation. Utan's faction left Mount Velik permanently, moving west to the Highport Mountains, where they eventually settled. The Orvasse River became a *de facto* border for the warring clans, and any dwarf from the opposing side that dared to cross was captured and killed.

The elves left Mount Velik without even saying goodbye. They returned to Brighthollow with their dragons one morning before the sun came up, refusing any telepathic communication from other spellcasters. Although the elves initially tried to assist the dwarves in settling their differences, they left in frustration when the infighting escalated.

Sela recovered fully from her injuries, except for the blindness in her left eye, which was permanent. She took over as Rali's regent in the desert. Even with Vosper dead, Parthos remained a target. Balborites and orcs made frequent attempts to breach the city's defenses. The attacks failed, but they lost many good men. During the last attack, Sela engaged an assassin in hand-to-hand combat. When the assassin laughed, Sela discovered that her attacker was a woman. Skera-Kina had survived, and she was stronger than ever.

Elias spent months traveling through the countryside, working as a healer. Elias earned the nickname *Gentle Hand*, because he was able to heal so many injuries without causing additional pain. As his reputation and skills grew, he chose to take on an apprentice, a young woman named *Haiba*. He and Nydeired visited the Elder Willow often in order to spend time with Chua and Starclaw, who still lived peacefully in the magical grove.

It was there that Tallin finally tracked Elias down, during one of the many visits to his father. Tallin and Duskeye arrived at dusk after Chua and Elias had settled down to eat. Elias sat on a short wicker stool and Chua lay nearby, reclining on a folded blanket. Haiba sat by a small fire, preparing plates of cooked mushrooms and fresh greens.

"Tallin? What a pleasant surprise," said Elias. "Please sit. Share our meal with us."

"Thank you, Elias, but this isn't a social visit," said Tallin.

"All right," said Elias. "What's on your mind?"

"Assassins have attacked Parthos four times this year. Sela identified one of the assassins as a woman. I'm sure it was Skera-Kina. She's eluded me twice already. She's directly responsible for the dwarf clans falling into war. She murdered two clan leaders, and her attack on Hergung has left him so withdrawn that his advisors have taken over leadership of Mount Velik, with disastrous results. Skera-Kina must be stopped, and I need all the dragon riders' help in order to succeed."

"What do you want to do?" said Elias.

"The assassins will never stop causing havoc on the continent," said Tallin grimly. "We need to stop this plague at its source. We need to go to Balbor Island and destroy the Balborite assassins... once and for all."

Continued in Book Four: The Balborite Curse

Sneak Peek Of Book 4: The Balborite Curse

allin the dragon rider gazed out upon the Death Sands, arms folded across his chest. Even in the spring, the desert was a harsh place, but he loved its stark beauty. Dry scrub and tufts of stubborn yellow cactus peppered the landscape, and beyond the horizon, there were endless tracts of gold-colored dunes. He could see a long way in the clear, dry air. The dawn had melted away into a dazzling noon, and it was already suffocatingly hot.

Beads of perspiration stood upon his brow, matting wisps of red hair against his forehead. Scorching wind, laden with dust, eddied against the wall, leaving coppery grit everywhere. The cloudless sky was intensely blue, shimmering like a sea of cornflowers.

Tallin was a dwarf halfling, born and raised with other dwarves at Mount Velik. Though he had spent his childhood with his own people, his adult years had brought him to the solitude of the desert, and he considered this place his home.

An orange and blue pennant swayed lazily in the breeze, displaying the official colors of the realm. The colors were woven into Tallin's clothing, too, stitched into the sleeves of his tunic and wrapped around his waist in a belt of knotted leather.

Tallin touched the ring on his finger with his thumb, a gift from the king some years ago. It was a band of gold crowned with a huge center sapphire. The center stone was surrounded by an intricate array of small citrines. A tiny black dragon was carved into the band, as well as embroidered on the corner of his left lapel: a symbol that stood for the unified kingdom of Parthos and Morholt.

The land was at peace, at least for now.

He leaned against the walls, looking out over the ramparts. A single road, edged with cobblestones, crested down from the dunes toward the main gate. The line of visitors stretched back a half-league, waiting to be searched in the long line that wound down to the entrance. Each person, cart, and animal entering the city was subject to scrutiny. The soldiers at the gate did their job methodically, in silence.

The guards searched the baskets of an older man, but let his young children pass through without question. Despite the wait and the oppressive heat, the travelers remained patient, and no one complained.

Tallin watched the crowd with a careful eye. He was a mage and had been monitoring the city gates for days. Duskeye, his companion, was a sapphire-blue dragon, his enormous body resting underneath a fabric canopy nearby. Duskeye raised his long neck and blinked his good eye lazily, peering out over the barren landscape.

Duskeye and Tallin were bound together as rider and dragon; the carved dragon-stone that glittered at the base of their throats verified their permanent bond. Like all dragon riders, Tallin and Duskeye had pledged to defend this city, as well as the surrounding desert. Parthos was a magnificent keep, carved right into the mountain. The design was an impressive feat of engineering, built to withstand both siege and the threat of constant erosion from the harsh environment.

A maze of covered aqueducts, fed by a deep underground spring, ensured that the city always had clean drinking water. Neat terraces of drought-resistant plants were cultivated up the craggy mountainside, maximizing arable land and reducing water loss. Camels grazed outside the walls, eating the thorny shrubs that sprouted up in the arid climate.

Nomadic women followed behind the herds with straw baskets, collecting dung. The nomads pressed the manure into neat bricks and sold them in the street market to be used as an efficient cooking fuel. The bricks were slow-burning and virtually smokeless, making firewood unnecessary.

Tallin turned his gaze to an old garrison outside the main wall, now doubling as a makeshift camp for foreign merchants who stayed here to trade. An array of tents and cook-fires dotted the sand.

Just then, there was a clamor at the city's entrance. An old man's voice shouted something unintelligible, and a hissing sound filled the air as one of the guards drew his sword.

Duskeye looked out over the ramparts and pointed into the wind. *"What is happening at the gate?"*

Tallin leaned over the wall for a better view. "Duskeye, let's go. Something unusual is happening."

Duskeye lowered his neck so Tallin could mount the leather saddle. The dragon took flight, circling down near the guard station.

Duskeye landed with a loud thump, his body stirring up sand. The crowd quieted immediately, parting to let them through. Many people turned their heads in respect, and a few girls giggled nervously and waved, trying to catch the rider's eye.

Tallin addressed a soldier at the gate. "What's going on?"

Off to the side, the soldiers held a man under guard, a nervous merchant who smelled like sweat and dust. "This man is a smuggler, sir," said one of the guardsmen. "We searched him and found this." The ebony-skinned guard passed Tallin a glass vial.

Tallin's eyebrows shot up. He recognized this type of glass—it was Balborite crystal, exquisite in its beauty and resilience, designed to hold the deadliest of poisons. It was also illegal.

Tallin accepted the vial from the guard and gripped it between his thumb and forefinger, holding it up to the sun. Light reflected off the oily liquid inside, which had a pearl-like sheen. He immediately knew what it was.

Curious onlookers craned their necks to see, even as they maintained a discreet distance. One old woman caught a glimpse of the vial, and her eyes rounded with surprise. "It's kudu oil! They found kudu!" she cried, and a collective gasp went through the crowd.

The woman was right—this was deadly kudu oil. A single drop was lethal, and a vial this large could kill a hundred men. A murmur of excitement mixed with fear swept through the crowd.

The accused man fell to his knees. "I'm innocent, I'm innocent! I didn't do anything, I swear!" he wailed.

Tallin gave the order to close the city and seal the gates. "Close the garrison doors. No one else may enter Parthos. Strip this merchant down, search his bags, and bring him inside the city. He is our prisoner now."

"W-what, but why?" the man sputtered, "and what about my camels?"

The captain gave the prisoner a withering look, then turned to the other guardsmen. "Slaughter his camels and search the entrails for ampules."

"My camels? You can't kill my camels!" he protested.

"As you command, my lord," said the guardsmen, ignoring the now-hysterical prisoner. The guard sounded a small animal horn, and four more sentries materialized in an instant, dragging the struggling prisoner by his arms.

The captain turned around to address the crowd. "Citizens and guests, raise your tents if you wish, but no one else shall pass through these doors today. The gates will be reopened at dawn tomorrow. If you need water for your animals, a guard shall bring it to you outside."

With a polite nod and a wave of dismissal, he sealed the doors. There were a few grumbles, but the waiting crowd dispersed quietly. Some unpacked their tents for the night, while others turned around to leave.

Inside the city, the prisoner refused to be dragged away. Two soldiers struggled to hold him as he fought. "Stop this!" he screamed. "This is outrageous. I demand an audience with the regent!"

"Keep quiet," said one of the guards, delivering a slap to the back of the man's head, which only made him fight harder.

"Don't touch me, you rotten blighters! Let me go! Let me go!" he screamed over and over, struggling as he fought to break free.

"Be still, you idiot!" yelled the guard, but the man continued on as if he hadn't heard.

Tallin had seen enough. "Stop," he ordered, and the soldiers paused. "I'll take care of him." He raised a glowing hand.

The prisoner froze, his eyes rounding in alarm. "What are you going to do to me?" he stammered.

Tallin ignored the question and flicked the man's ear. "*Hilfaquna!*" he said, uttering the simple spell. The prisoner went limp and toppled forward, striking his head against the curb. Each soldier grabbed one arm and dragged the unconscious man away, his toes scraping the ground.

Tallin knew that the other dragon riders needed to be warned. Closing his eyes, Tallin reached out with his mind across the distance, attempting to link his thoughts with Sela Matu, the leader of the dragon riders. He found her patrolling the northern border with her female dragon, Brinsop. He touched her consciousness gently, prodding her with his own mind.

She flinched, and Tallin immediately felt the drain on her power. Sela always struggled to link telepathically. He knew he would need to keep their communication brief.

"Sela, the guards caught another smuggler at the gate." Tallin sensed her alarm.

"Another kudu oil smuggler? That's the second one this month," Sela replied. "That settles it. This can't be a coincidence. Someone is attempting to attack Parthos from within."

"Shall I contact the other riders?" asked Tallin.

"No, I'll contact them myself. Segregate this smuggler from the other prisoners. I will question him. I am near the Dead Forest, and I'll return to the city as quickly as I can." Sela abruptly ended the contact.

The corners of Tallin's eyes wrinkled and dimples appeared on his cheeks. He chuckled—it was always like this with Sela. Despite any limitations she might have as a mage, she was the most commanding woman he knew. Her warmth and vitality inspired those around her, and her energy seemed boundless, even as she aged.

Acting as the king's regent, Sela ruled in Parthos, while her adult son, King Rali, ruled from the capital city of Morholt. Under their united leadership, Parthos and Morholt had experienced several years of peaceful, quiet rule.

Unfortunately, after a few years of peace, things were rapidly changing for the worse. The dwarf kingdom was crumbling into chaos in the midst of the worst clan schism in a thousand years. A single clan had already splintered off, abandoning their ancestral home on Mount Velik. The lowest caste of dwarves, the enormous Vardmiter Clan, had departed Mount Velik for a new stronghold. Tallin, being half-dwarf, had tried to broker a treaty between the warring factions, but it seemed that the schism was now permanent, and with both kingdoms weakened by infighting, the entire dwarf race was vulnerable. The divided clans would never be able to defend against an attack, especially one from orcs.

Tallin could almost see King Nar, the orc leader, rubbing his hands with glee as he planned his attack on the dwarves, his most hated and ancient foes.

Things had changed in the city, too. For decades, Parthos had operated like a city under siege. After a few years of peace, the heightened sense of security was gone. People got complacent and lazy. Tallin saw carelessness everywhere; even the city's soldiers had grown lax in their duties.

The number of foreign merchants had doubled. Dealer stalls were filled with merchandise from all over the continent. It was thrilling for some residents of Parthos, many of whom had never seen such exotic treasures. Where there had once been only one choice of fabric, now there were twenty.

Women could purchase silk gowns, lace, and jewels. Instead of just selling common food staples —like camel butter and dried meat—there were colorful spices and rare fruit. Most disconcerting of all, some merchants had begun to sell vividly colored, iridescent glassware. When Tallin inquired about its origin, the merchants had been defensive and vague, or uncertain about such details, saying only that it was imported from the north.

The glass looked suspiciously like Balborite crystal, and although glass weapons were banned throughout the continent, it had been impossible to ban the sale of the glassware completely. The demand for the exquisite crystal was astounding. Even at extravagant prices, Parthinian women were desperate to own the delicate glass and use it in their homes.

Tallin drew out the vial that he had taken from the merchant. He rolled it in his palm, eying the viscous fluid within. He didn't dare open the container, for the oil was dangerous even if it was not ingested. Duskeye craned his neck and peered at the deadly liquid with his good eye. He sniffed the air and wrinkled his nose. *"Even inside that glass tube, I can still smell it."*

"What does it smell like to you?" asked Tallin.

"Like spoiled fruit, but the odor is subtle. Kudu oil is poisonous for dragons, too. As soon as we can fly, our mothers train us to avoid the plant. My dam did the

same, and I remember it well."

Tallin nodded, intrigued. He hoped that Duskeye would go on. Although they had been bound together for many years, Duskeye rarely talked about his family, none of which had survived the Dragon Wars. For years, dragons and their riders had been slaughtered by the thousands, and now only a handful remained. "Tell me about it," said Tallin softly.

Duskeye paused, staring out into the desert. His gravelly voice grew quiet. *"Let's see... when I was just a hatchling, my dam took me and my clutchmates outside the cave. She showed us the kuduare plant, warning us never to touch it. A few plants grew wild at the very top of the mountain; the plant has waxy blue leaves and white flowers, shaped like little bells. One of my brothers disobeyed her, stomping the plant with his foot. He screamed like a frightened rabbit, for the oil stripped his foot-scales right off. He ended up howling on the riverbank for over an hour, soaking his foot in running water. Luckily, he was able to rinse his foot before the oil reached his bloodstream. Our mother rapped him soundly for his stupidity, and the oil left a permanent scar."*

"What was his name?" asked Tallin.

"Brundis," replied Duskeye softly. *"He was a blue dragon, like me, but lighter in color. He was so headstrong and stubborn. But he was the handsomest of all of us, by far, which is why my mother allowed him so much latitude. His underbelly was multi-colored; like a sea of wildflowers. My mother teased him that the Great Dragon of the sky had given him an excess of beauty but*

a scarcity of brains."

"What happened to him?" asked Tallin.

"Brundis was too proud to bind himself to a rider, even an elf, who once desired him for his beauty. He remained wild, chasing females and hunting prey. Mercenaries killed him during the war in the first wave of attacks. I searched for him and found his body in the Elburgian Mountains. The dragon hunters cut all his claws as war trophies. I mourned him, built his funeral pyre, and burned his body using my dragon breath."

"Is that customary? I've never seen a dragon funeral."

"It's a death ceremony. Before the war, when a dragon died, the females—mothers and sisters—usually performed the death ceremony. The ritual was private and usually held at night. Dragons have their own customs, just like humans and dwarves, but there simply aren't enough of us to carry them on anymore."

"I wonder—has Brinsop ever performed a death ceremony?" wondered Tallin out loud.

"She's an alpha female, so I'm sure she has sometime in her past."

"How do you know that Brinsop is an alpha female?"

Duskeye shrugged. "I just know. Before the war, she-dragons organized their families into prides. The prides hunted and raised their hatchlings together. Males are forced out of the pride when they're old enough to mate. When a dragon dies, the body is burned by the pride, with the alpha female leading the ceremony. After the Dragon Wars, there were so few dragons left that the *prides disbanded. Brinsop was the alpha female of the largest pride in the desert. That was a long time ago."*

"Sela never mentioned it," said Tallin.

"That's not surprising. Like me, Brinsop is the only survivor in her bloodline. The memory must be painful for her. It's possible that Brinsop never discussed it with Sela; it's a very private subject."

Tallin waited for Duskeye to continue his story, but he fell silent and did not speak again. The future of the dragon race was precarious. No one had discovered a wild dragon in years, and chances were slim that any other survivors remained. Tallin never stopped searching, but he was beginning to lose hope.

During the Dragon Wars, thousands of dragons had been mercilessly slaughtered. Even if there were a wild dragon out there to be found, Tallin could not be sure that they would welcome contact with outsiders. In fact, they might be outright hostile, having learned to shun anyone who might cause them harm.

Besides Tallin and Duskeye, Parthos hosted four other dragon riders: Elias and Nydeired, the only surviving white dragon; Galti and Holf and their two black dragons, Orshek and Karela; and Sela and her carnelian dragon, Brinsop.

There was one dragon rider in the east, Chua and his dragon, Starclaw. They lived in quiet solitude in the Elder Willow, a mystical grove of trees. Both had survived horrific physical torture during the war, and as a result, they were both blind and disabled.

Chua could not walk, and Starclaw would never fly again.

A few dragons lived in Brighthollow, the land of the elves. The elves refused to disclose how many dragons lived among them, but it wasn't more than a handful. Dragons were unable to reproduce in Brighthollow, since the enchantments that pervaded the elvish lands suppressed dragon fertility. There would be no new hatchlings from there.

Tallin's shoulders slumped. He had hoped that the dragons would begin their path to recovery by now. However, no female dragons had been willing to nest. Perhaps it was too soon, or they were still too uneasy. It weighed heavily on him.

Tallin tucked the vial of kudu oil back into his pocket, pondering what its presence in Parthos could mean. Had it been intended for him? For one of the other riders? Or one of the dragons themselves? He could only speculate, and none of the options was at all pleasant. There were so few dragons left already. Tallin felt a sense of dread. Was it too late, he wondered, for these noble creatures to recover their numbers after such a catastrophic decline?

Was it too late to save the dragons from extinction?

Continued in Book Four: The Balborite Curse

A SPECIAL THANK YOU

Thank you for reading. If you enjoyed this book, please help spread the word by leaving a review on Amazon. Your reviews help other people discover this series.

You can learn more about me and get information about new releases by joining my official mailing list here: *www.KristianAlva.com.*